Success isn't ~ much you h~ much you do for others!

Your Stories
Volume One

♡ *Taylor Joseph*

compiled and edited by
Taylor S. Joseph

★ ★ ★ ★
Four Star Publishing
Canton, Michigan

Published by:
Four Star Publishing
P. O. Box 871784
Canton, MI 48187
fourstarpublishing@comcast.net

ISBN: 978-0-9851990-0-5

Book design by Lee Lewis Walsh,
Words Plus Design, www.wordsplusdesign.com

Printed in the United States of America

Preface

Taylor S. Joseph

I spent two and a half years visiting 135 schools around the U.S., giving author presentations and trying to motivate students to be more active in reading and writing. Many times, after my presentations, students would come to me with a story that they had written, looking for encouragement.

I had a great idea to collect these stories and publish the best ones. Before I knew it, word had spread that I was collecting stories and I ended up with over eight hundred. I read every single one, narrowed it down to the best of the best, and *Your Stories, Volume 1* was born. Two new short stories from me are also included.

This book is a compilation of the work of some of the greatest young writers in the country. There are so many talented students out there waiting to blossom, and all they need is a chance and some encouraging words. I'm happy to give them wider exposure, and hope to produce *Your Stories, Volume 2* in the near future.

I would like to say "thank you very much" to all the librarians, teachers, principals, parents, and especially students who have made this book possible. After what I've seen at schools, I don't worry one bit about the next generation and its ability to succeed.

Taylor S. Joseph
March 2012

Contents

Seventh Grade Students

Eighth Grade Students

Ninth Grade Students

Tenth Grade Students

Number Ten
Taylor S. Joseph

The night was dark and the fog was thick. I was driving down Rural Highway 45, coming back from a sales call in southern Louisiana, better known as bayou country. They say that when the fog rolls in, you can't see two feet in front of you, and they're right.

I thought about pulling off to the side of the road until morning, but I thought again. I knew that there was no way that a twenty-five-year-old woman in her right mind, who was all alone, was going to stop and spend the night on a deserted highway in one of the most secluded swamps in Louisiana. So I slowed down, but continued to press on.

My stomach growled loudly, reminding me that I was an hour away from civilization, where I could get a hot meal and a room for the night. The farther I drove, the thicker the fog became and the more cautious I grew. Mesmerized by the road, I shut my eyes for an instant, then shook my head to wake up.

As I opened my eyes, I saw a dark figure dash into the middle of the road in front of me. My heart pounded and my stomach weakened as I slammed on my brakes and swerved into the other lane. I heard a loud bang, as if someone had fired a shot right at me from the side of the road. My car continued to swerve to the left as I gritted my teeth and gripped the wheel with all my might, trying to keep from going off the road. *Please don't let this be the end for me,* I thought as I steadied the wheel and tried to pull the car back to my side of the road.

Pain shot throughout my forearms as I felt another strong tug on the left side of my car, as if something were trying to pull me into the swamp. I stomped harder on my brake pedal, finally sliding to a complete stop with my knuckles still white from my death grip on the wheel.

I took a deep breath and thought, *Man, that was a close one. I wonder what that thing in the road was. It looked almost like a person.* I looked out the window and couldn't see anything except the thick, eerie Louisiana night.

Swallowing heavily, I reached for my cell phone and dialed 911. Nothing happened. I looked at my phone and panicked as I saw the tiny screen message: *No service.*

Desperate and scared, I knew I had to take a chance. As I stepped out of the car, the thick moist air hung around me as though I were underwater. I looked down at the driver's side front tire and saw strands of rubber shredded on the rim. *Oh no, a blowout. I'm not spending the night out here all alone!* I cautiously went to my trunk to get out the spare and felt the hair on the back of my neck stand up, as if someone or something was watching me. When I opened the trunk, I heard a faint whispering moan: "Rebecca, Rebecca, stay with me!"

I nearly jumped out of my skin. I jolted around with my fists raised, stricken with fright. "Who's... there?" I stuttered.

When no one answered, I frantically grabbed the tire iron and slammed the trunk, ran to the driver's door, jumped into the front seat and locked the doors. Shaking in fear and clinging to the tire iron, I gasped, "Please God, help me, please!"

Off in the distance I heard what sounded like scattered footsteps. Again, I heard the whispered moan: "Rebecca, Rebecca, stay with me."

Trembling, I closed my eyes, trying to shut out the vision of an axe murderer about to make me his next victim. I started to hyperventilate, but knew I had to remain calm, as helpless as I felt. I spent the next several hours in my car wide awake, frightened out of my wits and barely able to move, until morning came.

About an hour after the sun came up, the fog burned off. I mustered enough courage to get out of my car and change the tire, looking over my shoulder the entire time. I drove for an hour before I reached the main highway, pulling off at the first exit. I found a full-service gas station, and when the attendant approached me, I asked, "Can I get a new tire for my car?"

"I don't know if we can do that today," he replied. "There was a forty-car pileup on the highway last night from the fog, and all the mechanics were out towing cars half the night, helping the police. You'll have to wait a while until one of them comes in."

My eyes opened wide. "What time was the accident?"

"Around eleven."

"That's funny," I said. "I had my blowout around ten, and I was about an hour away from the highway."

"You were lucky," the attendant replied. "Nine people died last night near where Highway 45 meets Interstate 68."

A chill went down my spine and I felt faint. *Nine people died! I would've been on that highway when that accident occurred. I wonder what that thing in the road was that stopped me?*

I tried to put the events of the night together. *No one has called me Rebecca since Grandmother died five years ago. Everyone calls me Becky, everyone.* I shivered and felt a cold gust of air, as if a ghost were present.

I looked at the attendant and said confidently, "That's all right about the tire. I think I'll be fine on the spare." As he walked away, I looked up and murmured, "Thanks, Grandma," and drove off.

Nine victims, I thought, as I drove down the road. I couldn't shake the eerie feeling that if I had kept driving, I would have been in the accident, too. I would have been number ten.

We Meet Again

Taylor S. Joseph

We all do things in life when we are young that we regret when we get older. Most of them we forget about, unless they were huge, life-changing mistakes. And then there are the embarrassing moments of being humiliated in front of a group, moments that haunt us forever.

Ian Martin was no different, except that one of his mistakes did haunt him many years later.

"Hey, Ian," said his friend Kenny. "Do you want to go for Markus Anderson after school, or Michael Gilbert? Next year when we're in eighth grade, we'll rule, with it being our last year in middle school and all. "

"We'll go after both of them if we can," replied Ian. "They're both geeks, and I can't stand them. I'll talk to Phillip and Charles and see if they'll come too. If we can only get one of them, let's take Markus. He's my favorite one to pick on." Kenny grinned and nodded.

Ian stood five feet eight inches tall, bigger than anyone else in his grade. No one ever messed with him, because he was as mean as a hungry cougar. His friends followed his lead without question.

After school, Kenny and Charles caught up with Ian, saying, "Michael's mom picked him up already. Phillip has a dental appointment and can't come to help."

"That's all right," Ian shrugged. "We'll go after Markus. Let's go wait for him at the corner of Parker and Madison. He always walks that way home."

The three quickly made their way through the rush of homebound children to Parker Street and waited. Soon Markus turned up in the crowd; when he saw the trio of bullies, he cringed.

Ian, as always, was the first to speak. "Hey, dork. What did you learn in school today? Did you learn how to get hit by a dodge ball in gym class?"

Markus, smaller in stature than the other three, tried to ignore Ian and walk around him. Ian grabbed Markus' arm and growled, "I'm talking to you!"

"Please, leave me alone," pleaded Markus. "I've never done anything to you."

"You've never done anything to me?" Ian sneered. "You came to school today, and that's enough. You got an A on the math test, and looked like the sissy you always are in gym. Isn't that enough?"

By now a crowd of ten had gathered. Markus pulled his arm from Ian's grip and started to hurry away. Kenny grabbed and pushed him, snarling, "Not so fast." The book Markus had in his hand dropped to the ground, as well as his backpack. The growing crowd let out a yell of "Fight, fight, fight!"

Ian kicked the book into the street. "You're pathetic." As Markus scrambled after his book, Ian tripped him, got on top of him and held his face to the ground, gloating, "You're such a little baby."

A neighbor came running over from his garage, shouting, "Let go of him right now!" The crowd scattered in a hurry as Ian looked up, rubbed Markus' face into the grass one last time before letting go, and stood up.

"If I see you lay one more finger on him, you'll have to deal with me," the man growled.

As Ian, Kenny and Charles walked away, Ian called out over his shoulder, "I'll see you tomorrow in school, dork."

When Markus and the man were left standing alone, the man bent down to pick up Markus' book and handed it to him, then asked, "Are you all right?"

"I'm okay," Markus mumbled.

"What do those guys have against you?"

"I don't know," replied Markus. "They don't like that I'm one of the best students in school. It doesn't help not being very good in gym either."

"I know it isn't going to seem like much help right now," said the man. "But being a great student is going to really pay off in the future. And as far as gym goes, one day that won't matter much either."

"Were you bad in gym too?"

"No," returned the man. "I was a starter on my high school football team. I wish I'd done better in school, though. That's not the point. I didn't realize until later how important things in life are that don't seem important when you're in school just trying to survive. Trust me! I lived it! Keep doing what you're doing and one day you'll look back with no regrets, after you make a good life for yourself."

The man smiled and Markus thanked him as he walked away.

■ ■ ■

When Ian got home, his mom stood at the stove in the kitchen. As she turned to him, Ian saw a fresh bruise on her arm, which she quickly covered in shame. Ian looked away. "Did Dad… go to work last night?" he asked.

"Yes," his mother answered. "That midnight shift at the factory is really hitting him hard. He's been drinking since he got home again."

"Ian!" his father yelled. "Get in here!"

Ian gulped, then walked into the living room. "Yes, Dad."

"I want that garage cleaned out today," Ian's father slurred angrily. Ian nodded. "When I wake up later, it better be done. Don't forget what happened last time you didn't do what I told you." He pointed to his belt, which was sitting on the coffee table.

As his father closed his eyes again, Ian gulped, backed out of the room and went to begin cleaning out the garage.

■ ■ ■

The next day during school, at lunch, Ian approached Kenny. "I'm in a bad mood today and I'm not waiting until after school. Where's that wimp Markus Anderson?"

"Reading by himself in the corner over there," Kenny responded.

They approached Markus and Ian sat down next to him. "What are you reading, dork?" Ian asked. Markus didn't answer.

A nearby girl called out, "Leave him alone."

"And what if I don't?" barked Ian.

"Then I'm going to tell a teacher what you did yesterday," Charlotte said. "You'll have to go to the principal's office and explain it to him. You'll probably get suspended and have to explain it to your parents, too. We'll all be better off here with you at home for three days."

Ian paused at the thought of being at home for three days, stood up and said, "All right, dork. You lucked out this time, but next time you won't be so lucky."

For the rest of the seventh grade, Ian tormented Markus and a few other kids. Over the summer, Markus' father got a promotion and he and his family moved away. Ian never saw Markus again — until twenty-five years later.

■ ■ ■

Ian sat in the cardiology waiting room at the hospital with his wife Carrie. He looked up at her and asked, "Why is this happening? I promised myself that when I had a son, I'd be the best father I could, and I've tried. Working at that factory on the line all these years has been hard, and now this happens."

"Stop complaining," Carrie said. "You're a great father. I know how you were raised, and what you've overcome in your life. Look at you now. Your son adores you and so do I. We need to hope for the best."

A nurse opened a door and called, "Mr. and Mrs. Martin, can you please follow me?" Ian's stomach knotted up and his heart raced in fear as she escorted them into an examination room and left them there.

A few moments later, they were joined by a man in a white coat. "Hello, I'm Doctor Kersey," he greeted them. "I've reviewed Mason's test results and I wish I had better news. It's just as we thought. He has a duct that didn't close properly in his heart, which connects the aorta and the pulmonary artery. We call this condition *patent ductus arteriosus*. That's why he's been so tired lately.

"The duct can be thought of as a way for blood to bypass the lungs in an unborn baby, which isn't breathing yet. After birth, the baby starts breathing; the duct is no longer needed and closes. If it doesn't close properly, some blood that should go to the body ends up in the lungs. This damages the lungs and causes the heart to work too hard, becoming enlarged and damaging the lungs even more. The long-term outlook in that case is very grim.

"In most of these cases, the duct closes at birth on its own. Unfortunately Mason's didn't. I'm surprised his pediatrician didn't hear the murmur before now. Let's see; he's two years old. Most of the time the opening can be closed with a catheter. Unfortunately, his opening is one of the largest ones we've ever seen. Without surgery, I'm afraid he doesn't have a chance for a normal life."

Carrie shrieked, and Ian put his head in his hands. "What are his chances?" he asked.

"If we don't operate, his chances are slim to make it a few more years," Dr. Kersey said. "He needs this repaired as soon as possible."

A tear rolled down Carrie's cheek as she asked, "Are you sure?"

"I'm sure," Dr. Kersey said. "But if we do operate, his chances are good, because we have one of the best pediatric cardiology surgeons in the country right here in our hospital. Dr. Anderson is world-renowned for his work with children. He's brilliant! Mason is lucky."

"How long before he's operated on?" Ian asked.

"Dr. Anderson will be here in a moment to discuss your options," Dr. Kersey said.

There was a knock at the door, and a short man entered, wearing a lab coat. "I'm Dr. Anderson," he smiled.

Ian's mouth dropped opened. He was momentarily speechless. There stood Markus Anderson, whom Ian had picked on so ruthlessly in middle school. Ian turned away, but Dr. Anderson didn't bat an eye as he began to speak. "I'm sure Dr. Kersey went over most of the preliminaries."

Carrie nodded.

"There is a risk anytime you're involved with heart surgery," Dr. Anderson continued. "I'm confident we can close that duct, though. Do you have any questions?"

Ian still couldn't speak, so he shook his head.

"Well, if you think of any, Dr. Kersey will answer them. Make an appointment with the receptionist for surgery before you leave." Dr. Anderson shook both Ian's and Carrie's hands, then left.

"You have to forgive Dr. Anderson," Dr. Kersey said. "He's very busy. He's saved hundreds of children's lives over the years. He's definitely the best there is."

Ian looked at Carrie and still couldn't speak. Carrie thanked Dr. Kersey, and made an appointment for Mason to have surgery.

When they were in their car, Carrie turned to Ian and asked, "What happened to you in there?"

Ian swallowed heavily and said, "Dr. Anderson was one of the kids I used to pick on in seventh grade. I did the most horrible things to him you can imagine."

Carrie's eyes opened wide and her face went slack. "I knew you were troubled when you were young, but I didn't know you were like that."

"I'm so sorry for all the things I did to people when I was little." Ian covered his face in shame. "And now Mason's life depends on the man I tortured for so long. The only good thing is, I don't think he recognized me. If he does recognize me, you don't think he would do anything to hurt Mason, do you?"

"No," Carrie said, pulling Ian's hands from his face and holding them. "He's a doctor and has saved hundreds of children's lives. How bad could you have been to him anyway?"

Ian hung his head. "Bad, really bad."

"You're not like that anymore and I'm proud of you," Carrie said. "People change. He doesn't even remember you anyway."

"How could he forget?" Ian mumbled under his breath.

"Everything will be fine," Carrie said confidently. "He's the best there is, and we don't have the money to travel to another part of the country to find another doctor."

■ ■ ■

A month later, Carrie and Ian waited, distraught, in the waiting room as Dr. Anderson operated on Mason. The operation was supposed to take four hours, but after six hours, they still hadn't heard a thing. Ian moaned, "Whenever it takes longer than they say, it means there were complications. I just know it."

Carrie was about to reply when Dr. Anderson came into the room. "We had a complication closing the duct. It was even larger than we thought." Ian's legs went weak and his throat tightened. "It was difficult, but Mason is going to be all right. He'll be able to live a normal life. Your son is going to be fine."

Carrie jumped up, filled with joy, and hugged Dr. Anderson. Ian stood up, reached out and shook Dr. Anderson's hand. Then he started to cry. "I know you don't remember me, but I'm the person who tormented you so many times back in middle school and now you've saved my son's life. I'm so sorry for doing that to you."

"I knew who you were when I first saw you in the examination room," Dr. Anderson said. "How could I forget? I figured you had a horrible life back then. You obviously have changed."

"I have changed and I did have a horrible life back then," Ian agreed. "That was no excuse, though. Will you forgive me?"

"I forgave you years ago," Dr. Anderson said.

"Thank you for saving Mason's life," said Ian. "I'll never forget what you did."

Dr. Anderson smiled widely and said, "You can go see your son now." A nurse escorted the happy parents into the recovery room.

Ian never forgot what Dr. Anderson did for him. He became an activist against bullying to help make up for all he had done. He even spoke at several schools and told his story about how Dr. Anderson saved his son's life. He promised himself that he would teach Mason the very important lesson that he learned from Dr. Anderson: *Always treat everyone with respect, no matter who they are. One day you may need help and they may be the one you need to save your son's life.*

Fifth Grade Students

How to Control Your Pony

London Griesey

5th Grade, Noblesville Intermediate School, Noblesville, Indiana

Growing up on a farm and raising horses isn't as easy as it sounds. Certain horses can be like monsters and have a mind of their own. And when those horses are ponies, watch out.

Being a girl and an only child isn't exactly the perfect life, when there's always so much work to do. Dad had a lot of confidence in my ability, and it was never so apparent as the time he came to me when I was only ten years old. He said, "Ashley, one day this farm is going to be yours. That's why I've been working you so hard lately. You need to know everything about it by the time you're an adult."

"Thanks, Dad," I said. "I love this farm as much as you do."

"I know you do," Dad said. "In time you'll be better than I am at raising horses."

The next morning, I got up early and thought, *I can be as good as Dad one day with this farm, but first I have to learn how to control the ponies. Then, when they become horses, they'll always listen to me.*

My first challenge came with a pony named Duke. He was jet black, beautiful and a real sweetie pie — that is, when other people were around. When Dad stood and watched, I mounted him with no trouble and rode like the wind. But the first time I took him into the yard on my own, it was if a demon possessed him. I went to his side and tried to mount him and he abruptly turned around. He rammed his head right into my side as I was off balance and knocked me down. He stood up on his back legs and neighed, mocking me.

I got up, pulled on his reins and said, "You're going to do just as I tell you." He pulled back hard, forcing me to slip and almost fall. I let go of the reins, and went and got Dad. When Dad got there, Duke was as perfect as could be, and let me ride him around the yard. He did that to me every time we were alone after that. Fortunately we were in the business of selling horses, and two months later he was sold.

A few months later, we had a pony named Candy, and she was anything but sweet. Dad said, "This horse is the nicest horse we've had in over a year. Walk her over to the clearing, and let's see how she does when you try to ride her."

I walked her to the clearing, looked into her eyes and said, "I'm in control, and you're going to do just as I say. If you do, I'll give you an apple. And if you don't, I'll put you into the barn and not let you out for two days." I gritted my teeth and stared at Candy firmly, not backing down one inch.

I got on her and yelled, "Giddy up!" and kicked her side lightly with my heels. Candy didn't move, and stood there as if I didn't exist. I kicked her lightly again and mouthed, "Kic, kic." Candy bent down and started grazing. I got off her, put my hands on my hips and said, "Fine. I'm through with you." And I walked away.

The next pony I tried to control was named Starbucks and did his name ever fit him well. He was a cute brown pony, with more energy than someone who just had a double shot of black coffee. I took him into the yard, looked him squarely in the eyes and said, "You're going to listen to everything I tell you. Do you understand?"

Starbucks looked at me, snorted and turned away. I started walking him around the yard, and he pulled back and resisted. I pulled his reins hard, and he bucked and snorted again. After a few days of training, I was confident that he was finally broken of his bad habits and was ready to ride.

With Dad watching, I mounted Starbucks and rode toward the hill near the end of our property. Starbucks had one of his hyper-tantrums on the way and started bucking. I yelled, "Whoa!" and pulled on his reins. He had a burst of energy and bucked me off the back of him. I landed right on my bottom and then fell into a puddle, hurting my wrist. I stood up and spit out a mouthful of dirty water as Starbucks trotted away, stopping at the top of the hill. I glanced over at him, and I swear he had a grin on his face as he grazed, daring me to try again.

Dad came running up to me and asked, "Are you all right?"

"I think so," I said, and started wiping the mud off my face.

Dad held back his laughter and tried to say in a serious tone, "If you fall off a horse, the best thing to do is get right back on him."

I got back on Starbucks, and he bucked me off again. I stood up, threw my gloves on the ground and started to cry. I sniffled, "I'm done with ponies. Maybe I'm not made to run this farm. I've tried everything to control these ponies and nothing works." I kicked the ground and turned away.

Dad laughed, "That's your problem. Ponies are animals and have feelings. You need to train them and get them to trust you. You never can control a pony or any other animal!"

My eyes opened wide, as if a light had gone off in my head. *You can't control a pony,* I thought. *No wonder it's been so hard for me.*

Dad spent the next year teaching me how to gain the trust of animals. When I grew up, I took over the farm and became a top-notch breeder. I learned a very important lesson that year that I never forgot: animals are like people and you can't control them. You have to gain their trust and treat them with respect, and they'll be your friends forever.

Leave Well Enough Alone

Amber Rowland

5th Grade, Grandview Elementary, Livonia, Michigan

The annoying sound of my alarm clock in the morning was one of the most dreaded sounds I had ever heard. Another day of school meant another day of struggles in math. History was actually my favorite subject; I could never get enough. I was in sixth grade and eleven years old, and I knew more about history than any other student in the entire school.

I lay in bed, trying to squeeze in a few more seconds before I had to hit the snooze button again. My eyes popped open. I jolted out of bed and thought, *Today we're going to the museum on a field trip. I can't wait.* I rushed to get ready and went downstairs.

As I was leaving for the bus stop, Mom said, "Alex, there's ten dollars on the counter for you to spend at the museum today. Don't forget to grab it when you get your lunch out of the fridge."

"Thanks," I said.

"Don't wander off and stick together with you friends. I mean it! I know how you can be when you're at a place like that."

"Mom," I groaned. "You never give me credit for anything."

Once at school, I was so excited I could hardly stand still, as we waited to get on the bus to go to the museum. My friend Ryan stood next to me and said, "I'm glad today is Friday and we have this field trip."

"Me too," I said. 'I can't wait to get there. You know how much I love museums." The bus door flung open, and we all started getting on.

When we got to the museum, my eyes almost popped out of my head as soon as we walked in the door. There was an old airplane hanging from the ceiling, and a huge train from the Old West right in the middle of the room. "Wow!" I said. "I can't believe I've never been here."

"I can't believe it either," said Ryan.

My teacher, Mrs. O'Neil, said, "This place is huge, and you can get lost very easily. Since the entire sixth grade is here, I want you to pick a friend to stay with at all times. Stay with the group, and if you do get lost, find a museum employee. Remember, we have special permission to stay until the museum closes at five o'clock." I paired up with Ryan, who I knew would let me straggle behind if I found something interesting.

A woman in her late twenties, with long brown hair, walked to the front of our group. "My name is Samantha and I'll be your guide for the day. Stay together, and if you have any questions I'd be glad to answer them. Follow me, please."

The first room we went into had a replica of George Washington with an American flag in a small boat, with figures made out of wax. The tour guide asked, "Does anyone know what this exhibit depicts?"

I raised my hand and said, "Oh, oh, oh."

Samantha pointed to me and asked, "What's your name?"

"My name is Alex, and this exhibit shows George Washington crossing the Delaware. He and his men crossed on Christmas Day, 1776. Washington knew he was running out of supplies, so he had to act fast. The battle took place in Trenton, New Jersey."

"That's right," Samantha said. "You apparently know your history." I grinned and glanced at the exhibit once more before we left.

The second room we went into was a Civil War exhibit. There were wax soldiers set up to simulate a battle scene. Samantha asked, "Does anyone know what this battle depicts?"

I quickly raised my hand and Samantha said, "Yes, Alex."

Almost salivating, I said, "This scene is from the battle of Gettysburg. You can tell by the Pennsylvania flag. It occurred from July 1 to July 3 in 1863. It was the bloodiest battle of the war, with the most casualties."

"Right again," Samantha said.

As we went through the entire museum, I was almost in a daze. It was the most amazing place I had ever seen in my life. I was in the early American section, looking at wax figures of the Pilgrims' first landing in America, when I looked up and noticed my whole class was gone. Over the loudspeaker, I heard an announcement blast out: "The museum will be closing in five minutes."

I swallowed heavily and my palms started to sweat. I dashed out of the room, taking a wrong turn and ending up in the medieval section. There wasn't a person in there, so I panicked and started walking as fast as I could, not even paying attention to all the knights in armor on horses. When I got into the middle of the huge room, I abruptly stopped and spun completely around, looking for an exit sign. I took a deep breath, and let it all out when I saw an exit off in the distance. I took a step toward it and heard a slight clang on the floor.

I turned around and saw something small rolling toward me, approaching my feet. When it got to me, I bent down and picked it up. My face tightened in confusion as I looked at the item and realized it was a gold ring that looked like a cheap wedding band. Engraved on the outside of the band was the number 2 with the Roman numeral II next to it. I jumped back a full foot when I looked up and saw a man with long black hair standing there. He was wearing a purple costume with half-moons all over it, and he had a large grin on his face.

"Do you work here?" I asked.

He hesitated then said with an old-world accent, "Ah… yes, you could say that."

"Oh, I get it," I said. "You dress up for the people that come to the museum. Cool costume. It looks like it fits in perfectly with medieval times." He smiled and stood there silently.

"Do you know the way back to the front of the museum?" I asked. He pointed toward the exit sign. I asked him, "Did you drop this?"

The man said, "Yes."

I reached my hand out to hand him the ring. He shook his head and said, "If you keep it, you'll get two wishes."

"Come on, mister," I said. "You don't have to act anymore. The museum is about to close. Take it."

"It's yours," he replied.

"I don't have time to talk about it, so I will." I put the ring into my pocket and started to walk toward the exit sign.

"Don't forget. Two wishes."

I shook my head and mumbled, "Please, what do you think I am, stupid?" I walked rapidly out of the exhibit room, not looking back.

When I got into the hall, Ryan said, "I've been looking all over for you! We have to get back or we're going to be in big trouble." We hurried back to our group and barely made it as they were taking count. After we left, I didn't think about the ring again.

That evening, Dad went to the store before bedtime to get some milk for breakfast. When he came into the living room, he said, "The meanest man was in front of me in line. He practically told the cashier off. I can't stand it when people are like that."

"I can't either," I said. "I wish all people were never mean again." I felt lightheaded, and closed my eyes to clear my head. I opened my eyes again, felt dizzy and said, "I feel really weird. I think I'm going to go to bed." Dad nodded, and I went into my room and fell asleep.

The next morning, I slept in late because we didn't have school. I stayed in my room until shortly after noon. Mom came into my room and said, "I went online and checked your math grade and you have a D-. You haven't been studying."

Oh boy, I thought. *Here it comes.*

"I've decided not to punish you," Mom said. "That would be mean. Try harder next time." She walked out the door.

I stood there with my eyes glued to the door, thinking that this couldn't be happening, and that she was going to rush back in and ground me. When she didn't, I stood in a daze, almost in shock, still waiting. Confused, I walked into the living room.

Dad turned on the football game, which had already started. I heard the announcer say, "It's forty-nine to forty-nine in the first quarter."

What? I thought.

The announcer continued, "Neither team has made one tackle. That would be mean." I watched one of the teams kick off the ball. The receiving team caught the ball and ran right down the field without one player even trying to get in the runner's way. When he scored a touchdown, the other team went into the end zone and celebrated with the team that scored.

"What's going on?" I mumbled. Another score flashed on the screen: *64-64, first quarter.*

That ring, I thought. *I did wish no one would ever be mean. It can't be. It was just an innocent statement. I really didn't even mean to make a wish.* I shook my head and went into my bedroom. I reached into my pants pocket and pulled out the ring and stared at it. Instead of a number 2 on it, it now had a number 1. The Roman numeral II had changed to a I as well.

My vision blurred for a second, and I dropped the ring on the floor. *It can't be,* I thought. *If it is, though, that would be great. I'd never get in trouble again if I didn't want to do my homework, because Mom wouldn't want to be mean.*

I went into the den and turned on the news. The newscaster said, "The cockroach population this year will be out of hand. The exterminators are refusing to spray to kill them, because that would be mean. There has already been a report of one cockroach found in an omelet at a restaurant that the cook would not kill. We hope they don't get into all our foods. The mosquitoes and flies should be equally as bad."

Yuck, I thought. *I would hate to find bugs in my food.*

Mom came into the room and said, "Come on. Let's go to the store." We got into our car and started driving out of our subdivision. When we got on the main road, traffic was backed up, and we came to a complete stop.

After a few minutes, a policeman came to our window and said, "You might want to find another route. There has been an accident. A man didn't want to cut in front of a lady, so he drove off the road into a tree. Luckily, he's all right."

I was just about to say something mean like *can't you get the traffic cleared faster, because this is a pain,* when the words stopped right in my mouth. I tried again, and no mean words would come out.

The wish did come true, I thought. *I can't believe it. I have one more wish. I should wish to be rich or to be president or something. Hmm, I better choose wisely.*

A woman walked right in front of our car, and a tiger jumped in front of her and growled. I sat inside the car and started to shake. The police officer pulled his gun out and yelled to the woman, "Get down!" The police officer went to shoot his gun, and then dropped it on the ground. The woman slowly stepped backward, and the tiger lunged at her and clawed her. Then it ran off, and the woman fell to the ground, screaming in agony.

My eyes opened wide and I yelled, "No!"

Mom asked with a shaky voice, "Why was there a tiger loose, and why didn't you shoot it?"

The police officer said, "The zookeeper didn't want to lock the animal's cages anymore. They all were let loose in the city. As for shooting that tiger, I don't know what happened. I froze up and couldn't kill it." The police officer rushed to the woman that got clawed, who had now stood back up.

"Are you all right?" the police officer asked.

"I think I'll be all right, if I get to the hospital to get this bandaged up."

I gulped and thought, *What have I done?*

Mom said, "We'd better get home until this all gets straightened out." We drove home and went into the house. Dad was still watching the football game. I looked at the score and saw it was 497 to 497 in the third quarter.

I was getting ready to go into my room when I heard a large bang. We all ran to the front of the house and saw a car that had driven into the living room of our next-door neighbor's house. The driver got out and said, "Sorry, but there was a squirrel crossing the street and I didn't want to hit it. I have insurance."

Mrs. Fuller, our neighbor, was getting ready to tell the man off when she stopped and said, "That's all right. Be more careful next time."

I rushed back into the house and mumbled, "What have I done?"

The newscast came on the TV in the den, and we all ran in there. "All the animals at the local slaughterhouse were let go," the newscaster said. "The government is afraid there's going to be a food shortage if this keeps up."

I ran into my room and pulled the ring out of my pocket. I held it tightly, focused with all my mental strength and said, "I wish things were back to normal, the way they were before I made the first wish." The ring glowed and spun around once in my open hand. I felt dizzy again, stumbled backward, and almost fell down. I squinted in disbelief as I saw the number turn to 0 and the Roman numeral fade away right before my eyes. I gulped and said, "I hope it worked."

I walked into the living room and heard the football announcer say, "What a vicious hit. I bet he'll feel that one tomorrow."

My stomach settled, and I smiled and went into the den. The news was showing a police officer holding a rifle. He fired a tranquillizer dart, hitting a lion that had been on the loose. The lion fell to the ground and several people rushed at it, throwing a net over him. The newscaster said, "The authorities should have all the animals back in the zoo by late tomorrow afternoon."

I sighed and said under my breath, "Thank goodness everything is back to normal."

I took the ring and buried it behind my garage, six feet deep, where no one would ever find it. After I put the last shovelful of dirt back into the hole, I sat down to catch my breath. I said to myself, "I guess if something's not broken, don't try and fix it, or it might be worse than when you started. I now know to leave well enough alone."

Minnesota

Sandra Warne

5th Grade, Noblesville Intermediate School, Noblesville, Indiana

Summer was definitely my favorite time of the year, and my favorite part of summer was our annual trip to Minnesota to see my cousin Katie. Katie and I were better than best friends; we were relatives, and that old saying "blood is thicker than water" was true when it came to us. The fact that Katie and I were the same age was probably one of the reasons we got along so well.

My name is Nicole Sampson, and when I was thirteen years old, I had no idea that my trip to Minnesota in the summer of 1993 was going to be the most crazy, unbelievable thing that ever happened to me in my entire life. I don't expect anyone to believe my story, because I don't even know if I can believe it myself.

It was so beautiful where Katie lived in northern Minnesota. Her property was out in the middle of nowhere, with huge trees, and not another house for an eighth of a mile. Through the back of her land flowed a beautiful river, where her father fished and we threw stones all the time. Usually the only bad part of the entire trip was the ten-hour drive from Indiana to her front door. Eight hours into the drive, I turned to my sister Elizabeth, who was three years younger than I, and said, "I'm so bored. I wish we were there."

Mom said, "We'll be there in two hours. Just relax."

"I have to go to the bathroom," said Elizabeth.

"We're really in the middle of nowhere," Mom said. We looked out the window and saw the same sign we saw every year: *Souvenirs and gift shop, Chippewa Indian Reservation, next exit, three miles.* Mom looked at Dad and said, "Every year we pass by that reservation and never stop. Elizabeth has to use the bathroom, so I think it would be a good idea this year."

Dad growled, "It's probably a tourist trap."

"Dear, we have to stop," Mom pleaded. "Besides, it wouldn't hurt if the girls learned a little more about the heritage of our nation."

"All right," Dad said. "We'll pull off at that exit."

When we got to the exit, we pulled off the highway onto a small two-lane road and saw another sign, *Indian Reservation three miles*, with an arrow pointing the way we were going. Dad drove three miles and asked, "All right, where is it?" We looked out the window and saw another sign, *Indian Reservation two miles,* and an arrow pointing to a dirt road. Dad sighed and complained, "These tourist traps always do this. They say it's three miles, and it ends up being thirteen."

"Turn and stop complaining," Mom rebuked.

Dad turned and asked, "Do you want to drive, then?" Mom shook her head, and we kept driving. After two more miles we saw another sign, *Indian Reservation two miles*, with an arrow pointing toward a smaller one-lane road that looked more like a path. Dad turned his lower lip up, gave Mom a dirty look, and didn't say a word. He turned down the dirt path, and two miles later we were there.

When I got out of the car, I looked around and couldn't believe my eyes. There were cabins that looked like small houses on one side of the reservation, and tepees on the other. There were several horses tied up to posts, just like in the Old West. A small store made entirely of logs, which looked like it was from the 1800s, was conveniently placed in the front of the reservation. Tables were set up outside that spanned the entire wooden porch, with women sitting out dressed like old-time American Indians. After we all used the bathroom, we went toward the store, and Mom said, "This would be a great place to get a souvenir." Dad's eyebrows lifted, but he didn't say a word.

We all went into the store and looked around for a while, until Elizabeth found a necklace she thought about buying. She decided against it, and we all went outside. Dad said, "I'll be in the car. I want to look at a map and see where in the world we are." After Dad left, we looked at the turquoise jewelry they had sitting out on the tables until Elizabeth said, "I've decided I do want that necklace."

"Let's go back in," Mom said.

"I'm going to stay out here," I said, and continued to look around. I didn't see anything that interested me until I got to the very last table at the end of the porch. I glanced around the corner and saw an old man sitting in a rocking chair, rocking back and forth; he looked small and frail, as if he were ninety years old. His skin was wrinkled and chapped, but he appeared content and serene. He was dressed in an old leather shirt, a pair of cloth pants and moccasins. His silver-gray hair reminded me of an old coin. He had a headband on with a few feathers sticking out the back. There was a table in front of him with nothing on it. Being a sucker for old people because they were so kind and helpless, I went up to his table and said, "Hi. What's your name?"

"My name Running Wolf," he said weakly but confidently, "yours?"

"My name is Nicole Sampson," I responded. He came to a dead stop in his rocking chair; his eyes widened and lit up. He took a deep breath as if to speak, but no words came out.

"You don't have anything for sale?" I asked.

He reached behind his chair and set a small, old leather bag on the table. It had a thin leather strap like a shoestring from a moccasin holding the top together. "Magic stones," he said in a deep voice.

I gazed into his eyes and felt weak in my stomach. I saw a man who had lived a long hard life, for whom I had true compassion. I smiled, trying to appease him and asked, "How much?"

"Ten dollars," he said.

"For rocks?" I complained.

"Not rocks," he said quickly, "magic stones."

I picked up the bag, opened it, and pulled out one of the two stones that were inside. The pebble was no larger than a pea and was brown with slightly darker brown speckles on it. After moving it around in my hand and looking more closely, I frowned and said, "It looks like an ordinary rock." Shaking my head, I pulled out the other pebble, and that one looked the same. I put the pebbles back into the bag, set it on the table and asked, "Ten dollars for those rocks?"

"Not rocks," he said, "magic stones."

I smiled and my heart melted at his persistence. "How old are you?" I asked.

"One hundred eight years old," he said.

Filled with pity, I pulled a ten-dollar bill from my pocket and set it on the table. I picked up the leather bag, put it into my pocket and said, "Thank you."

He took the ten-dollar bill and put it into his pants pocket. He said, "*Awa cawapa*," just as an old woman came up.

She asked, "Grandpa, you weren't bothering this young lady, were you?"

That's her grandfather? I thought. *He looks almost the same age as her.*

The woman asked, "Why did you say '*Awa cawapa*, be careful' to her? I heard you right before I came up." She turned to me and asked, "He wasn't bothering you, was he?"

I shook my head and said, "Goodbye." When I was walking away I thought, *What a nice old man, a hundred and eight, wow!*

When we got back into the car, Mom asked, "Did you buy anything?"

In fear that Dad would say I was crazy for spending ten dollars on two rocks, I said, "No," and didn't think another thing about them.

When we got to Katie's house, she jumped on me right when I got out of the car. With Katie and me together, it was going to be the best part of the summer, or so I thought. After we got settled in, Katie said, "I didn't tell you. Remember that old tree in the back yard that my dad didn't cut down when we built our house, because he said it was so old?" I nodded. "He built a tree house for us out there."

"Awesome," I said. "Can we go see it?"

"Yeah," Katie said. "Let's hurry, before Elizabeth and my brother Zach want to come too."

We rushed out to the tree house, and when we got inside my mouth hung open. It was like a mini-house in there, with a TV and everything. It had wall-to-wall carpeting and even a window you could look out of.

"This is incredible!" I said. "You're so lucky."

I told Katie about our stop at the Indian reservation and about Running Wolf. When I told her about the stones, she laughed. "Let me see these so-called magic stones." I pulled one of the pebbles out of the bag and held it. She said, "It looks more like a tiny rock than a magic stone. You got taken."

I put the bag back into my pocket and said, "I know. I felt sorry for the guy, though. Indians are so cool. I wish we could go back in time and see how they lived."

I blinked as the rock started glowing in my hand. Everything started spinning, and I felt dizzy and unable to move. I looked at Katie; her body was disintegrating into particles right before my eyes.

I felt as if I didn't exist for a moment, then saw Katie and myself rematerialize and come back to life at the same time. We fell lightly onto the ground right on our behinds. I shook the cobwebs out of my head and looked at my hand. "Hey, the stone is gone," I said. I froze and sat motionless as my eyes focused on the tree we had been in and noticed it was only eight feet tall. When I turned back toward Katie, her face was blank. "What happened?" I asked.

"I d-d-d-don't know," she stuttered.

A loud Indian cry blasted out from behind us, "Ow wa wow a wow wa wa wow!" We turned to see three braves, riding at full speed right toward us. My heart felt like it would explode as two of them jumped off their horses in full stride and lunged at us. We both stood up and one of them grabbed me around my neck, holding a knife under my throat, while the other one grabbed Katie.

I trembled in fear, until they put their knives away and grabbed me by my hair. We kicked and screamed as two of them bound our hands with rope and tied us so we couldn't get away. They threw us on the backs of their horses, and as we were riding, Katie said, "Those stones must have been magic after all."

The brave that had Katie on his horse yelled out, "*Awak*," which we thought meant "quiet." We rode bareback for less than a mile, until we came to the Indians' settlement. The settlement was like something from a history book, with fifty-eight teepees and a larger hut. As the two braves pulled us off their horses, the other brave that was with us ran to the large hut.

He went inside, and came out shortly after with an Indian who was wearing a full chief's headdress. Luckily for us, the Indians had at least picked up some of the English language. The chief approached us, saying, "Who paleface squaws?"

The brave who had brought me yanked on my hair to jerk my face up so I had to look straight at the chief. He said, "Found palefaces in woods, must be spy, look at clothes."

The chief said, "Who are you? Why you wear spy clothes?"

Scared and still shaking, I said, "My name is Nicole Sampson and my friend's name is Katie Nelson."

"I Chief Burning Cloud, chief of Chippewas. You trespass on our land."

"No," Katie disagreed. "This is our land."

Oh no! I thought, *Wrong thing to say.*

Chief Burning Cloud's eyes burned with anger when he said, "No! Chippewas' land! You spy!"

"We are not spies," I pleaded.

A small boy who looked about four years old ran up to the chief. He tugged on his pants leg and asked, "Paleface friends, father?"

"No, Running Wolf, paleface enemy of Chippewa."

My eyes almost popped out of my head, and my heart felt like it skipped a beat. I looked at the little boy and saw the exact same eyes I had seen on the reservation earlier that day, but a hundred and four years younger. My mind added all the pieces together and I mumbled under my breath, "We went back in time a hundred and four years. The rocks were magic."

An Indian who must have been second in command rushed up and said, "Receive message. Three full moons from now when air is cold, Lakota-Sioux meet at Wounded Knee, fight paleface. Ask for help."

Chief Burning cloud said, "Angry Bear, tell Sioux we meet at Wounded Knee to help kill paleface."

"No!" I said. "We just studied that battle in American history. It was a total massacre. Your tribe will be killed."

Katie's face turned white as Angry Bear pulled a knife from his belt, grabbed me by the hair and said, "I kill paleface squaw now, wear her scalp."

"No," Burning Cloud said. "They die sunset tomorrow."

"Owhh, owhh, owhh, owhh!" the entire tribe howled. It got so loud I couldn't hear myself think. Running Wolf came to me and tugged on my pants leg. I looked down and felt slightly eased, seeing the same compassion I had felt for him earlier that day, but now in his small, bright-lit eyes. Angry Bear grabbed a rope and pushed Running Wolf lightly aside. He started tying me up, while another Indian tied up Katie.

As the rope was going around me, I yelled, "You can't go to Wounded Knee, Chief Burning Cloud! Your people will die. Please listen." Angry Bear stuffed a piece of cloth in my mouth, and they finished tying us up. They tied us to a post in the middle of the settlement and left us unguarded, figuring there was no way we could get away.

After they left, Katie and I worked the cloths out of our mouths and I said, "We're back in 1890. I remember reading about how terrible the battle at Wounded Knee was. The Cavalry shot and killed almost every Indian there. We must stop them from going there, or their people will be lost forever."

"I'm more worried about us getting out of here," Katie said. "You heard them, we die tomorrow at sunset."

"The chief's son is the man who sold me the rocks on the reservation a hundred and four years from now," I said. "I don't know what's going on. This can't be happening."

A tear rolled down Katie's cheek as she said, "I'm scared!"

"I am too." I thought for a few seconds and said, "I remember when we learned about the Chippewa; they are a very spiritual tribe. If somehow we could make them think they're getting a sign from above, they might not go to Wounded Knee and might let us go."

Katie and I spent the night outside tied to the pole, with no hope of escape.

The next morning, Chief Burning Cloud called his tribe together and brought us in front of them. He said, "I had dream from Great One from above last night. Dream told of how we not go to Wounded Knee. Paleface squaw right. Peace, not war for Chippewas. Untie palefaces, let go free."

A brave came up behind us and started cutting our ropes when Angry Bear spouted, "Paleface enemy of Chippewa." My hands went free and I reached into my pocket for the bag with the other stone in it. I opened the bag and hastily pulled out the pebble. The leather bag fell to the ground a few feet away. I looked down and saw Running Wolf come up and grab the bag. He stepped away just as Angry Bear said, "I kill paleface squaws and save Chippewa."

I opened my hand with the stone in it and said, "I wish Katie and I were back in our own time, in her tree house."

The stone started to glow as Angry Bear said, "Palefaces must die." Our bodies started to disintegrate while Angry Bear reached for his knife. He threw his knife at us, right as we disappeared. A few moments later, we were back in the tree house, standing there face to face.

I gulped and asked, "Was that real?"

"Yes, it was real," said Katie. "Look on the floor." I looked down and my whole body tingled. I bent over and picked up Angry Bear's knife that had come through when we came back. Katie and I stood looking at each other, speechless.

Finally, I said, "I saw Running Wolf with the leather bag in his hand before we left. Do you think somehow it could've been the same bag he gave me?"

"It must've been," Katie said. "When you drive back through there, talk your Dad into stopping so you can ask Running Wolf."

"I will," I said. We spent the next two weeks together as we normally would, except that we learned as much as we could about the Chippewa and shared it with one another.

Two weeks later, on the way home, we stopped back at the reservation. I went to the spot where I had first seen Running Wolf. His chair was there, but it was empty. His granddaughter was sitting at the table next to the chair. "Is Running Wolf here?" I asked.

"No," she said. "He died two weeks ago."

My stomach tightened and I felt breathless. "What day did he die?" I asked.

"Monday, the seventh of August."

I put both my hands to the side of my head and gasped. "What time did he die?"

"Around six o'clock at night," she responded.

I stumbled backward, almost falling down. *That's the same day and time Katie and I came back from 1890.* I thought. *I can't believe it.*

His granddaughter asked, "Are you all right?"

"I'm fine," I said, and walked away confused.

All the way home, I couldn't figure out how and why our trip back to 1890 happened. I kept thinking it was to save Running Wolf's tribe from extinction, but I wasn't really sure. Katie and I never told anyone about our trip back, because no one would have ever believed us. I learned as much as I could about the heritage and history of the American Indian. When we grew up, both Katie and I became lawyers and fought as hard as we could for Indian rights. And to this day, I can't explain how or why our trip back to 1890 happened, but I'm glad it did, because it changed my life forever.

Sixth Grade Students

The Enchanter

Peyton Bell

6th Grade, Rockwood South Middle School, Fenton, Missouri

With summer quickly approaching and the end of seventh grade awaiting me, I began to feel excited. I was a pretty good student of average height, with shoulder-length, light red hair, freckles, and blue-gray eyes. I finished breakfast and rushed out the door as I said to Mom, "I'll see you after school."

Mom said, "I love you, and have a great day."

I walked across my front lawn toward the bus stop and heard off in the distance, "Sarah dear, can you come here?"

I looked behind me, and my shoulders drooped like a plucked flower; it was my nosy widowed neighbor, Mrs. Jameson. I always tried to avoid her never-ending questions at all costs. She was a short old woman with gray hair, who was slightly hunched over when she walked.

Again she said, "Oh, Sarah dear, when I saw these earrings I couldn't resist them and thought they'd be perfect for you." She smiled strangely and put her hand out to give them to me. I sighed as guilt filled my body. My face weakened when I saw her waiting for me to respond.

Compelled by compassion, I took the box and said, "Thank you."

She said, "Try one on."

I looked at the red velvet box and noticed that it looked old and tattered. I blinked heavily, feeling a little lightheaded, and was getting ready to open the box when I heard in the background, "Come on, Sarah. We're going to be late for school." I looked over my shoulder and saw my friend Ted standing there with his hands on his hips, tapping his foot on the ground.

I turned back toward Mrs. Jameson and said, "I have to go now." I shoved the box into my coat pocket and said as I hurried away, "Thanks again."

Mrs. Jameson mumbled, "Wait, dear. Try one on." I purposely didn't pay attention to her and kept walking.

■ ■ ■

That afternoon, I met Ted at a downtown park near our house. The park was usually busy, but that day it wasn't. Ted and I sat down on a bench and talked for a minute, until I reached into my pocket and felt the box with the earrings in it. I pulled out the box and said, "I had forgotten about these. Mrs. Jameson gave them to me this morning."

"That old kook," said Ted. "She's weird. Go ahead and open the box, though."

My eyes lit up as I opened the box and saw that the earrings looked quite expensive. They were gold-colored and oval-shaped, with a glistening crystal hanging at the bottom. As I continued to stare at the earrings, I became dizzy and felt mesmerized.

"Wow," Ted said. "Those look like they cost a fortune. There's some writing on the inside of the box. What does it say?"

I snapped out of my trancelike state and looked at the exquisite gold lettering. It read, "If found, return to Brad Albert Dare."

"Don't pay attention to what's written on the box," a voice said calmly from behind us. We both whirled around to come face to face with a young woman who looked like a model. She was about twenty-five years old, had long blonde hair, and was tall and fit. Every feature she had was almost perfect, as if she were trying out for the Miss America Pageant.

Ted gulped at her beauty as I nervously questioned her. "Who are you, and what do you want?"

"My name is Elise, and I'm here to warn you about BAD," she replied.

"Who's BAD?" I questioned.

"B-A-D is Brad Albert Dare and his name is written on the box," Elise said. "He's an Enchanter."

Ted flung his head sideways and asked, "An Enchanter?"

"Yes, an Enchanter," Elise repeated. "He uses certain items, like those earrings, to control people and make them do his wicked deeds. If you return those earrings to him, you'll never be able to resist him, and he'll have power over you for the rest of your life. But if you put those earrings on, he'll never be able to control you and he'll move on to the next person. I'm telling you this because BAD has chosen you, Sarah."

I grinned and then laughed. "Oh, come on. Do you expect me to believe that?"

Elise peered into my eyes and my mind went blank. "Take the earrings in your hand, Sarah," she said.

My mind and body felt as if I was in a deep sleep, but I could see and was wide awake. I held both the earrings tightly in my hands, looked at them closely, and went into a deeper trance. All I could hear and see was Elise saying, "Put the earrings on and BAD will never be able to control you."

I nodded obediently and reached my hand toward my ear, when my hypnotic state was broken by Ted saying, "Wait! If this ridiculous story is true, then why can't you take the earrings and destroy them?"

"The Enchanter's powers are great and I can't destroy them," Elise said. "I'm only allowed a few more seconds with you, so put the earrings on; hurry, save yourself!"

I started to breathe heavily and moved my hand closer toward my ear, as Elise smiled. My hypnotic state was again broken by Ted saying, "Wait!" We both turned back toward Elise and she was gone.

Ted asked, "What happened to her?" I shook my head as if I was in a daze. "I don't know if Elise was telling the truth or not, but something definitely weird happened to you when she told you to put those earrings on," he said.

"What are you talking about?" I asked. "I feel great."

"You better give those earrings to me," Ted said.

I put the earrings back into the box and shoved them into my pocket. "No, I won't. These are mine and you're not taking them." I felt a little queasy as I got up and began to walk away. Ted followed me.

A short man with dark hair approached us. He was wearing a dress shirt that was stained dark with dirt, and pants that looked like they were from a hundred years ago. His skin was soiled and grimy, almost as if he were homeless. He said with a British accent, "My name is Brad Albert Dare, and you have something of mine."

"I know who you are," I said. "There's no way I'm giving you these earrings so you'll be able to control me the rest of my life."

BAD laughed and said, "I see the Deceiver has already visited you."

"Deceiver?" I asked. "What deceiver?"

"Elise is a Deceiver who works for the Enchanter," BAD said. "She tries to convince people to do something that will put them under the Enchanter's spell. I think you have a pair of earrings that have almost sealed your destiny. Please give them to me now!"

"No," I said. "Elise was pretty and nice. She would never hurt me. I don't believe you." I started to put on the earrings again.

BAD shouted, "No! If you put those on, you'll be doomed until the spell can be broken."

"Why should I believe you?" I asked. "Elise was beautiful and kind. You look like you haven't even had a bath in a year."

"Because I'm telling the truth," BAD said, and then he looked deep into my eyes. My eyes focused into his, as if we were one. I felt clearheaded, dropped my shoulders and felt my body relax as if nothing in the world mattered. "Besides," he added, "you can't always judge a book by its cover."

Ted quickly grabbed the earrings and said, "Here, I'll give them to you."

"It doesn't work like that," BAD said. "Sarah has to make a choice of whom to believe. If you give me the earrings, the spell will not be broken."

Ted gave the earrings back to me and BAD said, "Like Elise, I have but a short time with you. You must make a decision now." He reached out his hand.

A thought of my mother popped into my head, and I handed him the earrings. BAD grabbed them firmly, danced around and laughed loudly. "Finally, after all this time, they're mine. They're really mine!"

I winced and thought, *I just made the worst decision of my life. I'm going to be under the power of an evil Enchanter forever.* I stood there shaking, waiting for my horrible fate.

BAD dropped the earrings on the ground and held the heel of his boot over them. He pressed down on the earrings and an ungodly sound like ten cats wailing in pain filled the air. I felt a sudden pain in my head like a brain freeze from a Slurpee, so I tightly covered my ears. BAD rubbed his heel on the ground several times, crushing the earrings beneath his foot while he said, "By the power given to me, I deem all the Enchanter's earrings powerless."

BAD removed his foot and the sound stopped. I uncovered my ears, then looked down where the earrings had been, and nothing remained but a pile of dust. An evil hiss rang out, and a shadow that resembled a person formed and elevated to eye level. Ted and I stepped backward and I began to tremble. The hiss suddenly stopped, and the shadow rose, then disappeared into thin air.

BAD said, "You did it, Sarah. You're a hero. You were the first person in the last hundred years to break the Enchanter's spell. All the people over the last century who are still alive that were enticed and controlled by any of his earrings are now free, including your neighbor Mrs. Jameson. Elise was a Deceiver and I'm a Retriever. I go around trying to retrieve items the Enchanter uses to control people. The items must be given to me by the free will of the person who receives them, or the spell can't be broken. The earrings' power and the Enchanter's power grow every time he captivates a victim. His evil earrings had become so powerful that I thought I'd never break the spell. And if you had put them on, your life would've been miserable. "

I looked at Ted and said, "You saved me."

BAD said, "Regardless of whether Ted helped you, you had the strength and the faith to resist the earrings' power. I must leave now; thank you, and goodbye." BAD walked away and disappeared in the distance.

I took a deep breath and said, "I thought I was a goner after I gave the earrings to him and heard that evil sound. How did you know not to trust Elise?"

"I learned a few years ago from my dad that when something looks or seems perfect, it probably isn't as good as you think," said Ted. "And when something seems awful, it probably isn't as terrible as you think, either. Elise was too pretty and perfect to be true. Besides, I could see it in her eyes. How did you know to give the earrings back to BAD?"

"Mom always says that you can't judge a book by its cover. When BAD said that, a thought of her popped into my head, and I knew he was the honest one."

We both smiled and took a deep breath.

Ted said, "You know, no one will ever believe what happened."

"I know. I'm just glad it's over."

"Me too," Ted agreed.

A month later, at my birthday party, Mom gave me an expensive necklace as a gift. I turned, looked at Ted and gasped. I turned back toward Mom and said, "It's beautiful, but I'm not really into jewelry right now. Can you take it back?"

Mom's head jerked backward and she looked at me peculiarly. "Sure," she said. "We can get you something you like better."

Ted and I both learned a very important lesson from the earrings: things aren't always the way they seem.

One Wish Gone Bad

Armana Haque

6th Grade, Boyd Elementary School, Allen, Texas

"Carl!" Mom shouted. "You get in here right now!"

Oh no, I thought. *What did I do now?*

I reluctantly stomped into the room with my shoulders pinned back, ready to get scolded. Mom started on me again. "I just received your report card, mister. It's terrible! You're never going to pass eighth grade if you don't get those grades up. Do you want to go to summer school again for the third year in a row? You have two more card markings to improve, and I expect those grades to go way up. I have no choice but to ground you. That means no basketball camp over your break."

"No, Mom," I said. "Not that! You know basketball is my favorite thing in the whole world, please!"

Mom's face filled with pity and her tone weakened. "I know you love basketball, but I have no choice. If you put a stronger effort into school, than maybe you could go to a camp over the summer."

"You're so unfair!" I shouted and walked out the door.

Mom said in the distance, "Remember, you're grounded. Don't step one foot off the property." I gritted my teeth and nodded.

I walked to the back of our property, about a hundred yards away from our house. I sat down on a rock and stared into the creek, fuming. My anger and frustration boiled inside me when I picked up a rock and threw it into the water. I watched the water as the ripples evened out and the rock sank to the bottom. Something shining in the creek caught my eye and I went toward it. I reached my hand into the water and pulled out a golden rock about the size of a golf ball. I thought, *Oh my gosh! It's beautiful! It can't be real. If it was, though, I'd be rich.*

I stared at it in a daze. *If I was a millionaire, I could move away and never go to school again. That would show Mom. She'd be so sad that she'd cry every day because I was gone. Then she'd be sorry she was ever mean to me. No rules! What a life that would be.*

I turned the rock over and written on the back with what looked like magic marker was: "Wish rock. Throw back and make a wish." My blood pumped faster and my body was jolted with excitement. I thought, *It can't be real. But if it is, I'll teach Mom a lesson.*

I squeezed the rock tightly in my hand and said, "I wish I lived in a world without parents." I threw the rock into the creek close to the shore, where I could still see it, and thought, *Yeah, right. Like that's possible.* I walked back to my house without truly believing my wish would come true.

When I walked in, Mom was gone. There was no note or anything. I thought, *She probably went out or something.*

I walked over to my best friend's, two houses away, and knocked on the door. When Brent answered, I asked, "Are your parents home?"

He said, "No. I don't know where they went."

I smiled and said, "I better get back home, and don't tell my Mom I was here, because I'm grounded." When I got home I thought, *That wish couldn't have come true.* I called my friend Colin. "Are your parents home?"

He said, "No. My dad was out in the garage, but he must have left or something. No one is home but me."

I hung up, thinking, *I'll bet that rock was real! My wish did come true!* I grabbed a box of cereal out of the cupboard. *I can do whatever I want. No more rules, no more people telling me what to do. Finally, I can live the way I want to.* I poured the box of cereal on the table. *Why do I need a bowl? I hate doing dishes anyway. I don't ever have to clean up again.* I laughed.

The cereal tasted a little stale, so I went into the living room. I sat down and watched TV for a little while and called, "Mom, do you know what time the skateboarding contest is on today?" When she didn't answer, I thought, *Oh yeah. She's gone.* A little bored, I walked into my bedroom, played a video game and beat my high score. Excitedly, I walked out of my room to go tell Mom about the good news, and then remembered I had no one to tell.

So what, I thought. *I have no rules now. Life is going to be great.* I went into the kitchen and saw the cereal on the table and smiled. I opened the refrigerator door and saw a pack of uncooked chicken in there. *We're having bar-*

*becue chicken for dinner, my favorite! Oh wait. I can't ever have Mom's chicken
again. That's all right, though. I'll try and make it myself.*

I went into the yard and dribbled my basketball around and thought, *I
have a game tomorrow, sweet.* But then I thought differently. *I don't have a
game because I don't have anyone to take me. Besides, all the referees are parents
from the school. Without parents, I can never play a game again.*

I went inside and was bored for the next hour. My stomach turned sour
and I shook a little, thinking about never playing basketball again. I said,
"What've I done? Without Mom I can't do anything. I love her and miss her
already. What's it going to be like for the rest of my life?" I shook my head
and ran out the door to the creek, where I had originally found the rock.
After looking around for a few seconds, I began to panic and jumped into
the knee-deep water. "No!" I yelled. "I have to find that rock!"

My heart pounded as I looked around for almost a minute. Finally I saw
the rock, glimmering just below the waterline, and reached for it. The rock
started to move downstream, so I reached for it forcefully and mumbled,
"Oh, no you don't. I'm setting things straight."

I grasped the rock, pulled it out of the water, stood up and said, "I wish
things were back to normal, the way they were before I made my first wish."
I took a deep breath and threw the rock into the middle of the creek. It
bounced on top of the water and then fell to the bottom out of my sight. I
thought, *I hope things really are back to normal, because I couldn't find that rock
again even if I wanted to.*

I ran back to my house and through the back door. Mom was standing
there with her hands on her hips. I saw that there were two bags of groceries
on the counter. She turned red and asked, "How could you make such a
mess? You're going to pay for this little tantrum of yours. Dumping cereal on
the table is something a two-year-old would do. I can see that grounding you
isn't working. No video games or TV for a month." Mom stood firmly, waiting for the fight to take place.

I walked over to her, hugged her as hard as I could and said, "I'm glad
you're back."

Startled, she flinched and said, "What...? I was just at the grocery store."

I said, "I love you, and I don't know what I'd do without you."

Mom stood speechless, then finally said, "If you think you're getting out
of cleaning this up, you got another thing coming to you. It took longer at
the grocery store than I expected, and I'm behind with all I have to do."

A tear formed in my eye and I said, "I'm sorry for how mean I've been to you. I love you, and I promise I'll try as hard as I can in school. I know you're a good mom. It's been so hard since Dad left."

Mom sighed and sat down. "It's been hard on both of us. You have to understand that I do the best I can. School is very important in life. I know how smart you are, but you don't try anymore. If I let you fail, then your chances of having a good life are slim. Please understand that I don't like punishing you, but I have no choice."

"I love you and I will never take you for granted again," I said. "I will help you with everything I can."

Mom smiled and said, "I love you, Carl."

"I love you too," I said. "Let me help you carry in the groceries, and then I'll clean up that stupid mess I made." She smiled, and we went outside.

I kept my promise and helped her all I could after that. I worked as hard as I could, and didn't have to go to summer school. Our fights completely stopped, which made both Mom and me happy.

I never really knew if my wish came true that day or if she was really at the store. I learned two things about my wish going bad: be careful of what you wish for because it might come true, and don't ever take the simple things in life for granted.

The Gnome Planet

Nathan Jeffrey

6th Grade, Boyd Elementary School, Allen, Texas

Being in sixth grade and not being one of the popular kids was not easy. For people like me, having one good friend was all that could be expected out of life. Day after day, it hurt to see all the other kids picked first for everything, from sports to school projects. And without Tom, my best friend, I don't think I could have gone on.

It all started one Saturday morning when Tom knocked on my door. When I went outside, Tom greeted me and said, "Tomorrow is Halloween and I can't wait."

"Me either," I agreed.

"I'm going out trick-or-treating as an evil sorcerer," said Tom.

"I thought you were going out as a vampire."

"That was yesterday," Tom answered. "I'm going to have the best costume in the state." I shook my head and sighed. Tom continued, "Let's go over to the Cranston place today. Since it's going to be Halloween tomorrow, maybe we can see a ghost or something."

"No way!" I said. "I've heard too many stories about that place. They say a lot of people that lived there disappeared."

"Oh come on," Tom said. "You never want to do anything fun. You aren't scared, are you?"

"No, I'm not scared," I said. "It's just I have to get my costume ready. I'm going out as a cowboy and I need to make sure everything is right."

"You never go out as anything scary," Tom said. "You need to stop worrying so much about everything and try different things once in a while."

'I do try new things!" I exclaimed. "I tried Brussels sprouts yesterday, and I didn't like them."

"I'm going over to the Cranston place right now, with or without you," Tom said.

I took a deep breath and thought, *I'm not going over there, no way. He is my only friend, though, and I don't want to lose him. Besides, I don't want to spend the day alone and bored out of my wits again.* I swallowed hard and said, "I guess it wouldn't hurt to walk by the place, but only during the day."

"Let's go now," Tom insisted. I felt a lump in my throat as I nodded and got my coat.

When we got there, I looked at the place and froze with fear for an instant. Every time I had gone by the Cranston place before, I kept my head down and my eyes focused on anything but the house, as if the place didn't even exist. It was an old decrepit house, with faded paint and rotting wood everywhere. The shutters looked like they were hanging by a thread, and the roof looked as if it were going to collapse at any time. The dilapidated porch and overgrown yard made it look as though no one had lived there in fifty years. A sign in the yard said "No Trespassing" in large red letters.

Tom picked up a rock and threw it. I heard it clang against the house, and jumped back a step. "You shouldn't have done that," I protested.

"Please," Tom said. "The police would probably be happy if they found out I did it. Look at this place. It's awful."

I nearly jumped out of my skin when a hand grabbed each of us firmly on our shoulders from behind. A weak voice asked, "What are you kids doing here? You must leave right away."

We both jerked our heads around, our fists clenched. Standing there with his fists gripped on our shirts was an old man who must have been seventy-five years old. He was about five feet seven inches tall, with gray hair and a weird look in his eyes, as if he were determined to hurt us.

He asked again, "What are you kids doing here?"

I whined, "Nothing, mister. Please don't hurt us! We haven't done anything wrong."

Tom stood bravely and said, "Let us go! My dad is a very important man, and if you hurt us he'll see to it that you're put in prison."

The man laughed. "Prison! After what I've seen in my life, prison would be a blessing. Do you know why I'm here?" We both shook our heads. "My name is Jack Cranston and I used to live here." My stomach did a flip-flop and I shook as he continued. "I spent the last thirty years in an insane asylum, all because of this house. Every thirty years, precisely at six o'clock in the evening, a portal opens up in the house that transports whoever goes through it to another planet. It happens on the day before Halloween — Devil's Night.

"All those stories you've heard about this place and people disappearing are true. I lost my wife and children thirty years ago tonight. I'm going to stand out here to make sure no one goes into that house. I told them everything they wanted to hear at the asylum so they would believe I was cured and let me out. This house is evil, and I won't let it take anyone else. "

I almost bit my tongue with worry, when Tom started to say something. "Mister..."

A police car suddenly pulled up, slammed on its brakes, and two officers hopped out. Mr. Cranston let go of us as one of the officers said, "You were told not to come here today. We figured you would, though." The officer grabbed Mr. Cranston and said, "You're coming with us. A night in jail might be what you need to stop spreading those crazy stories of yours."

The other officer turned to us and asked, "Are you all right? He didn't hurt you, did he?" We both shook our heads and the officer said, "We're going to have to take you two home to your parents and let them have a little talk with you about trespassing and abiding by the law."

"We weren't trespassing," Tom complained. The two officers escorted Mr. Cranston to the car and Tom said, "Run, Seth, run!"

We both took off running and I heard one of the officers ask, "Do you want me to go after them?"

The other officer said, "No. Let them go. Kids are scared of their own shadow nowadays. It's not like when we were kids. I think we taught them a lesson."

We ran all the way back to my house without looking back once. When we got home, Tom said, "That was a close one. I wonder if what that old man said was true."

"Oh, course it's not true," I said. "He's crazy."

"There's only one way to find out," Tom said, and grinned.

"Oh, no!" I bellowed. "There is no way I'm going within a block of that house tonight."

"You're not?" Tom asked. "That's okay. I'll go ask Brandon and Colin to go with me."

I sighed and slouched a little. My heart filled with sadness and I thought, *I'm scared. I don't want to go back to that place, but if I don't, Tom will go with the other guys. I know Brandon and Colin will talk Tom into going with them for Halloween, and I'll be stuck alone.* "All right," I said. "I'll go, but if anything weird happens, I'm running away as fast as I can."

"Agreed," Tom said.

We went to the house just before six o'clock and stood right out front. Tom said, "Let's go in."

"No way," I said.

"All right," Tom said angrily. "Let's go home. You never want to do anything adventurous. I don't even know why I asked you to come."

"I'm scared," I said. "Maybe you should've asked those other guys to come instead."

Tom looked me right in the eyes and said, "Those other guys are all right, but you're my best friend and will be forever." My eyes lit up, and I stood up straight. I felt confident and warm inside, as if Tom would never let anything bad happen to me. "You need to stop being so scared of everything."

"You're right," I said. "I'll go in, but only for a minute."

The creaky porch reminded me of how scared I really was, and made my legs feel like they were filled with lead. Tom tried to open the door, but it was locked. There was a window at the end of the porch with rotted wood hanging down near the frame, which was partly boarded up. Tom walked over to it and pulled two planks down, leaving us just enough space to get in. He squeezed through first and said, "Come on. It's not that bad in here." I shook my head and Tom again said, "Come on, please!"

I took a deep breath and squeezed through with my eyes locked shut. Just as I placed my foot on the floor, a weak squeak pierced the air and a piece of paint no bigger than a quarter fell from the ceiling next to me. I looked around and noticed that the place was worse than I thought. All the paint was chipped throughout, and in some spots the plaster on the walls and ceiling was crumbling. There was no furniture in the house, and as the setting sun shone through the window, it seemed to magnify the dust in the air.

I took a step forward and felt a cobweb tickle my neck. I shook my head, stepped back and said, "Let's go!"

Right as Tom was about to say something, the room suddenly seemed to be spinning. I felt dizzy and lightheaded and thought I was going to fall down. I said, "Let's get out of here!" and started to make my way toward the window. My body felt like it was disintegrating and turning to dust. Everything went dark and I must have passed out.

The next thing I knew, I felt a poke at my ribs and heard a little voice say, "Wake up." I opened my eyes and saw a little man standing right over me, holding a stick. I slid away from the creature, scraping on the ground.

Tom woke up and said, "Get away from me or you'll be sorry!" He stood up and shuffled away from the creature. I looked again at the little man and saw he was about three feet tall. He had a gray beard and a red pointed hat. I shook my head hard, trying to bring myself to reality, as if the man weren't really there.

Another little man walked over to us; he was the same height but had no beard, and his pointed hat was blue. He squeaked gruffly, "They don't look like great warriors."

"No, they don't," said the man with the blue hat.

I stood up and Tom asked, "Where are we?"

"My name is Angor, and you're on the Gnome Planet. Welcome to our kingdom."

"This can't be happening," I said. "It must be a dream."

The gnome with the red hat said, "My name is Sangor, and this is no dream. I am the ruler of this planet. What are your names?"

"My name is Tom and his name is Seth."

"Come and meet our people," Sangor said. From behind trees and bushes, and from inside little houses, gnomes started to wobble toward us, cheering. They started to sing, "Tom and Seth are deliverers from evil. Hurrah for Tom and Seth! Hurrah for Tom and Seth!"

After the cheers died down, Tom asked, "How did we get here, and why do your people call us deliverers from evil?"

"Almost every thirty years, a great warrior is sent through the portal," Sangor said. "This time might be the right time, because they sent two of you."

"Right time for what?" I asked.

"The right time to defeat and kill the beast," Sangor said.

My eyes got as huge as bowling balls as I asked, "What beast?"

"Over a thousand years ago, an evil witch named Drusilla lived here, who wreaked havoc on our people," said Sangor. "She tortured many of our citizens and turned them into snakes, toads and insects. One day, a valiant gnome named Bangor disguised himself as a weary old gnome. When Drusilla wasn't looking, he pulled out our magical sword and stabbed her right through the heart. Before she died, she put an evil spell on a nearby rat, turning him into a beast who, once every thirty years, would attack and kill many of our people. His name is Raton. Drusilla also used her magic to kill Bangor as she died.

"As Bangor was taking his last breath, he used his own spell to create a portal linked to your world that would open every thirty years, the day the beast awakened. Sometimes no one comes through the portal, and we have to wait until the next time it opens for a great warrior to come and try to defeat the beast. Many more of our people die when no one comes. You two are the great warriors that were sent. The spell doesn't allow anyone from our land to kill Raton. It has to be you."

"Oh, no," I said. "We aren't great warriors. If no one has defeated the beast in over a thousand years, what makes you think we can? We're only in sixth grade! This can't be happening."

"I don't know what this sixth grade is you're talking about," Sangor said, frowning. "All I know is that Raton will be released soon, and the first thing he does will be to come for you two."

"You need to open that portal again so we can go back," I said. "I want to go home."

"There are only two ways to open the portal," said Sangor. "One is to kill the beast, and it will automatically open to transport you back."

"What's the other?" Tom asked.

"The other way is to wait thirty years until it opens again," Sangor said. "Unfortunately, you can't survive for more than a week on our planet before dying from illness. Your bodies can't adapt to our world."

"Then we shall fight and defeat the beast," Tom said.

The gnomes cheered wildly for over a minute. When they quieted down, Sangor said, "Your time is short. Raton lives under that bridge right there, just fifty feet away, and is protected during his sleep. When he first wakes, he is vulnerable to your attack. He grows stronger with every moment he is awake."

Sangor reached toward Angor and took a sword from his hands. The blade of the sword was over two feet long and double-edged. It had strange Gnome lettering on it that looked like a kindergartner's scribbles; it glistened in the sun, almost blinding us.

Sangor, almost hidden by the sword he held, which was as big as him, said, "To kill the beast, you must stab him through the heart with this sword, the same sword that killed the evil witch Drusilla. He can be hurt in other ways, but not killed. Be careful! He is a crafty one! You will never be able to kill him with your brute strength. You must outsmart him, or you will sure-ly perish."

"Not only will we outsmart him," Tom said. "We will send him to his grave and free your people from their agony." All the gnomes cheered again wildly.

A second later, we heard a great muffled roar that sounded worse than twenty lions roaring at once. Sangor dropped the sword to the ground and said, "The beast!" All the gnomes scurried about, looking for the best places to hide. Another roar, louder and stronger, projected from under the bridge, making my ears hurt and my hair stand on end.

I covered my ears and Tom grabbed the sword. "Come on!" said Tom, "We must kill him before his power grows!" Tom ran toward the bridge, sword in hand, with fearlessness in his eyes. I followed closely behind, wanting to turn back and hide with the gnomes. Right when Tom reached the bridge, Raton emerged and shook himself, as if he weren't fully awake.

An awful smell like rotten eggs engulfed us, and a liquid splattered through the air, like sweat but thicker. A few drops splashed on me and I stepped backward and said, "Yuck!" I wiped the smelly slime from my arms and looked over at Raton.

He stood seven feet tall and had dirty matted hair, resembling the rat he once was. He had long sharp claws that could easily kill us with one swipe. His face was hideous, with a long rat nose and large, crooked, protruding teeth. His long and pointed tail was like a rotted piece of rope. The drool from his mouth ran down upon his chest, and again the smell of a thousand rotten eggs engulfed us. I turned my head away in shock at his ugliness, feeling like I would throw up from the smell. I desperately wanted to run.

Tom raised the sword and bolted toward Raton. The beast stepped aside and yawned. I stood watching, shivering with fear, as Tom made another lunge at Raton. The beast whipped his tail, hitting Tom and sending him flying several feet away. The sword slid right beneath my feet. Raton wickedly laughed and then growled. "Every time, the warriors get weaker and weaker, while I grow with power. It hardly seems fair to send two little boys such as you."

Tom stood up and yelled, "We are great warriors, and will strike you dead!"

The beast yawned again and laughed. Tom said, "You're stalling for time. I know you are weak right now." Tom started moving toward the sword, and the beast's tail whipped him again. Tom went flying a few feet and landed on his side, bellowing in pain.

I fell to my knees and began to whimper in fear. I rolled flat on my belly and whined, "Oh, great beast, spare my life. My friend doesn't know how great you are, but I do. I will die in a week anyway if you let me live. If you spare me, at least I can live in peace for a short time. Oh Raton, your strength and power is too much for us. Please, great one, spare me!" I went into a full cry and rolled up into a ball. "I want to go home and see my mommy. Please let me go home to my mommy."

I cried even louder, and Tom yelled, "You're such a baby! You've always been a baby! I don't know why I was ever friends with you."

The beast laughed and said, "I'm great and you're weak. You two are no warriors! Today will be the last day you ever see!" Raton jumped and flew through the air to pounce on me. I rolled over with the sword in my hands and held it high into the air just as the beast landed on top of me.

The blade struck the beast right in his chest. He fell to the ground next to me, with one end of the sword lodged into his chest and his full body weight pushing the handle of the sword on the ground. The sword went right through his heart as he moaned, "Ahhhhhhh!" His black, slimy, disgusting tongue protruded from his mouth as his head shuddered back and forth. His eyes bulged out of his head as he choked out his last words. "Tom and Seth… grrrr."

I stood up and wiped a blob of slime from my clothes. Tom stood there frozen, with his mouth wide open in amazement; then he came to me and asked, "Are you all right?"

I nodded and said, "I remembered what Sangor said about outsmarting him and not being able to beat him with brute strength. I knew I had to make him think he was greater than me, to trick him into jumping at me. I had seen someone kill a bear that way before, in a movie, and I figured that beast was dumber than a bear."

Tom shook his head slowly in disbelief. "I'm sorry that I said I don't know why I was ever your friend. I never told you this, but I've always thought that you were really smart, and this proves you are. You were the only one for a thousand years who was able to outwit the beast, and now that you've defeated him, you're one of the bravest people of all time." Tom hugged me and said, "Friends forever."

I whispered, "Friends forever."

The gnomes rushed us, screaming in elation and shouting, "Tom and Seth! Tom and Seth!" They gathered around us to get a last glimpse of the heroes who had saved their world from never-ending terror. The portal opened and Sangor said, "You only have a few seconds. Thank you, Great Warrior Seth and Great Warrior Tom. I will name my next three children Seth, Jeff, and then Cleff after your greatness."

Bangor said, "And I will name my children Tom, Bom and Hom. Hurry, you must go now." He lightly pushed us toward the portal. We waved and stepped toward the portal as it was beginning to close.

Everything went black again, and we woke up back in the old house. I looked at Tom and asked, "Are you sure that really happened?"

"It happened," Tom said. "Come on. Let's go home. You're a hero!" I smiled and nodded.

When I got home, Mother asked, "What happened to you? You're filthy and you smell like rotten eggs."

"Oh, nothing," I said, feeling confident for once. "It was just another normal day. By the way, I've decided to go out as something scary this year for Halloween."

The Insane Asylum

Heather Miller

6th Grade, Noblesville Intermediate School, Noblesville, Indiana

As seniors in high school, with our last Halloween approaching before we all went off to college, my friends and I wanted to do something really scary. We stood on the deck in my backyard, pondering what to do. "I know!" Katelyn said. "Let's all get dressed up in scary costumes and jump out at the little kids in the neighborhood. That's always fun."

Jessica and I looked at each other and we both shook our heads. I dropped my arms by my sides and said, "I want to do something better this year, something really scary. Let's go into the deserted insane asylum."

Mom walked outside with her arms crossed over her chest and said, "I wasn't eavesdropping, but I heard what you said. There is no way you're going into that asylum, and that's final. Too many weird things have happened to people over the years. I've heard stories that people hung themselves inside there when they trespassed. I heard that one person disappeared and they never found them again."

"Come on, Mom!" I protested.

"It's out of the question, Haley, and that's final."

I crossed my fingers behind my back, winked at Jessica and groaned, "All right. But I never get to do anything."

"I know what I'm talking about," Mom said. "Don't go in there." I nodded, and we went over to Katelyn's.

When we got there, I said, "We're going into that asylum no matter what my mom said."

"I don't know," Katelyn said. "I've heard a lot of weird stories too."

"You're not chickening out," I forcefully said. "We'll meet right before dark tomorrow."

When we parked in the old deserted parking lot the next evening, just outside the asylum's doors, I stared out the window, trembling with excitement. The main building was about the size of an elementary school and was all red brick, with broken windows scattered about. Hanging above the main double doors was the original sign, which said: *Krips Mental Hospital, 1919.*

When we got out of the car, I noticed that the full moon's light was dimmed by the dark shadows of the clouds. There was a cool tinge in the air that made me shiver, so I put my coat on. "I guess you won't change your mind, will you?" Katelyn asked.

"Not a chance," I said, and smiled. I reached into the car, under the back seat, and pulled out a crowbar and three flashlights. "I figured the door would be locked, so we'd have to break in."

Katelyn sighed. "Great. If we do make it out, then we can spend the night in jail for trespassing."

We walked to the front door, and I clenched the rusted knob in my hand, but it wouldn't turn. We went around back and saw a door at the bottom of the stairs that must have been a delivery entrance. The wood was rotted around the frame, and the door handle looked ready to fall off. "Come on," I said. "We'll have to pry it open." I stuck the crowbar between the frame and the door and we all grabbed hold of it. We pried until the door flung wide open, jolting us backward.

"You go first," said Jessica.

"I will," I bravely said, and stepped forward. I turned on my flashlight, took three steps into the asylum, and was greeted by the feeling of cobwebs on my neck. I twitched, grabbed the cobwebs from my skin, and flicked them toward the ground. "I hate that feeling," I said.

A squeak from the other side of the room caused us all to turn with our flashlights pointed in that direction. "It's just a mouse, look," I said.

"Rodents," said Jessica. "I hate them."

"Look, you guys," I proudly gloated. "We're in one of the worst possible places in the scariest building in the state. Better yet, we're in the basement. How awesome!"

The walls were made of cinder blocks and were moist and crumbling. There were tables and chairs scattered throughout, and at the other end of the room was an old set of iron stairs. "Come on," I said. "Let's go up." Jessica and Katelyn both grabbed my arms and followed me as we walked up the stairs.

When we got to the top of the stairs, we went through a door and saw an old stove sitting in the corner of the room. There was a chopping block right in the center, and a walk-in refrigerator off to the side that looked like it was old enough to use ice blocks instead of electricity. "Come on," I said.

We went through a double set of doors and found ourselves standing in front of a long wooden table. There were cobwebs hanging from the ceiling and an old fireplace off in the corner. "This must have been the dining room," I said. "I want to go into the hospital area. That's where all the action was."

"Let's go home," Katelyn said. "I have a funny feeling about this place."

"Stop being such a baby," I complained. "The old hospital has to be that way." I pointed toward the opposite side of the room. We walked out of the kitchen and into a long hallway. Down the corridor, every ten feet or so, were rooms with open doors that had housed patients in the past. "This is really creepy," I said. "I like it." I grabbed Jessica's waist from behind with both hands and yelled, "Boo!"

She jumped two feet into the air and screamed. "Don't do that again or I'm leaving."

I laughed and said, "Look, there's something down at the end of the hall." We tiptoed to the end of the hall, where an old, rusted metal gate was latched to the wall. "It's an old elevator," I said. "They used gates like this before they had automatic doors."

The gate creaked as I opened it, sending chills up our spines. I pushed the elevator button and it lit up. We all jumped backward and Katelyn said, "That's impossible. The power has been off in this building for years." The elevator dinged, and the light went on inside. We all jumped back even farther and hugged each other in fear while Jessica screamed. The elevator was empty and the door sat open, inviting us to go in.

"Let's get out of here," Jessica said. We ran around the corner to a set of stairs and started running up.

"Wait," Katelyn said. "We have to go back the way we came if we want to get out of here."

"I'm not going back that way," said Jessica.

We got to the top of the stairs and bolted through the door into the hallway. I stumbled, falling to the ground, then stood up and said, "This must be where the main hospital was located. Look at all those rooms." We looked into one of the rooms and saw an old physician's examination table and a chair. Over in the corner of the room, a bedpan and a stethoscope sat on the counter. I swallowed heavily and said, "Maybe this wasn't such a good idea coming here after all. Let's get out of here."

We ran to the door, where the staircase was that we had just come up, and tried to open it. It was locked. Katelyn shrieked and said, "That's impossible! Try again." She stepped forward and yanked on the door handle with all her might, and it wouldn't open. As she let go, she said, "I knew we shouldn't have come here."

I looked at Katelyn and she looked as white as a ghost. A loud moan filled the air, "Ohhhhh..." Jessica and Katelyn jumped on me and hugged me, trembling.

"There must be some explanation for this!" I yelled. "Calm down. We have to find another way out." I started walking down the hall, with Jessica and Katelyn holding onto the back of my shirt like two scared puppies. When we got halfway down the hall, the door at the other end flung wide open. One by one the doors to all the hospital rooms slammed shut by themselves, sending us running back to the stairs where we came from. The door was still locked, so we turned the other way.

We stood huddled together, whimpering and shaking in fear. Down at the other end of the hall, a man stepped through the doorway. He was six feet tall and had dark hair; he wore a bloodstained, white doctor's coat. We couldn't make out his face, which was totally dark. In one hand he held a large knife, and in the other a clipboard. His voice boomed, "Are you three my new patients? I've been expecting you." He began to walk toward us.

I closed my eyes tightly while Jessica and Katelyn screamed. "This can't be happening!" I said. I opened my eyes, and the man stopped about twenty-five feet from us.

"New patients are always challenging," he growled evilly. "I think your first form of therapy should be to meet my pets. They haven't eaten since last Halloween. You're their next feast." He dropped the clipboard and raised the hand that wasn't holding the knife; dangling from his tight grip was an old rusted chain. From behind him sprang a large wolf with the head of bear. Its teeth were dripping in blood, its eyes were fire-red and it looked possessed. Another animal with steel-blue eyes jumped out from behind him; it had the body of a bear and the head of a wolf. Blood drooled from its mouth as it licked its lips, staring at us.

We fell to our knees, shivering in fear. "Please, mister, no," I cried.

The doctor asked, "You don't like my creations? They're going to like you. I wonder what a goat would look like with one of your heads? But we'll never find out because my pets are too hungry." He dropped the chains and yelled, "Feed! Feed!"

The beasts came streaking toward us, growling with a wicked roar. I screamed, "No!" as they leaped at us.

I woke up with Mom standing over me. She said, "You were having a bad nightmare. Are you okay?"

Panting, I wiped the sweat from my forehead and said, "I guess so. I had a dream that Katelyn, Jessica and I went into the old insane asylum and got locked in. An evil doctor had two wild animals that hadn't eaten in a year, and he let them attack us. We couldn't get away. It seemed so real. I can't believe it was a dream."

Mom raised her voice. "I want you to promise me you'll never go near that asylum. Too many strange things have happened there over the years. Promise me!"

I smiled and stuck my hand behind my back. I crossed my fingers and said, "All right. But I never get to do anything."

Once Upon a Time

Olivia Marquardt

6th Grade, Vandalia Junior High School,
Vandalia, Illinois

Once upon a time, long ago, in a land far away, there was a beautiful princess named Ardella. She was next in line to be queen of the richest, most powerful country in the world, named Allanar. On her eighteenth birthday, she married a handsome prince named Christlas. When Ardella turned twenty-two years old, her mother Queen Aerial died, leaving Ardella and Prince Christlas to be king and queen.

Two years later, Ardella gave birth to a baby girl named Jasmine. During the birth, something went horribly wrong, and Ardella was never able to have children again. A month after Jasmine was born, an evil advisor named Barnamen plotted to kidnap Jasmine, who was the only living heir in their bloodline to the throne. Barnamen was successful and paid an evil, wretched woman who lived on the edge of the kingdom, without children, to raise Jasmine as her own. The woman, named Agatha, changed Jasmine's name to Penelope, and kept the secret buried deep inside herself in fear for her life.

Barnamen killed everyone who knew of Penelope's whereabouts, except for his closest confidant, named Rabereth. Barnamen was sure that his evil cousin Damon, who was next in line to the throne, would one day rule the world. Barnamen was soon discovered as the person who had plotted the kidnapping, and was executed, denying the entire thing.

Queen Ardella and King Christlas had their men search every area of the kingdom, desperately trying to find the only heir to the throne. It was to no avail, and fifteen years later, right before Penelope's sixteenth birthday, Queen Ardella died. A year later, King Christlas became ill and bed-ridden.

Two of Christlas' top loyal advisors, named Charles and Jonathan, conferred together, and Charles said, "I know we have searched every corner of the kingdom for Jasmine, but we must find her. If we fail and King Christlas dies, the kingdom will be turned over to Damon, who will surely incite war. Many innocent people will be lost and our people will suffer. The neighboring countries will see a death toll like never in our history."

"I will double our efforts, sir," Jonathan said. "I will leave no stone unturned to find Jasmine."

"Go," Charles said, "And hurry. King Christlas has little time left." Jonathan searched the countryside like never before, in desperation offering ten years' wages as a reward for information about the lost princess.

Meanwhile, Penelope woke up early on her straw bed, on the morning of her seventeenth birthday. After she got dressed, she stumbled into the outer room, to hear her stepmother Agatha growl, "Get the cow milked right away."

"It's still dark, Mum," Penelope said.

"I don't care if it's the middle of the night. Get out there and get all the work done. You know I can't do any work. With my back and my age, I can only do small things."

"Yes, Mum," Penelope said. She put on her old worn-out boots and her tattered coat, and went out to the stable. On the way, a feeling of hopelessness filled her that she had felt many times before. She stopped before entering the stable and thought, *I feel so lost and out of place. I feel like I don't belong here. I've felt this way so many times, and I can't understand why. There must be something in life for me, other than this.*

Penelope loved the animals and was always kind to them, feeling like they were her only friends. After she entered the stable, she sat down with the bucket and said to the cow, "Good morning, Ginger," and started milking her. "Yes, Ginger, Agatha will lie in bed again all day, while I work until my hands are raw. I have decided to leave this place and go out on my own. Do you want to come with me?"

"Moo," Ginger sounded off.

"Have it your way," Penelope joked. "Don't blame me if Agatha is too lazy to ever milk you after I leave." Penelope finished milking Ginger while she plotted her departure to seek her own destiny.

Meanwhile, Rabereth became ill, and he, too, faced death. He called Charles to his bedside, wishing to clear his conscience. Rabereth said, "I regret only one thing in life. It was Barnamen who kidnapped Jasmine some sixteen years ago. He took her to the edge of the kingdom in the village of

Huckstable. He left her with a wretched woman named Agatha. To this day, she lives there as a servant." Rabereth coughed and breathed his last breath, getting the news out just in time.

Charles' eyes lit up with excitement. He sent for Jonathan and explained the situation. Jonathan left immediately, taking the finest carriages the kingdom had to bring Jasmine back home.

Penelope waited until Agatha went back to bed for her morning nap. She snuck into her room and gathered a few things, packed them into a bag and left. As she walked out the door, she thought, *I will go into town and stay the night where I can. The next day I will make the long journey to Luxington, and try to get a job as a seamstress or maid. I will work day and night if I have to, until I make a life for myself.* She left without looking back at her stepmother's shack.

Later that evening, Jonathan and twelve men stormed Agatha's house and broke in. Jonathan approached Agatha and asked, "Where is Princess Jasmine?"

Agatha gulped and said, "I do not know what you are talking about. I only have my daughter Penelope that lives with me."

Jonathan took his knife, held it to Agatha's throat and said, "My patience with you grows thin. I will slit your throat now unless you tell me where Jasmine is. We know she has lived here as a servant for the last sixteen years."

Agatha dropped to her knees and began to cry. "I am sorry to have kept the princess here all these years. Barnamen said he would kill me if I did not. I have been ill all these years, as well."

"Where is she?" Jonathan yelled, while pressing the knife harder to her throat.

"She left," Agatha whined. "She packed her things and was gone only today."

"Where did she go?" Jonathan impatiently asked.

"I do not know," Agatha pleaded.

"If one hair on the princess's head is harmed, you will endure torture beyond belief," Jonathan warned. "Guards, throw her in the back of the last carriage, and guard her with your life." The guards grabbed her and escorted her forcefully toward the carriages.

Agatha feared that if they found Jasmine, she would tell them how badly she had treated her and her life would be lost. As they got to the carriages, she struggled and tried to get away, pushing one guard down. One of the guards pulled his sword out and stabbed her through the heart. As Agatha fell dying to the ground, Jonathan ran up and yelled, "You fools! We need her to identify the princess. Now we only have one way to make sure she is the princess once she is found."

Jonathan and his men spent the entire evening combing the area, and sent word for an additional fifty men to be sent to help. After riding all night, the reinforcements arrived. They spent the entire day searching the village, with no luck and time running out. Near suppertime, a woman came to Jonathan and asked to speak to him. The woman asked, "Is there a reward for the girl you seek?"

Jonathan, frustrated and desperate, had little patience left. "If you know of her, speak!"

The woman hesitated and meekly asked again, "Is there a reward offered?"

Jonathan took his knife and pressed it against the woman's stomach and yelled, "I have no time for this! The entire nation is at stake! Speak now, or die where you stand!"

The woman's face turned white and she began to shake. Without hesitation she said, "I believe I know the girl you are speaking of. Last night she offered to clean my house for a clean bed and a warm meal. I agreed and treated her with the utmost respect. She left early this morning in the direction of Luxington."

Jonathan pulled the knife away from the woman's stomach and reached into his pocket. He pulled out a small purse with twenty silver pieces in it. He tossed it to the woman and motioned for her to leave while he turned to his captain. "Prepare to leave at once for Luxington."

His captain said, "Sir, it will be dark in a few minutes. The men haven't eaten or slept in two days, and the horses cannot go another minute without rest."

Jonathan made a fist and barked, "We leave two hours before daylight. Tell the men to enjoy the rest, because they may not get any more until our job is done. Remember, not a word about who we are searching for. If the wrong people find out, she may be kidnapped again and held for ransom." The captain nodded.

The next morning, the regiment set out for Luxington as planned. They split into groups and scoured the countryside. Two hours before sunset, Jonathan saw a woman walking on the side of the road. When she heard the carriages off in the distance, she jumped into the bushes as if in fear for her life. Jonathan had his driver stop the carriage, and got out to question the woman. He said, "I saw you go into the bushes. Come out, or my men will come in after you. We mean you no harm. We are looking for a girl."

The woman said, "If you are looking for a girl, you can find many of them in town. I am not like the girls you are used to. If you touch me, I will see you brought up on charges." Jonathan motioned for his men to bring her out. They grabbed her by the arms and dragged her out. The woman was young and wore servants' clothing. The scraggly state of her long brown hair showed clearly that she was a peasant, but it was beautiful in a sort of pitiful way. She had a light layer of dirt on her face from her long journey that day.

Jonathan said, "We are looking for a girl that was traveling this way. Her name is Penelope."

Penelope's eyes widened in fear. *Agatha must have told these men that I ran away. I must not let them know my true identity.* "My name is Anne, named after Anne, Queen of Scots," Penelope said. "Although I am traveling alone, my father is a blacksmith and a successful one at that. Leave me now, or I will tell him of your cruelty."

Jonathan laughed. "I am one of the kings' top advisors, and your father will not do a thing for you. You are a peasant and I have no use for you. Release her." The men released her while Jonathan and his men began to leave.

Desperate to not spend the night alone in the wilderness with her feet blistered and raw, Penelope asked, "I am heading toward Luxington. Can I bother you for a ride, good sir?"

"I don't make it a habit of transporting mere peasants," Jonathan said.

"My father will be in great debt to you if you do, kind sir."

Jonathan nodded and said, "Until Luxington, and that's it." After they got into the carriage, Penelope's stomach turned queasy for an instant, and then she felt at ease. She stared at Jonathan and felt almost as if she knew him.

Shortly after, two men were riding on the road in front of them and Jonathan's men stopped to question them. Jonathan got out and said, "We are looking for a girl named Penelope. Her age is seventeen."

"We have seen no girl," one of the men said.

"Where are you going?" Jonathan questioned.

"We are headed toward Huckstable," the same man said.

Jonathan waved the men on and got back into the carriage. He was now desperate, realizing he had to get the princess back before Christlas died, or Damon would become king. He put his hand on his head and sighed. Penelope looked into Jonathan's eyes and a warm feeling came over her. She felt as if Jonathan would never hurt her. "What has this girl done that it would warrant a search with so many men?" she asked.

"It's none of your concern," Jonathan said. "All I can say is that we must find her before long or all of Allanar will be at risk."

Why would all of Allanar be at risk just because I left my stepmother? Penelope thought. *And why do I feel so strangely at home with this man?*

Jonathan looked into Penelope's eyes and felt mesmerized. He stared deeply, seeing his former queen for a moment. "What... did you say your name was?" Jonathan asked.

Penelope stared deeply back into Jonathan's eyes and began to cry. "I can no longer go on living a lie. I am the Penelope that you so desperately seek. I ran from my stepmother's house only yesterday. If you must punish me or kill me, do so now."

Jonathan sat straight up and his body filled with hope. "May I see your bare leg?" Jonathan insisted.

"You may punish me as you wish, but I will not allow that because I am not that kind of girl," said Penelope.

"I must see if you have a birthmark on your thigh, just above your knee. Princess Jasmine had a blotch there at birth."

Penelope's mouth dropped open, and she pulled up her dress. On her leg was the most beautiful sight Jonathan had ever seen — a birthmark that was in the same exact spot as Princess Jasmine's seventeen years earlier.

Jonathan fell to his knees and bowed. "Princess Jasmine, I have finally found you. You were stolen at birth and you must return to claim the throne. Your father, King Christlas, is sick and only has days left. You will be the queen of all Allanar if you return."

"My name is Jasmine?" she said in confusion. "I knew something wasn't right my entire life. I felt it inside. I will return, to help my father and claim the throne."

Princess Jasmine did return to claim the throne. She married a wonderful prince named Edward and they had seven children, never having to worry about an heir to the throne again. And all of Allanar lived happily ever after — that is, except for Damon, who never became king.

A Christmas Miracle

Sarah Peterson

6th Grade, Rockwood South Middle School, Fenton, Missouri

"One horse open sleigh," rang out from the radio in the next room. The beautiful, cheery music was interrupted by the PA. "Dr. Larson, report to room 207." I sighed, thinking, *I can't wait until Christmas, only two more days.* Being twelve years old and having my second cancer operation in two years had really taken its toll on me. Going in and out of hospitals, losing my hair with the chemotherapy, and the bad news all the time made me want to give up. I probably would have, if it weren't for my parents.

I cupped my hand to my ear to hear the song better, and heard a knock at my door instead. In came Nurse Johnson and Doctor Pang. I had seen so many doctors and nurses over the last two years, I could barely remember their names. Dr. Pang said, "Good morning, Chelsea. How's my favorite patient today?"

"I'm fine, I guess."

"I have good news for you," Dr. Pang said.

"Am I going home for Christmas?" I asked wide-eyed, sitting up.

"I don't know about that," Dr. Pang said. "I got the test results back and they look pretty good, though. No sign of cancer. You have one more week of chemo and then I think you can go home."

I smiled slightly and asked, "Can't I go home for Christmas?"

"That's not possible," Dr. Pang said. "But look what I got." He pulled out a St. Louis Blues hat from under his coat. "I heard the Blues are your favorite team. You can wear this until your hair grows back in a couple of months."

"I wish I could go home for Christmas," I said. "Not even for one day?" Dr. Pang frowned and shook his head.

"I know how much you want to be with your family," Nurse Johnson said. "I'm sure you can talk to them on the phone a good part of the day."

"Keep up the good work, Chelsea," Dr. Pang said. "I'll see you a little later." They left the room with the door cracked open.

I snuck over to the door and quietly peered through the crack while they stood in the hallway talking. "It's a shame that Chelsea's parents couldn't be here for Christmas," Nurse Johnson said. "But with her in and out of the hospital over the last two years, they can't afford it. Her father and mother took every day off from work they could during the operations and have massive medical bills. They have two other children and are almost bankrupt. I wish there was something we could do."

"Yeah, me too," Dr. Pang said. "Seeing a great kid like Chelsea go through so much is the hardest part of this job. At least she's cancer-free right now." Nurse Johnson smiled and they both walked away.

I ran to my bed, jumped in it and pulled the covers over my head. My body felt empty and I started to cry. I said softly, "I'm sorry, Mom and Dad, for costing you so much money. I didn't mean to hurt you so much." I prayed, "Please God, help my mom and dad have a good Christmas. And please help me to go home and see my family during the holidays. I don't want anything but that. I know the doctor said it was impossible, but I know you can do it. You can do anything. You got me through both operations and you can get me home. Please help me get back to St. Louis." Then I faded off to sleep.

The next morning, Nurse Johnson came in while I was lying on my bed. I kept mumbling, "I know you can do it, I know you can."

She interrupted me. "Wake up, sleepyhead. Today is Christmas Eve."

"Yeah," I sighed, "Christmas Eve."

"We're having a party tonight night and Santa might make an appearance."

"Ah," I moaned. "If it's all right, I'd like to stay in my room instead of going to the party."

She grinned from ear to ear and said "Come on! You have to be happy this time of year." She stared at me, waiting for a smile.

"I really don't feel much like talking," I said.

"I'll tell you what. I'll come back in a little while."

After she left, I kept mumbling, "I know you can do it. I know you can."

The rest of the day was a blur until Nurse Johnson came into my room and said, "The party is in an hour. Get ready. There are some clean clothes on the dresser that your parents sent. No hospital clothes tonight."

I halfheartedly got up, mumbling, "I know you can do it. You can do anything."

When I entered the cafeteria, my eyes bugged out and my mouth dropped wide open. The entire room was decorated in red and white, with a Christmas tree in the corner. There were presents everywhere, and Santa was sitting with a small girl on his lap, with her parents by her side. There were eleven other children there, all unable to return home because of their illnesses, with their parents by their sides. Nurse Johnson and Dr. Pang were there, wearing street clothes because they were off duty.

Nurse Johnson said, "Chelsea, we have a surprise for you."

My heart leaped and I froze like a statue when Mom, Dad, my brother Steven and my sister Kennedy walked in. A tear formed in my eye as I looked up toward the ceiling and choked out, "I knew you could do it. You can do anything. Thank you." Steven and Kennedy ran to me, almost tackling me. Mom and Dad joined in and we all hugged, holding back our tears.

After our emotional greeting was over, I said, "I don't understand. I heard Nurse Johnson and Dr. Pang saying you were broke because of me and you weren't going to be able to see me this Christmas. I'm so sorry I cost you so much money, Mom and Dad."

Dad and Mom squeezed me tightly and Nurse Johnson said, "The entire staff took up a collection so your family could come to see you. I heard you praying and I knew I had to do something. I woke up in the middle of the night with the idea, almost as if it were a dream. God works in mysterious ways!"

"Yes, he does," Mom said while smiling and holding me close. She sniffled and added, "Don't ever think that money is important to us. Having you with us is the most important thing in the world."

I turned to Nurse Johnson and Dr. Pang then said, "Thank you. It's a miracle, a Christmas miracle."

Nurse Johnson's eyes turned misty and she hugged me too. "Merry Christmas," she cheerfully said.

We all said "Merry Christmas!" together, sang Christmas songs and had a great time. In fact, it was the best Christmas I ever had.

■　■　■

Two years later, Dr. Pang told me I was still cancer-free. I was cured! Despite our family still being in financial peril, four months before Christmas I went to my mother and asked, "Can we take up a collection to try and pay for another family to see their sick child at Christmas?"

Mom's face glowed and she said, "That's a great idea!" Mom, Dad, Steven, Kennedy and I all did garage sales, bake sales and other fundraisers to try and raise enough money for a family to travel to see their sick child that year. Word spread like wildfire that we were trying to help families of sick children and many generous people agreed to help. We were able to raise enough money for two families to go spend Christmas with their sick children at the hospital.

Ten years later, at the age of twenty-four, I'm still cancer-free and we are still at it. We were able to raise enough money for twenty families to visit their children at Christmas and have their Christmas miracles, too. Next year our goal is to raise enough money for twenty-three.

Oreo

Kaylee Rostkowski

6th Grade, Central Middle School, Plymouth, Michigan

I opened my eyes to an odd voice saying, "Welcome to this world, little one."

The air tickled my lungs as I took my first breath and cried back, "Who are you, and what is this strange place?"

"I'm your mother, and this is your home, little one."

I snorted the taste of the stable air in and out. "What is this funny, dry, yellow stuff?" I asked, as I tried to stand up.

"That's straw," she gently responded. "The humans use it to keep our stalls clean." I wobbled and fell to the ground, and she carefully laughed. "Take your time. You'll have plenty of chances in the future to run like the wind."

The cool floor felt foreign as I stayed flush to the ground for a moment. My blurry eyes came into focus as I tried standing again, this time succeeding. I peered across the stall, looking into the eyes of my mother, and realizing she was strong and confident. Her beautiful, pure black coat shone clearly, reflecting the bright lights overhead. I gazed down at my wobbly legs and asked, "Why don't I look like you? You're black and shiny, and I have all these strange white spots on me."

"Every horse is different," she said. "Some are brown, some are white, and some have spots like you. In time your spots may go away, or they may stay for the rest of your life. Rest now, for you have many great times ahead of you."

A few days later, I was up and about as well as any newborn colt around. Mama came to me and said, "Today will be your first day in the yard. You'll go outside and meet all the horses on the farm. You'll spend many days in the yard with your friends, until every inch of the ground is as common as the nose on your face."

I took my first step outside, and the fresh clean air expanded my lungs with a rush of energy. Smiling, I trotted next to my mother, proud and brave, like a soldier going into battle. We approached the first set of horses and Mama said, "This is Seacrest, everyone."

The largest horse, named Thunder, lifted her head and said, "We know who he is. He's been the talk of the farm."

Mama raised her head high and asked, "How so?"

Another horse chimed in. "We heard your son was born with weird spots. I guess the rumors were true."

My head lowered and I looked at the ground as Mama said, "His spots aren't weird. I like them the way they are. They're different."

A smaller horse named Sassy said, "They're different all, right. They're so different I don't know if I can stand to look at them. You should've named him Spotcrest instead." All the horses laughed in unison.

Mama's mane stood straight up and her tail lifted. She snorted and jolted back on her hind legs. She grunted and lunged forward, hitting Sassy on the side with her front hoofs. The thud echoed throughout the yard as Sassy stepped backward, losing her balance. Mama remained standing, tall and proud, looking around as if to say, "Is there anyone who wants more?"

Thunder stepped in and said, "That's enough of that. There's not going to be a fight out here just because your son has ugly spots." Mama grunted, ready to strike again, when three more horses fell in right behind Thunder. Mama tilted her head abruptly toward the ground, turned her body in the other direction, and started to trot away, with me following closely.

My stomach twisted in pain with every step I took, listening to the other horses' whispers about me in the background. The last thing I heard before we went into the barn was one horse saying, "Can you believe she thinks those spots are normal?"

When we got back to our stall, I felt a lump in my throat, as if I couldn't swallow. A tear formed in my already misted eyes as I asked, "How come the other horses hate me? I never did anything to hurt them."

"They don't hate you," Mama said. "They just don't know you."

"But they said I'm weird because I have these stupid spots."

"Always remember that beauty is in the eyes of the beholder," said Mama. "I love your spots and I love you. Many times horses make fun of other horses because they're different. Sometimes it's because they're jealous and sometimes it's because they're scared of things they aren't sure about. You shouldn't judge horses by the way they look. It's what's inside them that counts. I'd rather be friends with the ugliest, nicest horse in the world than the prettiest, meanest one any day."

"Am I the ugliest horse in the world? Everyone thinks I am."

Mama's eyes misted and a tear formed. "No! You're one of the most beautiful horses in the world. Now you have to learn to be one of the nicest as well."

A month passed and the teasing continued every time I went into the yard, until one day Mama had had enough. We moseyed along, minding our business, when Thunder and some other horses trotted over to where we were grazing. Thunder asked, "Why don't you stay in the corner of the yard so we don't have to look at those spots?" The other horses stood behind her and laughed.

Mama stood on her hind legs and shuffled toward Thunder, hoofs raised. Thunder snorted loudly, shuffled backward and cried, "Oh, no you don't. I'm too smart for that." She rose up on her hind legs and flung her hoof out while shifting her weight forward, hitting Mama with all her might.

Mama's knees buckled like an old wooden bridge during a flood. My legs trembled as she hit the ground and groaned. My heart raced as rage enveloped my body. I lunged at Thunder with all my might.

She laughed and held her hoof up, smacking me on my backside. With the momentum, I fell to the ground next to Mama. Thunder announced loudly, "Next time, I won't be so kind! Stay on your side of the yard and keep those spots away from us!" All the horses laughed and trotted away.

That night before bed, I went to the corner of my stall and cried. Mama asked, "What's wrong, dear?"

"Why am I so ugly?"

"You're not, my precious one. All the horses don't understand us, but one day they will."

"I hate my spots," I cried. "I wish I was never born, and I wish I didn't have these ugly spots."

"Your spots are beautiful, and one day everyone will see that." I cried myself to sleep, wishing I was anyone but myself.

The next morning, a truck pulled up in front of the barn and two people I had never seen got out. The girl was short like me, with thick red hair flowing down to the middle of her back. She had freckles on her face and a warm, vibrant smile. The man was tall and strong, with dark hair and straight firm shoulders. They walked around the entire farm, finally approaching our stall. Our owner said, "This one's about two months old. He comes from a good line, but I understand if you don't want him. He looks a little different."

The girl's voice was full of life as she enthusiastically said, "Daddy, he's the one!"

Her father's eyebrows widened with true skepticism. "Are you sure, Molly?"

"I'm sure, Daddy. This is the one!"

"There are a lot of other horses still to see," her father said. "There's brown ones, white ones, and even a few really pretty black ones."

"Oh no!" Molly said, her freckles turning into dimples as she smiled. "This one is the most beautiful horse I've ever seen! Look at his spots." She pointed to the freckles on her face. "He's kind of like me, different but beautiful."

Molly's father's serious face turned to a smile of complete jubilance. "I guess he is different and beautiful, like you."

"I'll bet you couldn't find another special horse like him in the whole world," Molly said. "I love him. You said I could pick out any horse I wanted. I want this one!" She stood with her hands on her hips and her eyes on fire looking like she was ready for a fight.

Her father grinned with pleasure and said, "He's yours."

Molly jumped into the air with her arms flying and screeched, "Oh thank you, Daddy! I love you." She walked over toward me and I backed up in fear. "Don't be afraid, boy." She pulled a piece of an apple out of her pocket and held it in her open hand. I carefully edged toward her and chomped the apple down.

She hugged me around the neck and said, "We're going to be best friends. You'll see." My heart melted and a feeling of warmth filled my body as she held me tightly and wouldn't let go.

"We have a lot of work to do," her father said. "He's young and it'll be at least two years before you can compete."

"I don't care," Molly said as she released her grip. "I love my new horse. Can I name him Oreo?"

"He kind of looks like an Oreo," her father laughed. "Black with white in the middle." I stood warily with my head up, ready to defend myself, wondering if he was going to tease me too. "I like him. Sure, his name is Oreo."

Mama bowed in gratitude, and then half snorted and half cried. "Your new name is Oreo, son."

Later that day in the yard, Thunder trotted toward us with her head held high and her shoulders firm and steady. Expecting a fight, I clenched my muscles and gritted my teeth.

"I heard Oreo was bought by one of the top equestrian trainers in the country," Thunder said. "The man and his daughter are going to be training your son for extreme competition." Her muffled breath barely got out the next few words. "Congratulations and I hope he does well." She trotted away with her head down and her eyes focused on the ground.

Mama's head lifted high into the air. Her loud joyous snorts were heard throughout the entire farm, as she galloped around the yard twice. Finally, she proudly turned to me and said, "I told you your spots were beautiful!" I nodded and couldn't speak, with my tongue in the back of my throat.

My name was on the lips of every horse at the farm after that, all because I was different and had beautiful spots. From that day on, no one ever teased Mama or me again. Mama was right. Beauty is in the eye of the beholder, and Molly thought I was the most beautiful horse in the world. Besides the fact that Molly and I became best friends, she and I won two national championships. And I always remembered what Mama taught me: "Don't judge horses by the way they look." And I never did.

Friends Again

Meghan Rettig

6th Grade, Rockwood South Middle School, Fenton, Missouri

My stomach churned as I eagerly pulled our family's silver minivan into Camp Cedar Hill. Since I hadn't made the U.S. Dive Team, I figured I'd spend a good part of the summer doing what I'd always wanted to do: being a camp counselor and helping children. A memory flashed through my mind of how I had given the best performance of my life in the final round of the tryouts for the U.S. team. I gritted my teeth, clenched the steering wheel harder, and remembered that I promised myself I wouldn't think about it again.

I parked the van and got out, invigorated by the sound of birds chirping in the background. The smell of fresh pine and wildflowers filled the air, plastering a smile on my face. As I gazed off in the distance and saw the bright sunshine reflecting off the small ripples in the lake, a serene feeling of hope filled my body. *This may be just what I need to forget about what happened,* I thought.

I walked toward a refurbished wood cabin, no larger than my bedroom at home, that had a blue hand-painted sign reading, "Cedar Hill Office." I giggled under my breath. *This ought to be interesting.*

When I walked into the office, a middle-aged woman sitting behind a small wooden desk looked up from the stack of papers she was rummaging through and said, "My name is Lilly Harms, and I'm the head camp counselor. Welcome to Cedar Hill."

"Thank you," I returned. "My name is Katie Williams."

"Oh yes," she said. "We've been expecting you."

Ms. Lilly showed me around the camp, until we ended up right in front of a cabin that was no larger than thirty by thirty feet. She smiled and said, "This is the cabin that you and another counselor will share with eight ten-year-olds. You can get your things and pick a bunk. When the other counselor arrives, we'll go over everything. The girls should be arriving any time now."

"Thank you," I said.

Ms. Lilly smiled and said, "If you need me, I'll be in my office."

When I walked into the cabin, the smell of fresh-cut wood tickled my nose. A calm sense of relief came over me when I noticed that it was larger than it looked from the outside. The finely varnished knotty pine walls and planked floor gave me a feeling of the great outdoors. The bunks were made of cedar and looked much better than what I had expected. There were cheery, colorful, hand-drawn pictures on the walls from past campers, giving the cabin a lived-in feeling. *Not bad,* I thought. *At least it's clean.* I settled in and eagerly waited for the girls to arrive.

A little later that afternoon, I was out by the lake when I looked up and saw a huge Cadillac SUV pulling into the camp. The SUV parked next to my van and someone got out. My jaw dropped and I almost fell to the ground when I thought, *Oh no! It can't be! What is* she *doing here?*

I bit my lip and tapped my foot as I watched Carrie walk toward the office. "It can't be. It just can't be," I said under my breath. I went back to my cabin and shut the door, plopping down on my bed, frustrated and wanting to go home.

A few minutes later, Ms. Lilly and Carrie walked in. "Carrie," she said, "this is Katie, and she will be the other counselor you'll be working with."

My stomach burned with anger as I said, "There must be some kind of mistake! Not her."

Ms. Lilly sensed the hostility in my voice and asked, "Do you two know each other?"

"Yes, we know each other," I complained. "We used to be best friends until she cheated me out of a spot on the U.S. Dive Team. Can you assign me to another partner, please?"

Ms. Lilly's eyes got wide and she shook her head. "I can't. You two are the only ones I have until next week. I don't know what happened between you girls, and I don't care. All I know is that in the next few minutes, eight girls are going to be walking through that door who expect to have the time of their lives. It's up to you to make sure they do."

"I can't stay," I said. "I came here to forget about life for a while. I can't work with her."

Ms. Lilly sat down and said, "Many of these girls come here to forget about life for a while, too. Do you think you're the only one that has problems? You two will be off to college after this summer, and you don't ever have to talk to each other again. In the meantime, you'll just have to get along."

"After what she accused me of and said to me," Carrie replied, "I don't know if I can either."

"You have to," Ms. Lilly said, and she walked out.

I kicked my bunk and said, "Don't talk to me all week, so we can at least get through this."

"Fine!" Carrie agreed.

The door swung open and two girls piled into the cabin, with smiles as big as mountains on their faces. One punched her hand into the air and said, as fast as a chipmunk, "Hi! My name is Abby and my friend's name is Courtney. We're best friends. We live in the same neighborhood and we're even in the same class at school. We do everything together. Am I talking too much? My mom always says I talk too much. I don't talk too much, do I, Courtney?"

Courtney shook her head and was about to say something, and Abby cut her off. "I knew I didn't talk too much. My mom isn't always right. Well, maybe I do talk too much. I don't know." She smiled, opened her eyes wide and waited for me to respond.

"My name is Katie," I said. I lowered my voice and added, "And this is Carrie."

"Are you best friends too?" Abby asked, as fast as she had before. "If you are, then we can all be best friends." Before we could respond, five more girls burst in, scurrying around and screaming about who would get what bunk. They lined up and one by one they said, "My name is Maddi, my name is Sarah, my name is Kristy, my name is Liz, and my name is Tricia."

A girl walked in with her head down and set her things on the floor. She had medium-length brown hair and glasses.

I asked, "What's your name?"

"Emily," she said in a soft voice, looking away.

"Okay, girls," Carrie said. "After you put your stuff away, who wants to go for a nature walk?"

The girls all yelled, "Yeah!"

After they quieted down, I turned my nose up and said, "How about we go to the lake for a swim instead?"

The girls screamed louder and we all got our suits on. Emily said, "I can't swim well, so I'll just watch."

"Nonsense," I said. "I'll teach you."

We all went swimming, with me helping Emily the entire time.

Later that evening, Carrie said, "Let's sing songs around the campfire." The girls all cheered.

"I've got a better idea," I said. "Let's tell ghost stories." The girls cheered louder.

"I'm tired of you doing that to me every time I want to do something," Carrie complained. "You guys tell your ghost stories and I'll go to bed."

"Fine," I hissed as Carrie walked away.

The next afternoon we all went out for a long nature walk, until we got into a spot where the path split into three directions. I said, "All right, girls, it's this way back."

"No," Carrie said. "It's that way."

"No, it's this way," I said. "You don't know anything. You never did."

"Well, I'm going this way," Carrie said. "Who's going with me?"

The girls one by one hesitantly followed her until I sighed and said, "Whatever."

Carrie was right, and when we got back to camp I took a head count. I turned to her and said, "Emily isn't here. Did you see her?"

"No," said Carrie. "I don't know what happened to her."

My stomach felt like it had a nest of butterflies in it and my heart raced as if it was going to explode. I looked at Carrie, panic stricken, and asked, "What are we going to do?"

"Let's stay together and go look for her," Carrie said.

We took all the girls and retraced our steps, calling out Emily's name the entire way. I was about ready to say that we needed to go back and get help, when I heard Emily cry out, "I'm over here. I'm lost."

We all ran to her where she was sitting on a rock, crying. I asked, "What happened? We were so worried."

"When you were arguing, I thought I could find my way back on my own, so I went the other way," Emily said. "I couldn't stand to hear you two fight anymore. I came to camp in hopes that I wouldn't hear any more fighting. Please don't fight." She burst into open sobs. "That's all my Mom and Dad do, argue. If I have to hear them fight anymore, I'll pull my hair out." She grabbed her hair and tugged on it.

My anger for Carrie melted away as I hugged Emily and said, "I'm so sorry." I turned to Carrie and opened my eyes wide. I said, "I'm sorry for everything I said to you." I turned, ran down the path back to the cabin and started to cry.

Carrie and the girls came back to the cabin, and Carrie asked the girls to wait outside. She approached my bunk, and I sat up and said, "It's not fair. All I ever wanted out of life was to make the U.S. Dive Team. I overheard your father giving money to one of the coaches to pick you. I should've made the team, not you."

Carrie said, "I know you should've. I heard my dad talking to one of the coaches on the phone. I know what he did."

"How could you?" I yelled. "How could you let him pay off one of the coaches?"

"I couldn't," Carrie said. "If you had let me explain instead of calling me names and storming off, you would've known that I quit the team. You were always better than me. That's why I'm not there training now. I told my dad off and haven't said more than two words to him since I found out. He's such a jerk. He thinks he can buy anything with money, but he can't buy me. That's why I came to camp, to get away from home for a while. I'm going away to college soon, and I'll be on my own. I forgave him, and in time I will talk to him again, but not now."

I sat with my mouth open and my arms crossed, not knowing what to say. Carrie said, "If you still want a spot on the team, call the coaches. There might be an opening."

"I don't know," I mumbled.

"Maybe neither of us was destined to make the team," said Carrie. "I'm a big believer in destiny."

I swallowed hard and felt as small as a flea. I reached my hand out and said, "I'm sorry. I thought you were in on it with your dad. I should've given you a chance to explain. Will you forgive me?"

She grabbed me, hugged me and said, "Friends again?"

I said, "Definitely, friends again." Then all the girls, who had been eaves-dropping right outside the door, burst in screeching and jumped on top of us on my bed. They giggled as they got up.

Abby turned to Emily and rapidly said, "You're going to be Courtney's and my best friend the whole time we're here." Emily smiled and started to say something, when Abby cut her off. "We're going to swim together, go horseback riding, canoeing and everything. Am I talking too fast?" Emily couldn't get a word in edgewise so she shook her head no. Abby continued, "Good, because I didn't think I was. After canoeing we're going to do archery and roast marshmallows. You like marshmallows, don't you? I love marshmallows. They're my favorite. I like to roast three at once. Can you roast three at once?"

Emily opened her eyes wide, took a deep breath and nodded. Abby put her arm around Emily's shoulder and said, "Come on. Let's go outside. I've got a lot to tell you."

The rest of the week went perfectly, and we all had the time of our lives. I learned two very important lessons at Camp Cedar Hill that summer. Get all the facts straight before you jump to conclusions; and just because you want something badly, it doesn't mean it will or should happen. In life, you are where you are supposed to be because there is a thing called destiny, and sometimes you can't change it.

The Dream Key

Erin Beaudry

7th Grade, Mason Middle School,
Mason, Ohio

When it's in the palm of your hand, the serenity of the key settles you; at other times, it sends terror throughout your body. Once the enticement and power of the dream key is felt, it's almost impossible to overcome its seduction. The obsession will ultimately do nothing but bring you to your knees in agony.

It was a typical cold September afternoon in Massachusetts. I had finished all my homework, and called my friend Jade and asked, "Did you get that social studies assignment in Mrs. Crupt's class done?"

"Yeah, Victoria," Jade said. "It's done. If I'd known seventh grade was going to be so hard, I would've stayed in sixth."

"Very funny!" I laughed. "I'll meet you in front of the cemetery in thirty minutes. We can cut through to the park and kick the ball around. We have a couple of games coming up, and we both could use the practice."

"Can't we go the long way around?" Jade pleaded. "You know that place gives me the creeps."

"Stop being a baby," I said. "Thirty minutes, and don't be late." Then I hung up.

When I got to the cemetery, Jade was already there, sitting on the curb out front. I snuck up behind her, grabbed her shoulder and yelled, "Boo!"

She jerked her head around, jumped right up, and turned her entire body toward me. "Victoria! Don't do that ever again, especially here."

I laughed and said, "You should've seen your face. I thought you were going to die on the spot. Come on. Let's cut through."

I dropped the soccer ball I was holding and started to dribble it toward the cemetery gate when Jade said, "All right, but let's hurry."

Halfway through the cemetery, I said, "I've been working on this new move, watch." I put my right foot on top of the ball and rolled it over. It moved toward my left foot and I tapped it lightly once, then kicked it. The ball went off the side of my foot, flying sideways off the main path, and bounced off one of the tombstones, making a weird clanking noise. I looked at Jade and said, "Oops! I haven't perfected it yet, but I will." I went after the ball and said, "Come on."

Jade shook her head and said, "I'm staying right here. I'm not going by those graves."

I took Jade's hand and said, "I'll hold your hand if you want me to."

She stiffened, pulled her hand away, and said, "Go on. I'll be right behind you."

We walked down a row of six graves; my ball was sitting at the end, right on top of one of the gravesites. Next to it was a bit of crusted stone with something sticking out of the end. I looked at the tombstone and saw where a little piece of the granite was missing. I picked up the crusted stone and put it up to the tombstone. "That's what that clanking noise must've been. Look, it fits right in there."

Jade said, "I don't like this at all. Let's get out of here."

"Wait," I said. "The tombstone reads, *Jane Wilkinson, born 1670, died 1704*. Boy, people didn't live very long back then."

"Get the ball and let's go," Jade said. "I have a weird feeling about this place."

"There's something inside this stone," I replied. I started rubbing it clean, and after I crumbled the excess rock away, I turned to Jade and said, "Look! It's a key. I wonder what it opens." My eyes went strangely out of focus as I looked closely at it. I shook my head hard, looked away, and my vision became clear again. I held the key up and said, "One side of the key is black and the other is silver and sparkling."

I held it tightly in my hand, and Jade said, "Leave that here and let's get going to the park! Remember our games we need to practice for?"

"I'm going to keep it," I said, and put it into my pocket.

Jade shook her head and said, "Come on."

After we practiced, I was tired and we went home. I set the key on the table, silver side up, next to my bed, and didn't think anything about it. After I went to sleep, I had one of the clearest dreams of my life. I dreamed that I got an A on my math test, and my friend Tory got caught cheating.

The next day, when I was taking my math test, my teacher, Mr. Kelly, went over to Tory and took her paper away and said, "You get a zero on the exam. I saw you looking at Victoria's paper. I have zero tolerance for that."

Mr. Kelly graded our tests and handed them back before the class ended. As I looked at my paper, my stomach was in knots. My knees got weak as I read, "A. Good job, Victoria!"

I thought, *It can't be. It must be a coincidence.* I shook my head in disbelief and went on with my day. When I got home, I went into my room and picked up the key. I looked at it and went into a daze. The next thing I knew, Mom was calling me, two hours later. "Victoria. Come down for dinner." I set the key down black side up, and felt invigorated and full of life. I sat down to eat but didn't touch my food, because all I could think about was the key.

That night I had another extremely clear dream, where I fell down during my soccer game and skinned my knee. I woke up feeling groggy and lethargic, when I should have felt refreshed after such a deep sleep.

During the first half of my game that afternoon, the ball came to me right in front of our bench. I turned with it and was ready to kick it downfield to one of our forwards. A girl came up behind me and hit me with her shoulder from the side. I went flying forward, right onto my knees. After I stood up and looked down, I saw a scrape on my right knee with blood oozing out.

My body went weak and I froze like a statue. *The key!* I thought. *It had to be the key.*

I sat out the rest of the game in a blur until Jade walked over to where I was sitting and said, "We're going out for ice cream. Do you want to go?"

"I'm not hungry," I said, shaking my head.

"I hope your knee is all right. I'll see you tomorrow."

I nodded and didn't say a word.

That night before bed I thought, *I get it. The silver side up is for good dreams and the black side up is for bad ones. Who would ever want the black side up?*

A week earlier, I had asked my mom for twenty dollars to get a shirt at the mall, and she had said, "You don't need that shirt; you have enough clothes." That night, I dreamed I found twenty dollars at school and went to the mall and bought the shirt.

The next morning, I jumped out of bed and went to school. The day seemed odd to me, as if I weren't really there or didn't even exist. I walked through the hallway on my way to fifth hour like a zombie, until I looked down at the ground. My palms were sweating, and my body was as stiff as a mannequin in a store window — until I saw a twenty-dollar bill lying on the floor.

I bent down and picked it up. When I grasped the bill it was if I could feel every ridge and corner of the paper. I looked closely at the bill and felt a jolt throughout my body. My mind became clear and I felt invigorated, as if I had just had a great night's sleep. Right after school, I went to the mall and bought the shirt.

Later that day, Jade came over and asked, "What's wrong with you? You didn't even talk in school, and you missed practice today."

I said slowly, "That key I found helps me see the future."

"Yeah right," she said.

"It's true," I mumbled. "When I sleep with the silver side up, I have good dreams, and they come true. When I sleep with the black side up, I have bad dreams, and they come true."

"I don't know about that," said Jade. "All I know is you've been really weird lately."

That night after Jade left, Mom came into my room and asked, "Is everything all right? You haven't eaten in at least two days and you seem so different."

"Everything is fine," I said, as I gazed off in the distance.

"I'm going to make an appointment with Dr. Grayson," Mom said, "just in case." After she left, I made sure the silver side was up before I went to sleep, and couldn't wait for my good fortune the next day.

I had a horrible dream that my bike was stolen and I was shoved to the ground by a dirty-looking man in his early twenties. I jumped out of bed the next morning and went into the bathroom. My head was spinning, and I threw up. I felt a little better and got ready for school.

I spent the entire day bemused until I was on my way home from school. I stopped at an intersection on my bike to cross the street. I looked both ways and out of the corner of my eye until I saw the outline of a person coming up behind me. I got off my bike and wheeled it around. My mouth hung open and I began to tremble when I saw a dirty-looking guy say, "Hello."

The man looked about twenty-three years old and had greasy dark hair; he was wearing an old ripped concert shirt and a dirty pair of jeans. I turned away so I wouldn't gag from the smell, which reminded me of riding behind a garbage truck. I began to hyperventilate a little when he looked at me.

I moved away, and he pushed me on my shoulder. I tripped and fell to the ground, landing on my side. He jumped on my bike and rode away. I wasn't hurt, so I sat up and put my head between my hands. I went home crying and told Mom what had happened.

She said, "I'll call the police." After the police came and we filed a report, I went into my room and sat on my bed. I picked up the key and thought, *What's your deal? I had a bad dream with the silver side up last night. Is it a good dream and a bad one every other night or is there a different trick to it? I'm not sure what it is yet. But I know one thing, I'll find out, because I love being able to see the future.*

The rest of the night was a blur again and I went to sleep excited about it being a good dream night. I dreamed I was selected to a special team of all-stars to play in a soccer tournament out of state.

The next day when my coach approached me, I wasn't surprised. Coach Hamilton said, "I got a call from the director of travel soccer in Boston. He saw you play a game two weeks ago, and he wants you to guest on his team for a tournament in Ohio. Here's the form your parents will have to fill out. You're a great player, but don't miss any more practices." I smiled and she walked away.

That key is the best thing that ever happened to me, I thought. *I need to learn how to control it so all my days will be like this.*

That afternoon I went into my room and held the key in my hand. I thought, *How do you work? Teach me how you work. Please show me your secret.*

Jade soon came over, and Mom let her into my room. Jade saw me in a daze and said, "I knew there was something wrong with you, and I guess it is that key. I spent four hours researching dream keys on the Internet. Legend has it that there were seven dream keys issued to the seven tribal leaders of the Inca Indians. These keys were given by a great leader from above as a gift to the tribal chiefs, so they could see into the future to prevent Westerners from raiding their temples and stealing their gold.

"Legend says that they were passed down from generation to generation. One evil leader used the keys for wrongdoing and they began giving bad and good dreams. The person whose grave that key came from was a woman who went crazy. It didn't say how she died, but she was from Salem, Massachusetts. After doing more research, I found out that everyone who gets one of those keys goes crazy. I have no idea how that key got here, but the pictures are identical, look."

I sat staring at the key, and Jade said, "The only way to break the control that key has over you is by you, and only you, putting it back exactly where you got it. You have to put it back, you have to."

"I'll never put it back," I said. "I'll learn how to control it! You'll see!"

"You can't control it. It can only control you."

"No!" I said, and I stared at the key again more intensely.

Jade's face turned red with anger, and for the first time that I remember, she stood firm and unafraid. She growled, "Come here!" She grabbed me by the hair and my head snapped forward. I came out of my trance as she pulled me into the bathroom. She shoved my face in front of the mirror and said, "Look at yourself! You haven't eaten or showered in days. Your hair is scraggly and you have no makeup on. Look! Is this the way you want to be?"

She let go of me, and I looked deep into the mirror and stepped back in fright. My stomach turned as I saw what looked like half me and half a skanky skeleton. I yelled, "No! I can't keep the key. How could I have been so blind?"

Jade touched my arm gently and said, "You're my best friend and I love you. Please put the key back!"

I nodded and said, "It's so hard, though."

"Come on," Jade said.

We went over to Jade's house and into her garage. She pulled out a bag of cement and a bucket and said, "I've helped my dad enough times with stuff like this to know what to do." She poured half a bucket of cement and filled it with water. She mixed the cement with a putty knife, smiled confidently and said, "We're going to the cemetery, right now."

We walked over to the cemetery and stood in front of the tombstone where we found the key. Jade filled the hole where the key fell from half full with cement. She turned to me and said, "You have to put it in; only you can break its spell."

I looked at the key and felt its power pulling me toward it again. Jade grasped my arm and said firmly, "Put it in, please."

I jerked my head around and shook my body, trying to bring myself back to coherency. I reached toward the hole, gripping the key tightly in my unsteady hand. My heart raced and my mind went blank as I set the key into the fresh, clammy cement. I tried to pull my hand away and a feeling of desire came over me. The thought entered my head, *Take the key. Keep it forever.*

Jade touched my arm and softly said, "Let go." I let go of the key, and a shock of awareness engrossed my body. My stomach felt normal for the first time in days, and my head cleared. I took a deep breath and felt as free as a bird on an endless flight.

Jade quickly covered the rest of the hole, patching the key firmly inside the tombstone. We walked away without looking back once. Two days later, I was back to normal with a smile on my face and eating like a horse.

The next day, we walked to the store together, laughing as best friends again. When we got to the store, we noticed a set of keys in the parking lot, next to a car. I looked at Jade and she looked back. We frowned in fear and shook our heads. We immediately went the other way, and never talked about the dream key again.

Singing with an Angel

Elizabeth Bolaji

7th Grade, Colleyville Middle School, Colleyville, Texas

I'm not crazy. I know I'm not. But after finding me passed out on the bathroom floor several times, my mother said she had no choice but to seek professional help. Two years of extensive therapy and six different prescriptions later, they all have come to the same conclusion: I am crazy.

Doctor after doctor keeps telling me that I don't hear angels. They keep saying that I am sick, and that my mind is playing tricks on me, but they are wrong. I finally found it much easier to agree and say I don't hear things anymore. And then there is the pity, and the comments. "Poor Mrs. Seemson with her twisted daughter Jessie," one neighbor says. "I feel so sorry for the mom," says another.

This is how it all started. Three months after I was born, Nana came to watch me five days a week when Mom went back to work. She soothed me when I was sick, sang to me when I needed comforting, and even read to me when I got a little older.

Just before I walked into school for my first day, I said to Mom and Nana, "I'm scared. I don't want to go in."

Nana squatted down so we were at eye level, and said, "You're going to love school. You'll make a lot of friends, you'll get to do artwork, and you'll even be able to run around on the playground at recess." I looked down at the ground and pouted. She went on, "I'll make a deal with you. If you don't like school, I'll take you out and get the biggest ice cream cone you ever had in your life when you get home."

She stuck her hand out to shake mine and said, "Deal?"

I shook her hand and said, "Deal." I loved school, just like she had said, and she took me out for ice cream anyway.

Nana was there every day after school when I got home, and helped me with my homework. We ate together, laughed together and even sometimes cried together. And when Nana wasn't there, Mom was as nice as could be too.

When I was ten years old, Nana came to me and said, "I love you, dear, with all my heart. But there's something you need to know. I've been diagnosed with cancer and have a short time to live."

My feet went numb and my head started to spin. "No, it must be some kind of mistake," I said.

"It's no mistake," Nana said. "I love you, Jessie. Sometimes people have to leave earth because they're needed to do other things."

"What other things?" I asked.

"Oh, I don't know," Nana said. "You know how I told you to live the right way, and then when you die you'll get a huge reward?" I nodded. "Think of it as my time to get a huge reward." Nana and I cried together, finding comfort in each other's arms.

Six months later, right before Nana died, she whispered to me from her bed, "I will always be with you. Whenever you sing the songs we used to sing, I will be in your heart." I cried the entire day when she died.

A month passed, and I was still distraught. I began to fail in school and became withdrawn. Every day after school, I would count the sixty-three and a half steps from my front door to my bed, and then sit and sing the songs that Nana and I used to, until something unbelievable happened. Nana spoke to me silently in my mind. She said, "I'm here with you, Jessie. I'll be here with you every day you sing." From then on, I heard her voice every day.

I told Mom about it, and she immediately thought I was crazy. She took me to the doctors and they thought I was delusional too. I didn't care anymore. All I wanted to do was sing with my angel, Nana.

I sang every day with Nana over the next year, and Mom kept taking me to doctor after doctor. Then one day Mom rushed into the bathroom and yelled, "Are you all right? Wake up, Jessie!" I was passed out in the bathroom face down and couldn't remember a thing. Mom fell to her knees and said, "Please, Jessie, stop this. I can't take it anymore. Your grandmother is gone and you have to come back to me." I sat there blankly, singing.

"Please, Jessie, come back to me. You've been kicked out of school and I can't afford the doctor bills anymore, all because you can't accept her death. I know she isn't talking to you, so you have to stop, please." I kept singing.

Mom curled up in a ball in the corner and cried, "Somebody help us, please."

Two weeks later, Mom was on the verge of a nervous breakdown. She went to the local church asking for help, one last time. A priest named Father Charles, who was visiting from out of town, said, "I've heard about things like this. I have a friend who might be able to help you. He investigates things like stigmata and people who claim they hear voices."

"Oh, no," Mom said. "I'm not having someone come over and tell me my daughter is possessed."

"It's not like that," said Father Charles. "Look, probably one of the greatest women to ever walk the earth claimed she heard voices. Joan of Arc claimed she was talked to by angels, and I believe her. They thought she was crazy, but afterward she became a saint in the Church's eyes."

Mom took a deep breath and asked, "Wasn't she burned at the stake for treason?"

Father Charles said, "That was a long time ago. Give it a try. What will it hurt?"

"All right," Mom agreed.

A week later I went into my room and thought, *They feel so sorry for me. But I feel so sorry for them, not knowing and feeling the joy I do, the joy of singing with an angel. When we sing, it's like the accusations of me making it all up and the heavy medication don't matter. It's like I'm at peace with myself and with the world. I'll never admit it isn't true to the doctors again.*

Mom and a man walked in a moment later, and I started singing "Joy to the World."

The man nodded, raised his hand and waved Mom out of the room. "I'm Father Michael Brenner," he said. "I'm here to help you."

I stopped singing and asked, "Are you here to tell me I'm crazy too?"

"No," Father Michael said. "I believe you that you can sing with angels. I wish I could sing with them too."

I sat straight up in my bed and opened my eyes as wide as I could. I stared him down, and noticed he was a handsome man with short dark hair, probably in his late thirties. He was thin and frail, with strong, calming blue eyes. He had his black priest uniform on with a white square on his collar. "You believe me?" I asked.

"Sure I do. I know you wouldn't make it up."

"You're the first person to believe me," I said. "You look at me differently too."

"I've dealt with this for a number of years," Father Michael said.

"You're not here to stop this, are you?" I asked. "I won't allow it. It's the greatest feeling I've ever had."

"I'm sure it's the greatest feeling you ever had," he agreed. "People that experience things like this always say that it's unbelievable. And no, I'm not here to stop it. I'm here to help you understand it. Tell me about what you hear."

"There's not much to it," I said. "After Nana died, she told me she would always be with me, and she is."

"Is it your nana's voice you hear?"

"At first it was only her," I said. "After a while, other angels started talking and singing too. Sometimes I don't even know how many angels I'm singing with. All I know is that when I'm singing with the angels, nothing else matters. "

"When you hear Nana and the other angels, what do they say?" Father Michael asked.

"After Nana died, they told me that she was one of them. They said she was all right, and that they would be watching over me. They tell me they are always watching over me."

"And do you believe that?" Father Michael asked.

"Absolutely," I said. "Do you believe it?"

"Yes, I do," he said. I looked deep into his eyes, which calmed me. I believed and trusted him, and knew he was there to help me. "Are they here now?" he asked.

"I will see." I started singing again and nodded, letting Father Michael know the angels were there.

As I continued singing, Father Michael said, "I believe in you. I believe you're here right now. I know I have no right to ask, but please tell me what your intentions are with Jessie. Please help me find out what it is you want."

The angels stopped singing, and so did I. I heard a voice in my mind say, "We are here to protect her."

Surprisingly, Father Michael heard too, and asked, "Protect her from what?"

"Protect her from herself," the voice said. "When Jessie's grandmother died, she went into a depression she wouldn't have come out of. We have watched over her all this time."

"Is she able to function now by herself?" Father Michael asked. The voice didn't respond. "Help her function and have a normal life, if it is your will. She is a good person and needs to have a normal life, as her grandmother did."

Michael awaited an answer. I heard Nana's voice say, "I will always love you, Jessie. I must go now. I want you to live a good life, and one day we will be together again. Live a normal life, like I did."

The voice stopped, and I sat on the bed shaking. Father Michael came to me and held my hand. I smiled at him and said, "It's over. Nana told me to go live a normal life." I paused and asked, "Do you think I'm crazy?"

"I know you're not crazy, Jessie. I heard it too. Now do as your Nana asked. Go live a normal life. You know what to do now. "

I took a deep breath, and felt as if the weight of the world had been lifted off my shoulders. I smiled at Father Michael and said in a disappointed tone, "I guess I won't be singing with angels anymore."

Father Michael said, "I've got a feeling you'll be singing with all kinds of angels for all of eternity. You've been given a great gift. You were given the chance to sing with angels and know that there is an afterlife waiting for you. Now that you know angels exist, live your life as if they are watching you at all times."

He smiled and hugged me. I lived my life with unshakable faith after that, waiting for the day that Nana and I would be together again.

Hell, Not Jail

Kennedy Boren

7th Grade, North Oaks Middle School, Haltom City, Texas

I stood with a twelve-inch kitchen knife in my hand and thought, *I have to do it. I have to! Anything is better than living like this anymore. Besides, he deserves it. Six years of marriage and this is what I get.*

I walked into the living room, hypnotized by the glistening blade. I crept up behind Jake, my heart racing with excitement and fear. Adrenalin pumped throughout my body as I gripped the knife with all my strength. My mind went blank as I lunged at him, watching the tip of the knife enter his side while he stood unsuspecting. "You got what you deserve," I said, and pulled the knife out of his body as he shrieked in pain.

He moaned, "Why, Bailey, why?" He fell to the floor unconscious amid a growing puddle of blood. I let him lie for a minute while I stood in a daze. I sighed as a tear rolled down my cheek and I thought, *It serves you right.*

I grabbed a roll of plastic wrap and wrapped his body in it until it was like a sardine in a sealed can. After I duct-taped him securely, I dragged him to the garage, put him into the trunk of my Lexus and thought, *So far, so good.*

I went back inside and cleaned up every drop of blood and put every shred of evidence into a secure plastic case. After I threw the case into the trunk and cleaned myself up, I sat on the couch and thought, *Part one is done. Keep it together and remain strong. It'll all be over soon.*

Waiting in the living room until his phone went off was the hardest part. I read the text message that said, "Will you meet me again tonight at nine? I love you."

I texted back, "I'll be there. I love you too."

Rage filled my body as I thought, *You're next, you no-good cheat. How dare you take my man?* I went into my bedroom and pulled out the gun I had bought just for this occasion. When I looked at the blue-gray barrel, my heart was on fire, and jealousy was the flame. *You're going to get what you deserve too, you wench.*

I waited until just before nine o'clock, went over to April's house and rang the doorbell. She opened the door with a smile, thinking it was Jake. I pulled the gun from my purse and commanded, "Go back into the house!" Her eyes bulged out of her head as she slowly backed up into her foyer, unsure what to do.

I cocked the gun and said, "I know about you and Jake. I've been following you for over a month. Who do you think you are, taking my husband from me?"

April's face turned white and she began to tremble. "No, Bailey, please! Jake and I are in love. Please understand."

"Jake and you are in love?" I mocked. "Jake is dead in the trunk of my car and you're going to join him."

"Don't do it," April pleaded. "If you do, you'll go to a place where you'll never know love again."

"It can't be any worse than what I'm feeling now," I said. "And I'm not going to jail. I'm too smart for that."

I felt a lump in my throat and ground my teeth. Anger filled my heart, as if a hand were squeezing it and wouldn't let go. I hesitated for an instant, feeling the cold trigger of the gun on my moist finger, then thought, *I have to.*

I fired the gun, hitting April in the chest, and again in the stomach. She jolted backward, falling on top of her expensive coffee table. I walked over to her and pushed her limp body to the floor with my foot.

As she lay there bleeding, I thought, *It's done. Now all I have to do is bury them in the woods and no one will ever find them.*

I wrapped April heavily in plastic. Just as I was ready to drag her body to my car, two police officers burst into her house with their guns drawn. One of them yelled, "Freeze!"

I said, "I'm not going to jail for these two cheats," and reached for the gun on the table. I grabbed the gun and both officers fired. It felt like a hot fireplace poker had stabbed me in the stomach as the first bullet penetrated my skin. The second bullet went all the way through my arm. I fell to the ground screaming in pain. I heard one of the officers say, "It's a good thing the neighbor heard the shot and called us."

"Yeah," the other officer agreed. "I'm glad we saw her through the window when we snuck up to the house, or that could've been one of us lying there. An ambulance is on the way, but she's not going to make it."

Everything went black and cold after that.

■ ■ ■

I woke up standing in front of several people, whom I couldn't see well because of a blinding light. I asked, "Is this heaven?"

A loud hideous laugh filled the air, and a raspy voice said, "This isn't heaven. This is hell. How sweet it was that you thought you'd be saved. Now I have you for all of eternity."

My body was engulfed in flames and I moaned in pain. I was trapped in a furnace that was burning me alive. As the piercing pain shot throughout my body, I cried, "Please stop. Please show mercy!"

The voice wickedly laughed, "This is your destiny. You are here forever."

I thought, *How could I have been so stupid? I let my jealousy ruin my life. And how did April know that I would go to a place where I could never feel love again? How could I have ever picked hell, not jail?*

Warriors of Light

Luke Basha

7th Grade, Norco Intermediate School, Norco, California

You always hear people complain how awful their day was when things don't go well. Nothing compares to the shock I got the day after my twenty-first birthday.

My name is John Storm, and I was a normal six-foot-tall guy with a medium build, living on my own in New York City. My desire to become a writer and to do something extraordinary with my life propelled me to take a job with a major publisher, starting out in the mail room. After a long day at work, I started home as if it were an ordinary night. The sounds of horns and people yelling down taxis were now common to me, and I barely paid attention during the short walk to my apartment.

I cut through the alleyway toward my building, and halfway through, I was startled by the sound of trash cans being knocked down. I nervously turned around to see a man standing there with his entire body except for his face covered in a cloak. His eyes had a bright blue tint to them, and he seemed rushed and anxious. I took a step away from him, and he followed by stepping toward me. "Who are you?" I asked.

He covered his lips with his index finger and sounded "Shhhh." He motioned with his hand and said, "We don't have much time. Come with me." He put his hand on my shoulder and a gut-wrenching feeling filled my body.

"Close your eyes," he said. I stepped back in fear and heard a loud crashing noise from the other side of the alley. The cloaked man grabbed me by the arm and guided me along to a wall where a tunnel opened up. We stepped through and he said, "We should be safe for a little while."

The tunnel entrance closed as I asked, "Safe from what?"

"Safe from lurking evil in every corner of your world."

I grabbed my phone from my pocket and began to dial 911. "You're crazy," I said. My phone shattered into a thousand pieces right before my eyes. I stepped backwards and shook my head in disbelief.

The man removed the hood of his cloak and said, "Let me explain. Your ancestors were magical knights called 'The Warriors of Light.' They defended the mortal world from the Dark Alliance. When a Warrior of Light dies, a new one is born. When he turns twenty-one, we must find him and inform him of his impending future. If we don't, the dark side will surely find him and kill him, once they are sure he is a Warrior. You, John, are a Warrior, and my name is Nathaniel. I will be helping you through your transition."

"This can't be happening," I said.

"It is," Nathaniel said. "I assure you."

"Send me back to my apartment," I pleaded.

"If I do that, then the Dark Alliance will most likely kill you," he said.

Boom sounded throughout the tunnel, making me jump a foot into the air. It reminded me of a stick of dynamite going off, sending reverberations from the force of the explosion throughout my body.

"Maybe we aren't safe here after all," Nathanial said. "The dark side seems to get more powerful all the time." The walls of the dark, damp tunnel started to crumble, and Nathaniel yelled, "Hurry!" He began to run, and I followed closely behind. We reached the end of the tunnel right when it collapsed, coming out into a brightly lit world. I looked around in amazement to see beautiful green hills and bright sunshine reflecting off a pond that lay before a majestic mountain.

"I don't understand," I said.

"This is the world you belong to now," Nathaniel said. "You were in the other world for your own safety. The dark side would've surely killed you by now if you had lived here."

"What… is the name of this place?" I asked.

"We call it Samorah," Nathaniel said. A loud screech blasted throughout the air, causing Nathaniel to turn around abruptly. My eyes almost fell out of my head as I looked across the meadow and saw a large winged beast flying toward us. It was the size of a school bus, and its wings were red like blood, with eyes the same color. The beast's wings flapped wildly, sending a loud powerful gust of wind throughout the air. Its talons were long and bony and each claw was the size of my hand; it surely could have killed both of us with one strike.

"Run!" I screamed, as the creature let out another loud screech as if to torment us.

Nathaniel raised his right hand and firmly said, "Don't move. A protector will be along any time now." Seconds later, a piece of the earth began to move about thirty yards in front of us. A girl who stood no more than five feet five inches tall emerged from a hole. She had medium-length brown hair and wore an outfit that resembled an old world knight's armor, with leather boots and a helmet that had the ears and eyes cut out. "Jessica," Nathaniel murmured.

The creature headed toward Jessica, while she stood firm and brave, as if luring it in. The beast flew full force toward her with a look of death in its eyes. It let out a huge piercing roar and blasted an eruption of fire from its mouth that looked like it could incinerate an entire ten-story building.

Jessica lifted her hand, pointed her palm outward and yelled, "Absorption!" The fire was stopped from coming any closer to her. She squinted, winced and yelled, "Repulsion!" The huge wall of fire changed its course and headed right back toward the dragonlike creature. Jessica raised her other hand, looked up to the clear sky and said loudly something in a different language that sounded like, "*Aba caba walla shhhow.*"

A loud *boom* rang throughout the land, and the creature was incinerated instantly in a cloud of dust.

"We must hurry," Nathaniel announced, and motioned for us to move across the field, toward the largest hill off in the distance. Jessica joined us, and we ran with all our might across the field, until we got to the side of the hill. In front of us were two golden doors with oversize knobs. In the background we heard another screech, this one louder and more eerie than the first. "A war hawk," Nathaniel said. "They must be desperate to prevent you from entering."

"Entering where?" I asked.

Jessica turned and said, "No time to explain. Tell him of his fate so he can make his decision."

Nathaniel gazed at me with piercing eyes and said, "If you choose the door on the left, you'll return to your normal life. You will no longer be a threat to the Dark Alliance, because you will never have the opportunity to return here. Other than trying to recruit you for evil, they will probably leave you alone. If you choose the door on the right, you'll never be able to go back to the old world you know as New York City, unless you are sent to combat evil. Your old life will be over. You will become one of the most prestigious Warriors of Light, just like your ancestors before you. If you do choose to be a Warrior of Light, life will not be easy. You will be thrust into constant battles with evil at every turn. You may even give your life for the cause."

"Caw, caw," blistered throughout the air as the war hawk swooped in. Jessica raised her hand and said, "Hurry. You know I can't hold off a war hawk for long." The war hawk roared and blasted a lightning bolt at Jessica. With her hands still raised, she yelled, "Repulsion!" The lightning bolt split; part of it blasted the ground in the other direction a few hundred yards away, with Jessica and the war hawk taking the rest of the hit. She went flying four feet into the air, hit the side of the hill, fell to the ground and moaned in pain. The war hawk fluttered and took a nose dive toward the ground, then regained consciousness and circled upward.

"You must choose, now!" Nathaniel warned.

"I want to be a writer," I said. "But if I choose that, then your world and mine will suffer, now that I know they are interconnected. I need more time. I can't decide!" The war hawk turned and made a run toward us with his talons extended, ready to strike.

Jessica stumbled to her feet and moved between us and the war hawk to protect us. "I need more time!" I screamed.

"You have none!" Nathaniel yelled.

A boom of thunder filled the air and another bolt of lightning blasted toward us. Jessica raised both her hands and yelled, "Repulsion and reflection!" I looked into Jessica's beautiful, fearless brown eyes and a feeling of hope came over me. I felt a peaceful sensation of belonging and a total sense of pride. It was as if my life suddenly had meaning and everything made sense to me now.

My body prickled with adrenaline and I yelled, "I choose the Warriors of Light!" I grabbed the door handle on the right, and we all rushed through. I quickly slammed the door and the lightning bolt hit the door behind us, bounced back and hit the war hawk.

"Ehhheeh," bellowed from behind the door, and then a loud bang was followed by a rumble that shook the ground. "You chose just in time," said Nathaniel. "The beast died upon impact, which is rare. You must be the one we've been waiting for."

I looked across the room to see a huge round wooden table, the size of a classroom, with many older men, and some younger ones, sitting silently.

A man dressed in a hooded purple cloak stood up and walked toward us. He unveiled his face and said, "Welcome, my son."

My eyes narrowed, then opened wide as if they would pop out of their sockets. I had never known my father, but now an undeniable bond overwhelmed me. "Dad…" I said. "I thought you died twenty years ago."

"My son, oh, my fearless son. I had to choose just as you did; that's why you thought I died. I couldn't reveal myself to you until now. I am a Warrior of Light, and now you are too. You had to choose between good and evil of your own free will. You chose well, son. Come and join me, your grandfather, and great-grandfather, so we can keep your new world and your old one safe from evil. I love you and I'm proud of you. Now your journey begins as a Warrior of Light."

I smiled and said, "Thanks, Dad."

Soldier of Hope

Vince Bella

7th Grade, Gahanna East Middle School,
Gahanna, Ohio

The midday sun reflected brightly off my double-edged sword that was finally raised. A bead of sweat rolled down my cheek, and my grip tightened as the captain yelled, "Prepare for battle!" I stood with my heart racing, third row back, impatiently waiting for the chance to strike our enemy dead. Honor and the well-being of every man, woman and child in our country was our only thought, all five thousand of us. Anything less than a victory would be worse than death itself.

A thought of my grandfather popped into my head, of the day when he sat me down as a small boy and said, "Gerald, your father and I are no strangers to the battlefields. My father and his father won many great battles so that one day you wouldn't have to fight. By the time you are a man, all the battles will be won, and you and your children will live in peace."

I shook my head, and thought, *If we win this battle, then my son Kenneth, who is at home with his mother, and his future sons, will surely know peace.*

The captain shouted his final speech, "Stand tall and protect the motherland at all costs! Fight for all that is good in the world, and never let our enemy hide in the cracks of evil again. This is our destiny. We will go down as the greatest soldiers known to man." The violent roar of the men overrode the captain as he raised his sword and yelled, "Charge!"

The first line of a thousand charged while yelling a defiant war cry, "Death to our enemies!" and now it would ring in my ears forever. The land looked like a dust cloud, with both sides only a hundred yards apart. With our archers preparing to fire, the last thing in my mind was that we were outnumbered by a few hundred. I waited for the captain to call the second assault.

The sound of metal clashing and men shouting and falling to the ground was shortened by the captain yelling, "Second line, charge!" The second line ran toward the enemy with the same intense battle cry, unsure if this day would be their last. I stepped forward, tightened the grip on my sword and thought, *We will prevail; good always does.*

The captain surveyed the battlefield and shouted, "Third line, prepare for battle!" I swallowed deeply as if my tongue was halfway down my throat. "Third line, charge!"

I bolted toward the enemy with all my might, screaming. As I ran toward death or victory, the dust formed a film on my teeth, reminding me of the other four battles I had survived. When I approached the front lines, the familiar clash of metal sounded strong and loud. The distinct sound of arrows filling the air made me believe they were coming from all sides.

In my sights was my first victim. I ran up behind an enemy soldier who was engaged with one of our own, and stabbed him in the back. He fell to the ground with a thud, while my eyes met those of the man I saved. I pulled my sword from the enemy's back and turned to find one of his comrades charging me.

My heart pounded as I stepped backward and slashed at his throat. I missed and he countered with a wild swing. I shuffled away and then lunged at his stomach with my sword. He fell to the ground like a branch from a tree during a storm.

I turned away again, to find yet another enemy charging in my direction. The sudden rush of force made me flinch as an arrow whizzed past my right ear and into the chest of the oncoming fighter. I took a deep breath and charged at an enemy from behind, striking him in the back. He fell to the ground dead, and I turned for more.

Two hours later, I stood covered in blood, looking across the battlefield with five hundred men from our side. The countryside looked like a river of red, with bodies lying everywhere. We marched into their land and stormed the castle later that evening. I was the first to enter the king's chambers.

I held my sword high and said, "Surrender or die, King Andrew."

King Andrew said, "I will not surrender to a lowly soldier."

"I am not just a soldier!" I exclaimed. "I am a soldier of hope, a soldier who has won a battle for his country with honor and dignity! A soldier of hope who now can live his life in peace. My children and their children will never have to live with the pain I have from killing on the battlefield."

"Your children and their children," the king mocked. "There have been wars and battles since the beginning of time. Your children and their children will never know peace, and they'll never know you." He grabbed his sword and lunged at me. I slid backward and swung my sword perfectly. He fell to the ground bleeding, moaning in pain. A dozen of our soldiers rushed to my side, congratulating me.

The captain came in and I explained exactly what had happened. He said, "You are a hero, my friend. Your name will be on the lips of every person in the kingdom."

"Thank you, sir."

I left the room and fell to my knees exhausted, thinking, *The battle is won, and now there can be peace!*

■ ■ ■

Forty years later, my grandson stood in the fourth row back as the captain yelled, "Prepare for battle!"

His mind raced as he thought, *If we can just win this battle, then my son and his son will know peace. I am a soldier of hope, and I will fight to my death for my son not to have to feel the pain on the battlefield that I know all too well. If this battle is won, then there will finally be peace!*

Leave the Past Alone

Aisha Espinosa

7th Grade, Coppell Middle School East, Coppell, Texas

I woke to the sound of a snowball splattering on my window. I jumped out of bed, opened the window and looked out. My best friend Kyle was standing there, with another snowball in one hand and his snowboard in the other. "Come on, Luke," Kyle said. "You sleep way too late during winter break."

"Quiet," I mouthed. "You'll wake up my little sister, Kate. You know how much of a pain she is to ditch when she follows us. I'll be down in a minute." I threw my clothes on, grabbed a granola bar from the counter and bolted out the door.

Kyle greeted me with, "Hurry up. I want to get over to the park before anyone else gets there. Is your dad at work?"

"Yeah," I said. "He's working on some special case or something."

"Cool," Kyle said. "Then we can board all morning."

I took my snowboard from the garage and we started walking toward the park. The freshly fallen snow glistened in the morning sun, blinding me for a second. I put my sun goggles on and asked, "Did you get that project started yet?"

"Are you kidding?" Kyle asked. "I'm not doing that thing until the last day. Besides, my older brother said he did the same project for Mrs. Kensington when he was in eighth grade. He said I could use his old one as a guide to make my own."

"You're so lucky," I said.

"Hey," Kyle said. "Let's not talk about school. We have a whole week to snowboard, so forget about it."

When we got to the park, he said, "Awesome. We're the first ones here. We'll probably get at least a half an hour in before anyone else shows up."

I took a deep breath and tasted the fresh air in the back of my mouth and thought, *Everything looks so clean and pure after that fresh snow. I love living here and coming to this park.*

We started walking up the trail to the top of the hill in the heavily wooded area. I could smell the evergreen trees as the snow flew off the branches that swung back at me as Kyle led the way. When we got to the top of the hill, I said, "Me first." I took a deep breath and my heart started to speed. I jumped on my snowboard and pushed off. I swerved back and forth, gaining speed, yelling, "Yeah!"

When I got to the bottom and stopped, I yelled up, "It's sort of slow today. After we pack it all down and the sun melts it a little, it'll be great. I'll be right up." I glanced up and saw Kyle messing with his boots, so I hurried up the path, hoping I could meet him before he made a run down.

About thirty feet up the path, I felt a calloused hand cover my mouth. The person's other hand felt like it was poking me in the back with something. I mustered a panicked, muffled scream, which didn't amount to much. I heard Kyle yelling "Woo!" in the background, making his first run down the hill.

Another burly man jumped from the bushes and pulled me backward by my coat. They threw me to the ground, jumped on me, and started tying my hands with thick, coarse rope. Just as my hands were secured, Kyle started up the path toward the top of the hill. The man who had tied my hands pushed my face down in the snow and put his knee in the small of my back.

Meanwhile, the burly man grabbed Kyle and threw him to the ground. Kyle bounced off the ground and tried to get up. My heart pounded as the man jumped on him, trying to control him. Kyle struggled, trying to roll over and get away, but the man was too strong. He held him down and said, "You better stop struggling, or I'm going to beat you until you do."

Kyle simmered down, and the man bound his hands just like mine. My heart felt like it was going to explode and I said, "We didn't do anything. What do you want?"

The smaller man said, "Shut up," and struck me with his open hand across the face. "You'll know soon enough." My face felt like it had been stung by twenty bees, as they gagged us with washcloths and duct tape.

The burly man said to Kyle, "You wait right there, or I'm going to stomp your face!" He put rubber gloves on, picked up Kyle's and my snowboard and threw them deep into the brush away from the path. They went through Kyle's pockets and mine, pulled out our cell phones and took the batteries out. They threw our phones and batteries deep into the bushes, just like our snowboards.

The two men stood us both on our feet and started walking us into the woods, holding us by the back of our coats. The smaller man pulled out a knife and wielded it toward our faces so we could both see it. I felt like I was going to throw up when I glanced at him and noticed he had a wicked grin, as if waiting for an excuse to use the knife.

My dad had taught me if I was ever abducted to learn as much about the captors as possible to help plan my escape. I was finally able to get a good look at the two and saw the burly man was six feet tall and very muscular. He had on a dark ski cap that was folded over as a hat. His face was plump and he was missing two teeth up front. The smaller man was about five feet nine inches tall and had on the same type of hat, plus a dark parka and snowmobile boots.

My heart pounded more and more with each step we took farther from the trail and our only hope of being spotted. I glanced out of the corner of my eye and saw Kate off in the distance, behind a tree about sixty yards away, with her head sticking out around it. I gulped and looked down at the ground so as not to draw attention to her, hoping that she wouldn't get spotted. I looked back toward her again with a terror-stricken gaze as if to say, "Go get help!"

A twig snapped over in the direction where Kate was hiding and almost made me choke on my own breath, knowing she was our only chance. I immediately moaned and began to struggle, to distract our captors so she could have a chance to slip away. Luckily the distraction worked, because no one else heard or saw her, which gave me a ray of hope.

We walked another hundred yards, until the burly man growled, "Far enough." He threw Kyle on the ground, while the other man shoved me up against a tree. My stomach burned with fear when the burly man walked over to me and abruptly pulled the duct tape away from my mouth. I yelled, "Ouch!"

He said, "Oh, stop it, you baby." I swallowed hard, and he asked, "Are you Luke Peterson?" I nodded. He grabbed me by the coat and asked, "Well, are you?"

My body felt numb and I was filled with terror. I barely managed to say, "Yes, why?"

"Are you the Luke Peterson whose dad is an FBI agent?" he asked.

"Yes," I said.

"Your dad ruined both our lives," he said. "We were working together in a harmless business, and your dad put us in jail."

I looked over at Kyle, who was still gagged, and started breathing heavily. I knew the only chance we had was to stall and hope Kate could get help. "You must be mistaken," I said. "My dad has worked at a desk for the last fifteen years."

The smaller man took hold of my hair, threw my head back and snarled, "Liar." He waved his knife in front of my face and pleaded, "Let me kill him now!"

"No," the burly man growled. "I want him to know exactly what happened to us before we kill him." My eyes popped out and I shook with fear. "We had a nice thing going, bringing product into the city from overseas and selling it. I mean, who were we hurting? I was making half a million a year. Your dad headed up the investigation against us. Drug trafficking is what they charged me with. I spent six years in prison. Do you know what it's like in there? Well, do ya?"

I shook my head and he said, "They took my son away from me because I was in jail, and his mother moved away. Do you know what that did to me?"

I shook my head again and said, "I'm sure there must've been some mistake."

"There's no mistake," the other man said. "Your dad is going to regret the day he arrested me for the rest of his life."

"He was only doing his job," I said.

"He doesn't know who he was messing with," the burly man said.

I tried to stall as long as I could by squabbling some more, until the burly man finally yelled, "Enough!"

"What about my friend?" I asked. "He had nothing to do with this."

"We're going to kill him too," the burly man said, "to make your dad even madder."

"Can't you leave the past alone?" I pleaded. "You can't change what happened."

"I can't change what happened," he said, grinning spitefully. "But I can sure feel better about getting your dad back for what he did." He took the knife from the smaller man and said, "Your father took the most important thing away from me — my son. Now it's payback time. He's going to see what it's like to lose his son, too."

"Revenge never makes a person feel better," I said. "It only makes things worse."

"Well, I'm going to find out firsthand," he said. He stepped toward me, and I shivered as I saw the sun reflecting on the blade.

He laughed, and I heard a voice yell, "Freeze!" Both the men turned around and saw two county police officers holding guns pointed right at them. The burly man took a step toward me and one officer said, "One more step and you're dead." The burly man dropped the knife and put his hands in the air.

The other officer said, "Get on the ground, with your hands behind your back!" Both of the men did. The officers arrested both the men, and then untied us.

After we were safely in the police station, Dad finally arrived, and said, "I'm so sorry, son. I love you. Are you all right?"

"I'm a little shaken up, but I'll be okay," I said.

"We don't have to worry about them ever bothering us again," Dad said. "With their records and an attempted murder charge pending, it'll be thirty years before they get out."

Kate ran up and hugged me and said, "I was so scared, I didn't know what to do."

"You did the right thing by getting help," Dad said. "You're a hero. I guess I raised two smart kids."

"I learned one very important thing," I said. Dad turned his head a little, and his eyes widened. "Leave the past alone because you can't change it, and if you dwell on it, it won't do any good. They should've moved on with their lives."

I turned to Kate and said, "I'm so sorry for all the times I was mean to you and yelled at you for following me. You can follow me or come with me anytime you want."

Kate smiled and said, "I'm going to remember that you said that."

My sister and I became best friends after that, and I never complained about her coming with me again.

Love Potion

Sarah Libassi

7th Grade, Morton Middle School, Vandalia, Ohio

Science was never my best subject, so I grabbed my science book and started studying for my final. A moment later I heard Mother yell, "How dare you accuse me of that! You're the one that's never home."

"Yeah, well, at least I actually earn a living!" Father shouted back. "You spend money faster than I can make it!"

"That's because I have a husband that's never around, and I have nothing to do," Mother retorted.

"Maybe I should leave for good," Father said.

"Maybe you should," Mother replied.

I took hold of my iPod and heard a door slam loudly. *Why can't they get along?* I thought. *They fight almost daily. It's a good thing I'm an only child and no one else has to hear this all the time.*

My name is Erica Reed and I'm fourteen years old. I'm five feet two inches tall and have long, straight dark hair. And this is my story.

Eighth grade had been the worst year of my life, with the divorce pending in a couple of months. My grades dropped a full letter, and my parents couldn't understand why. I guess hearing them yell the meanest things possible at each other wasn't supposed to affect me at all.

I turned up my iPod all the way, trying to block everything out. I started singing loudly and moved my head back and forth to the sound of the music to mask the emptiness I felt inside. I made my all-too-familiar wish, *I wish I could go into my closet and come out as somebody else.*

The loud rap on my door startled me at first and I don't know why. It had been the same routine every day: a fight by my parents, then a knock at my door with Mom walking in to see if I was all right. Mom asked, "Do you need any help with your homework?"

"No," I said. "I'm fine."

"I'm going grocery shopping," Mom said. "It shouldn't take more than an hour. Your father left, so if you need anything, call me on my cell." I nodded and cranked my iPod up again.

After Mom left, my mind wandered. *I really don't care about my science grade. I'm not going to be a scientist anyway. I don't care about any of my grades. Who really cares about anything?* I lolled around for ten minutes and was bored stiff. I thought, *I'm going to go to the mall for a couple of hours. It's only two miles away, and knowing Mom, she won't be back by then anyway.* I left a note on the table and got on my bike and left.

I tried to clear my mind as I pedaled my bike, feverishly hoping for any relief from being me. I stopped at a crosswalk, gripped my handlebars tighter and waited for the light to change. I looked over at traffic and saw Mr. Spellman, my science teacher, stopped at the light. I lifted my hand and started to wave to him, when the light changed and he pulled away.

I started pedaling as hard as I could, thinking, *I need to ask him a few questions about the final. Maybe he'll cut me a break if I see him outside of school.* I followed him for a quarter mile until he pulled into a subdivision.

Just as I turned into his subdivision, he pulled up into a driveway about ten houses away and then into its back yard. He immediately got out of his car and hurried back to what looked like a little garage. I tried to catch him, but he went inside before I could say a word.

I parked my bike and looked around. His lot was large and heavily wooded, almost giving the feeling of being in the country. I walked toward the garage, which was about thirty feet long and twenty feet wide and entirely made of wood; it looked like it had not been painted in years. There were no windows on the entire building, and the door looked like it had been reinforced with heavier wood and a heavy-duty lock.

I hesitated a moment, feeling strange and out of place. Instead of going to the door, I went to the side of the building. I saw a slight crack in the rotted wood and nervously peered in. My throat felt heavy and I gulped as I saw Mr. Spellman inside, looking in an old book. I could barely make out what he was saying, but it sounded like, "*Abble dabble dobbie dure*, change this liquid into a cure." He finished talking and pointed what looked like an old, bent, whittled stick at a small bottle, which was sitting on the table. A puff of smoke went over him and the bottle shook.

I almost jumped out of my skin backwards, and shrieked. Mr. Spellman asked, "Who's there? I heard you!" He rushed out of the garage to find me standing there stunned, with my hands frozen at my sides. I started to walk away and he said, "Hold it right there, Erica."

I stopped and said with a shaky voice, "I was just seeing if you could help me with the science exam."

"Were you following me?" he demanded.

"No, honest," I pleaded. "I saw you at the intersection on the corner and thought I could ask you a few questions."

"How much did you see in there?"

"Oh, nothing," I said, and started creeping away.

He grabbed my arm and said, "Wait a minute! How much did you see?"

Knowing I had no choice, I took a deep breath, let it out and said, "I saw you do something to a bottle and say some words. That's all!"

He tightened his grip, grinned wickedly and said, "You've seen too much. Now I'm going to have to kill you!"

My eyes bugged out and I started to pull away in a panic. "Please, no! Mr. Spellman, I won't tell anyone."

Mr. Spellman laughed and said, "You should've seen your face, Erica. I thought you were going to die right there." He laughed again and said, "I'm not going to hurt you. I knew this day was going to come sooner or later. I didn't expect it so soon, and I didn't expect you'd be the one." I stood there as blank as a sheet of paper. "I knew someone would catch on to me and uncover my secret. Come on in and I'll show you my workshop."

He let go of my arm and we walked inside. My eyes widened and my jaw dropped. The entire workshop was dark and dusty and looked like it had never been cleaned. There were old signs up everywhere; some looked over a hundred years old. One said "Health Potions" and another said "Clean-up Potions." He had what looked like a library of shelves with potions for everything imaginable. I turned to him and asked, "What...?"

Before I could say anything else, he said, "I'm a wizard." I lost my balance and almost fell to the floor. As I stood astonished, he continued, "Not a wizard like you see in books; a modern-day wizard. When I was eighteen years old and in college, my love for science was apparent to one of my professors. He took me under his wing and taught me everything he knew about magic; it was passed down to him from an old wizard he knew named Raliky. When each wizard dies, someone has to take over. These spells have been passed down for thousands of years."

"So you do black magic with spells?" I asked.

"Oh no," Mr. Spellman said. "I only do what we call white magic. You never want to get involved with black magic. You'd have a terrible fate worse than death."

"White magic?" I asked, perplexed.

"Yes, white magic," he said. "There's good and bad wizards. I only do good works to help humanity."

"Good works?" I asked.

"Remember the Gulf oil spill a few years back?" he asked. I nodded and he went on. "Didn't you ever wonder why there wasn't more destruction than there was? After they plugged the hole, I put a potion in the water, and a week later almost all the oil was gone. And do you know why there hasn't been an eruption of a volcano in so long? It was me, with another potion. And when the bird flu broke out, it was me, of course, who prevented it from becoming an epidemic."

I turned my head and squinted at him, still confused.

"Look," he said. "Mankind has been messing things up since the dawn of time and there's always been one of us to fix things. Do you think the earth could take all we give it and still survive? I have to do stuff like this or all of mankind and all the animals would be extinct."

"If you do as you say, then how come there are hurricanes and things like that?" I asked.

"I'm not perfect," he said. "Sometimes things get past me. Besides, you have to let some bad things happen, so mankind doesn't get complacent and even worse than they are."

"Yeah, but you're a science teacher," I said.

"Science and magic each have their place in the world," he said. "They're actually closely related. The science teacher thing is something I do as a cover, and to make a living."

My face tightened as he said, "I see you still don't believe me. Come over here."

He went to his shelf and picked up a bottle that was old and dusty. It looked like a fancy perfume bottle from two hundred years ago, and had weird Greek writing on it. He said, "This is the oldest potion in my work-shop. This potion was used over a thousand years ago when Genghis Khan tried to conquer the world. Some was slipped into his drink, and he was as tame as a kitten after that. And this potion here was used when the North American buffalo and the bald eagle were nearly extinct. Today they're both thriving."

"Wow!" I exclaimed. "I guess you are a wizard."

"Now comes the hard part," he said. "What do I do with you? I guess I could put a spell on you and turn you into a cockroach. Everyone hates those." My tongue hung out and I felt like throwing up. "I'm just kidding. I can't turn you into anything. I haven't figured out how to do that yet, but I'm working on it." He smiled and said, "If you tell on me, no one would believe you and you'd be thought of as an idiot. But then I'd have to move my workshop to prove you were insane. It would be time-consuming, and detrimental for you.

"All right," he finally said. "What is it you want to keep my secret quiet? Let me guess, riches, gold, silver, money?"

I thought long and hard and said, "No, none of that." Mr. Spellman's eyes widened in surprise. "I'll take a love potion."

"Oh," he sighed. "I don't know. That's very dangerous. You know what happened with Cleopatra from history class. And just because you like a boy, it doesn't mean he's the right one. I try and let love take its own course."

My eye misted. I sniffled and said, "It's not for me. It's for my parents. They've been fighting so much lately, and they filed for divorce. I love them both, and I can't take it anymore. Sometimes they put me in the middle of their fights, and I can't take sides. I don't know what to do. Please, Mr. Spellman, help me, please." A tear rolled down my cheek.

"It's against my better judgment," said Mr. Spellman, "but all right. I'm going to trust you. If you mess this up it could take me months to fix, so get it right." He walked over to a shelf on the other side of the room. He squinted, grabbed a bottle and muttered, "Here it is," and then handed it to me. "It's very powerful, so be careful."

"What do I do?" I asked.

"Pour half of the bottle into your mother's drink," he said. "Pour the other half into your father's drink. Make sure they are the first ones they see after they drink it. They will fall madly in love with the first person of the opposite sex that they see after they drink the potion. If they see someone else first, your life will be a disaster."

I took the bottle and said, "Thank you."

He cracked a slight smile, grabbed my hand and said, "Remember, the first person they see will be the one they fall in love with. One other thing: bring the bottle back to me when you're done. On a science teacher's salary, I can't be replacing all these bottles all the time." I smiled and left.

Later that day, I asked Mom if we could have dinner like we used to when I was little, with all three of us as a family. She talked to my dad, and he agreed. I set the table, and before they sat down I pulled the bottle out of my pocket. My stomach was doing flip-flops as I looked around. I poured half of the potion in each glass, just like Mr. Spellman told me to. Mom walked in right when I was done, startling me. I dropped the bottle on the floor and a drop spilled. Carver, my dog, came over and licked the drop that spilled. I grabbed the bottle and put it into my pocket just in time for Mom not to notice. I sighed and thought, *That was close.*

When we sat down for dinner, the fighting started. Mom said to Dad, "So, did you get that paperwork done like I asked, or did you procrastinate like you always do?"

"I don't want to talk to you if you're going to start that again," Dad said.

I quickly said, "I have an announcement to make. I am officially getting an A in science. I know you two have been worried about my grades; well, all the hard work has paid off." Both of them smiled in shock. "This calls for a toast." I picked up my glass and said, "To hard work and good grades."

My parents couldn't believe their ears. They picked up their glasses, and each took a long drink. Dad said, "I'm proud of you." Right when he got the last word out of his mouth, the doorbell rang.

Mom asked, "I wonder who that could be?" She walked toward the door and I yelled, "No! We're eating dinner!"

"Relax," Mom said. "It's probably just the neighbor."

My heart raced as I bolted toward the door. *She can't see anyone else!* Before I could get there, Mom opened the door, leaving me standing there frozen in my tracks. Sitting there on the porch was a package, with the UPS driver already in his truck driving away. I sighed heavily as Mom picked up the package and brought it in.

Dad asked, "What garbage did you buy now?"

Mom was ready to blast him with her words when their eyes met. They both paused, as if they were in a trance. Mom shook her head fast, as if to clear her mind, and said, "Oh, Frank. Your eyes are so blue today. I never really noticed how bright they are."

Dad said, "Your skin is so soft-looking, dear. You're beautiful."

"You're just saying that," Mom returned, and blushed.

"No, I'm not," he said. "I really haven't noticed you enough lately."

I thought, *Yuck. I guess it's better than them fighting all the time, though.* Carver barked to go outside, so I let him out. The next thing I knew, my parent were holding hands like they were on their first date. The potion worked, and they fell in love all over again.

Carver saw the ugliest dog you could ever imagine walk by, a real mutt. He fell in love with her and was impossible to live with after that. I figured it was a small price to pay to get my parents back together. They cancelled their divorce, and eventually toned their love down to a reasonable level after the potion settled in.

My life was back to normal and I couldn't be happier. I showed a great interest in science after that, and got all A's. Mr. Spellman realized that, because I showed that I didn't care about riches and all the evil things the world had to offer, I was a great candidate to take over for him one day. He said my heart was in the right place, because I wanted to help my parents before myself. He and I became great friends, and I became a science teacher just like him. My parents stayed married for the rest of their lives and never fought again.

Elevator Talk

Anni McNamara

7th Grade, Mason Middle School, Mason, Ohio

Some of them talk about their night out with their new lover, while they hope that their spouse never finds out. Others talk about their shopping lists and what they're going to cook for dinner. As they all press the cold plastic buttons, they have no idea that their most private, coveted secrets are my own entertainment. My own entertainment, which I wouldn't think twice of gossiping about to someone else to ruin their lives. After all, they deserve it. All those people, with their smiles, new clothes and good jobs, think they're better than me. They're not, though, because I'm smarter than them. I hear every word they say, and they never know I'm listening.

As I walked to the ventilation system room, which serviced the elevator in our high rise apartment building, I smiled spitefully, hoping for some ripe gossip. When I walked in, I turned my flashlight on and looked around at the dark, musty room that I knew all too well. As a high school student who was stuck in the building all the time, I had to pass the time somehow.

I closed my mouth and pushed my ear against the cold steel grating of the elevator ventilation shaft. A tiny cloud of dust filled the closet-sized room. *A small price to pay for the fun I'm about to have,* I thought. The elevator door's squeaking made me stand on my toes, and I heard the rumbling of feet. *Yes. My first victim. I hope someone is with them so they'll spill their guts.*

The deep rumble of the first man's voice was apparent when he asked, "Are you going to be all right, Pete?"

Mr. Kennedy, I thought. *I've never really heard him talk to anyone before except for a short hello to another tenant. He lives in 18-R, I think.*

"I'll be all right," Pete said. "I wish I didn't have to kill him. He deserved it though. I have to admit that with all that blood everywhere, I did feel a little queasy."

"Yeah," Mr. Kennedy said. "It comes with the territory."

"If Jim the Butcher ever finds out I killed his brother, I'll have to move out of state," Pete said.

"He won't find out it was you," Mr. Kennedy said. "No one knows but us."

I quickly turned my head, flicking my hair against the grating. I stepped backwards as another cloud of dust grew in the air. I felt like I was going to choke on my tongue. I coughed once, right into the ventilation shaft, and then sneezed. Pete quickly asked, "Did you hear that?"

Mr. Kennedy said, "I heard it. Where did it come from?"

Pete pointed upward and said, "Look. Where does that duct run?"

"I don't know," said Mr. Kennedy. "But we're going to find out!"

My head jerked up and my eyes got as big as balloons. I felt my hands shake, and my legs went numb. *Oh no. What if they find out it was me? They'll kill me to keep me quiet.* I ran out of the ventilation closet and into the hall. My legs felt like lead anchors with each step I took. I ran up two flights of stairs and into my apartment, slamming the door behind me.

I hurried into the living room where Mom was watching TV. She asked, "Whoa, what's the rush, Monica?"

I gave her an innocent look and words wouldn't come out of my mouth. I finally said, "No rush. I just want to go into my room and listen to some music." Mom nodded and waved her hand in approval.

When I got into my room, I sat for a moment and thought, *I can't tell anyone about this. If I do, those guys that killed that man will find out and they'll come after me. I can't tell anyone... except my best friend Carly and maybe Brianna.*

I dialed Carly's number, and when she answered I said, "Get over here right away."

"I'm doing my homework right now," said Carly.

"I don't care what you're doing. Get over here," and I hung up. I called Brianna next, and she said she'd be right over. When all three of us were safely in my room, I told them the entire story about how Mr. Kennedy and the man named Pete that had killed a man. I also told them about how they had heard me. Finally I said, "You both have to promise you won't tell anyone."

"I promise I won't," Brianna said.

"I promise too," Carly said. "Are you going to go to the police?"

"No," I said. "Then they'll find out I heard them for sure. I don't know what I'm going to do next. I'm scared."

"I would be too," Carly said. We talked for a little longer, and then both my friends left.

■ ■ ■

When Carly got home, she called her cousin Jenna to come over, and told her sister and Jenna to come into her room. After they sat down, Carly said, "You have to promise me you won't tell anyone what I'm about to say."

"I promise," both girls said. Jenna told both of them about what Monica had heard.

Meanwhile, Brianna called her friend Becky and Becky's brother Josh and told them to come over to her house. Brianna's parents weren't home, so they went into the kitchen and Brianna said, "You have to promise me that you won't tell anyone what I'm about to tell you." Both of them promised. "Monica overheard someone talking in the elevator about some guy named Pete who killed three men."

"I don't believe it," Josh said.

"It is true," Briana said. "I heard the story myself."

Both their faces dropped to the floor. Becky said, "Oh my gosh! Is it someone in our building?"

"Mr. Kennedy lives here, but I don't know about the other guy," Brianna said. "I heard the guy named Pete is a really bad dude and likes to see their faces right before he kills them."

Becky's brother Josh said, "Wow! He must be really mean."

"Oh, he is," Brianna said. "I heard he can't wait until he kills another person. I think he's a hit man or something." Becky turned white and stared at Brianna. They talked for a little while longer; then Becky and Josh left.

Later that day Becky talked to her friend Marisa, and asked, "Do you promise you won't tell anyone what I'm about to tell you?"

"I promise," Marisa said.

"I heard that Monica Johnson heard two guys talking in her building. One of the guys is a serial killer. He was telling the other guy all the details about how he killed six people and can't wait until he makes it ten. I guess he's a real psycho. I heard he drinks the victim's blood and everything."

Marisa's stepped back and her face went blank. She said, "That's gross! Tell me some more."

"The guy preys on older women and he chops up their bodies."

"Oooh!" Marisa said. They talked for a little while, and then Marisa left. Marisa called her friend Sara and said, "I heard that Monica Johnson knows a serial killer who drinks the blood of his victims. He's plotting his next killing right now. He chops up the bodies and has them stored in his freezer in her apartment building."

"I don't believe it," Sara said.

"It's true!" Marissa said. "I heard it from Becky so it has to be true."

"Well, I guess if you heard it from her, it is true," Sara said.

■ ■ ■

A week later, I was sitting in my living room with my parents' right before dinner. The doorbell rang, and my father opened the door. I peered over his shoulder, and my heart almost stopped when I saw Mr. Kennedy and two other men standing there with their hands on their hips. I stepped backward and shouted, "Watch out, Dad! Call the police."

I quickly turned and started to run toward the phone, and tripped on my own feet. I fell in our living room and hit my shoulder on the arm of the couch in a panic. I turned over and started to stand when I saw Mr. Kennedy quickly reach into his breast pocket for a gun. I jumped behind the couch for cover thinking it was the end for my parents and me. I heard Mr. Kennedy say, "I'm agent Phil Kennedy, and this is agent Pete Bronson. This is Jerry Retski, my supervisor. We all work for the FBI."

I looked over the back of the couch to where the three men were standing, and all I could see was bright lights from overhead reflecting off their badges back at me. "Is your daughter Monica Johnson?" Agent Kennedy asked.

I let every ounce of air out of my lungs and dropped my head then stood up. My Father asked, "What has Monica done?"

"I hate to tell you this," said Supervisor Retski. "Your daughter may be in great danger. Apparently, she was listening to a conversation my two agents had on the elevator in this building. Even though she didn't hear any major details about a shooting that occurred, apparently people on the street think otherwise. Both agents Kennedy and Bronson have been working on this case for over a year. I can't tell you everything, except that the people they're investigating are connected to organized crime. Agent Bronson shot one of the mob members during the bust. Monica, if these people even think you might know something about the shooting, they may come after you. Who did you tell about the agents' conversations?"

My arms dropped by my sides and I looked away. "Nobody knows about the conversation. I didn't tell anyone... anyone except Brianna and Carly. Those two wouldn't say anything, they promised."

"The word on the street says differently," Agent Bronson said. "We've heard everything from 'you overheard a serial killer wanting to drain the blood from his next victim' to 'you heard a former soldier who killed seventy-five civilians on a mission.' The only thing we've got going for us is that the story has been changed so many times with each time it's told, that who knows if it'll ever get back to the mob."

I had a lump in my throat as big as an apple. My stomach went queasy and I couldn't speak. "See, the problem is that if the mob ever finds out the truth that you overheard the agents, they will come after you," said Agent Kennedy. "They'll want to know who shot one of their members, and Agent Bronson's life could be in danger."

Mom crossed her arms and raised her eyebrows. "Monica Johnson! How many times have I told you to mind your own business and stop gossiping? Now look what you've gotten yourself into."

I sat down on the couch and started to cry. "I never planned for this to happen. I'm so sorry."

"Sorry won't help," Supervisor Retski said. "Have you ever heard the term 'loose lips sink ships'?" I shook my head. "That means that you have to watch what you say. Wars over the years have been started because of misinformation, gossip and rumors. Thousands of people have died on the battlefield in years past, all because someone twisted around what someone else said and gossiped the wrong information. Your listening to their conversations has really put us into a terrible predicament. If you stay here, you could get a visit from a mob boss one day — or you may not. I suggest that you move away and not tell anyone where you go. We can't give you protection for something like that."

"No," I complained. "I didn't mean for this to happen."

"All those years that I told you not to gossip, and you didn't listen," Mom said. "Do you realize how many people's lives you've hurt when you couldn't keep your mouth shut? I guess that old saying is right. 'What goes around comes around.' I hope you've learned your lesson." The tears were now rolling down my puffed-up cheeks.

Dad said, "We're going to have to move. We're not taking any chances."

"That's probably best," Supervisor Retski said.

A month later we moved out of the city, about forty miles away. I lost my home, my friends, and I even had to change schools, all because I liked to hear gossip and couldn't keep my mouth shut. I even had to go to counseling to break free from the addiction of talking about others and spreading rumors. I definitely learned my lesson the hard way, and tried to never gossip again. And I never forgot what the saying "loose lips sink ships" meant.

Stuck in My Own Skin

Carly Middleton

7th Grade, Williamstown Junior-Senior High School, Williamstown, Kentucky

I woke to the sound of my mother yelling from downstairs, "Get up, Sydney! You're late again." I rolled over and lethargically pulled the covers over my head, then sighed. *If I have to sit through another boring day of school like yesterday, I'm going to die. Seventh grade is the worst.* I pushed my feet toward the floor and stood up. *Nothing exciting ever happens to me.* I got ready for school, unaware that everything in my life was about to be turned upside down.

When I got into first hour, I put my head on my desk, covered my ears and closed my eyes. I sat, trying to fall asleep, wishing I was anywhere but school. Near the end of the period, Mr. Delany said, "Don't forget that the Halloween dance is tomorrow night." I raised my head, opened my eyes and sat up straight. "There will be huge prizes for the top three costumes, including a family four-pack of tickets to Six Flags Amusement Park for the winner, with overnight accommodations, donated by our Parents' Booster Club."

I tapped my desk lightly with my index finger. *If I could win first place, people would see me differently. Maybe I would have more friends and not feel so lonely. Plus, Mom and Dad would have no choice but to take me to Six Flags. Life would be great, at least for a weekend.* The bell rang, and I bolted out of my chair. *I'm going to win first place. I have to.*

When I got into the hall, my excitement was cut short as I looked down the corridor and saw her. There she stood in the corner, with her long blonde hair and beautifully straight teeth. Three boys walked by and did a double-

113

take as she threw her hair back. One of the boys said, "Wow! Brittney sure looks good today."

One of the other boys said, "You aren't kidding."

My five-foot-five-inch-tall, skinny frame and brown curly hair just couldn't compete with Brittany. I looked right at the three boys as if to scream, "Look at me. I'm alive too." They all kept walking as if I didn't even exist.

Two of Brittney's friends, Melissa and Chelsea, walked over to Brittney with eyes glowing and smiles plastered on their faces. I put my head down, turned aside and started to walk past them, when Melissa asked, "Did you hear about the prize for the best costume tomorrow?"

Brittney bragged, "Yeah, I heard about it. I'm going to win first place again this year."

"Any ideas for a costume?" Chelsea asked.

"Does it really matter?" Brittney asked. "Who's going to beat me? I guess I'll go out as a zombie cheerleader. I'll use last year's head cheerleader outfit and throw on some makeup. They have to give it to me. No one else has a chance."

"Yeah," Chelsea agreed. "We'll help you with your makeup and do your hair. You'll look even better than last year."

I rolled my eyes and shook my head while biting my lip. *I have to beat her this year. I have to come up with a great costume.* Doubt set in as my confidence dropped. *Who am I kidding? She's so pretty, and everyone likes her so much. And look at me. How could I ever compete against her? You know what? I'm going to beat her this year. I'm tired of being a nobody. Prepare for war, Brittney!*

Later that day, I approached my only friend, Mia, and asked, "Are you going to the dance tomorrow night?"

Mia said, "I'm going, but I don't think I'm going to dress up."

"I am," I said. "I'm going to beat Brittney for best costume this year." Mia went into a full laugh. "You can't be serious. She wins at everything."

"Not this year," I said. "Meet me after school to go to look at costumes, four o'clock at the park."

"I will, but I'm not sure if you should be wasting your time."

I raised my eyebrows and shook my head. "Just be there." Mia nodded, and we both went to class.

Later that day, the park was fairly crowded so I sat down at one of the picnic tables. I glanced two tables over and saw a man in his late thirties reading the newspaper. I paid little attention to him and started reading the things that people had carved into the wood on the picnic table. Mia rode

"A man at the park told me that you have the best Halloween costumes around," I said. "I have a party to go to tomorrow night, and there's this girl who wins best costume every year, and I have to beat her. I'll pay you well. Please help me."

Wanda stood up and limped from behind the counter toward us. Mia asked, "Are you all right?"

"I'm fine. I have an injury from when I was younger that never healed. I've learned to cope with it. You want a really good costume... hmm...." She dug through a cedar chest that looked like it was two hundred years old and said, "This should fit well." She handed me a folded-up costume.

I unfolded it and asked, "What is it?"

"It's a jack-o-lantern costume. You wear that, and I guarantee you'll beat Brittney."

"It looks really old and not very scary," I complained. "And how did you know it was Brittney I was trying to beat? I never mentioned that."

"Oh... I keep up on who wins the costume contests at all the schools for Halloween. After all, I'm in the business, you know. As the night goes on, the costume will look better and better. There's only one catch. You must take it off before it becomes one minute after twelve. I assume you go to the middle school. I know the dance ends at midnight, so I'll be there at fifteen after twelve to pick it up."

Mia looked at me with her nose turned down and face puckered. "That's weird," I said. "But if you're guaranteeing a win, then I guess that'll be fine. How much do I owe you?"

"Twelve dollars should do," said Wanda. I quickly pulled the money out of my pocket and handed it to her, worried she would change her mind about the price. She gladly took the money and we headed for the door. "Remember, dear. You have to take it off by midnight."

"I know, I know," I said, and we hurried out the door. After we got back to our bikes, I said, "That lady is never going to move out of that cellar if she only charges twelve dollars for a costume like this. I would've paid at least thirty." We got on our bikes and rode home.

The next day at school, the only thing I could think about was how Britney was going to look and feel when I won first place. I wanted her to pay for all the times I had felt so inept, and to know exactly how it felt to be unpopular and disappointed. The minutes seemed like hours, until finally it was time to get ready for the dance.

A half hour before the dance, I went into my room and pulled out the costume. After I unfolded it, I noticed that the tag said, "Do not wear after midnight." I rolled my eyes, then shook my head. *What is this, Cinderella?* I thought. I put my leg into the costume, and felt as if a light electrical shock went through my body. I put the rest of the costume on and felt another slight shock. A second later it felt as if the costume tightened to conform to my body.

When I walked over to the mirror, my head snapped back as I gazed at myself. The costume was perfect! The entire thing was orange fabric with a black belt and black shoes. My skin was all wrinkled as if it had changed into an old rotten pumpkin. The mask adhered to my face perfectly and looked like a carved, scary, jack-o-lantern — but real.

I stepped back, feeling a little scared. A slight tingle ran through my body. I felt almost euphoric and thought, *Wanda was right. I am going to win the contest. This costume looks as real as can be. I can't wait to see the disappointment on Brittney's face when I win.*

When I got to the dance, I walked over to Mia and my voice rasped without even trying. "Hi. How do you like it?"

"Is that you?" she asked. "It hardly looks like you, Sydney. That's the best costume I have ever seen."

"Thanks," I said. "I'm going to win for sure."

Brittney walked by and said, "Wow! Who are you? Your costume is incredible. It looks so lifelike."

"It's me, Sydney Hamilton," I rasped.

"Your voice sounds perfect too," Brittney said. "How can you talk like that?"

"I don't know," I said. "I guess it's because I'm talking through the mask."

"Well, good luck," she said. "I thought I had a chance to win this year for sure, but after seeing you, nobody is going to beat you." A fulfilled smile animated my face as she walked away.

Later that evening, another popular girl named Ashley, who I hadn't thought even knew I existed, walked over to me and said, "Great costume. Maybe we could hang out sometime after school or something."

"That would be great," I rasped, my voice even deeper.

The rest of the night, people kept coming over to me and telling me how they loved my costume. Right before they announced the winner for best costume, I thought, *This has been the best night of my life. So this is what it feels like to be popular. I love it. I wish this night would never end.*

A few minutes later, Mr. McDonald, our principal, announced, "The winner for best costume this year is Sydney Hamilton!"

I jumped into the air, lifted my head high and strutted up onto the stage. I took the trophy and the gifts, then growled, "Thank you very much."

I grinned vengefully at Brittney, wanting to see pain and anguish on her face, as I had had so many times when she was around. Instead she was clapping and cheering wildly. I thought, *That's not right. She's supposed to feel jealous and angry like I do all the time when she gets all the attention.*

After I took the prizes, I went into the bathroom and looked into the mirror. The costume looked so real, I couldn't even recognize myself. I turned my head away from the mirror and thought, *Only ten more minutes left, and it's back to normal for me. I'm going to make the most of it.*

I went back into the dance, walked to where Brittney and her friends were standing, and thought about what to say. To try to make Brittney feel inadequate, I gloated, "I think I'll win the contest every year, that is, if I feel like going next year."

"If you wear a costume like that again, no one will ever beat you," Brittney said. My throat felt like it had a hot coal resting on my tonsils from the raspy voice I had had all night, so I nodded and walked away. *She is supposed to be mad,* I thought. *What happened?* At that moment the clock struck midnight and I thought, *It won't hurt to wear this thing a little longer. I'm so popular right now, and I want people to remember me Monday at school.*

We hung out for a few more minutes, until everyone broke up and went outside. When I walked through the door, Wanda was standing there, with her eyes as big as frying pans. "Are you crazy!" she exclaimed. "You were supposed to take that costume off at midnight!"

"It's no big deal," I said. "I'll take it off right now."

"You don't understand," she said. "You can't take it off now! You can't ever take it off!"

"Don't be silly," I said. I tried to pull the mask off and it wouldn't budge. It felt like it was glued onto my body. I tried to pull off the pants and they wouldn't come off either. I asked, "What is this?"

Wanda smirked and her voice turned raspy like mine had been. "We had an agreement that you would take the costume off at midnight. It won't come off now. You're stuck in your own skin forever."

"Don't be ridiculous," I said. "I'll take it off tonight and bring it by tomorrow."

"You can't," Wanda triumphed. "I was hoping this would happen. It always does to whiny, jealous people like you. Poor little Sydney, who couldn't follow instructions and wanted to be the most important person in the world. None of you ever follow the instructions, and then you come begging to me the next day. I'll see you tomorrow when you have nowhere else to go. Then you'll be my slave forever, ha, ha, ha," she laughed ominously.

That woman is crazy, I thought, and I got into Mom's car. I didn't take Wanda seriously, so I told Mom all about the greatest night of my life and how popular I was. She was skeptical and warned me, "Popularity isn't all it's cracked up to be. You should be happy with who you are."

When I got into my room I felt a little dizzy. My skin felt itchy, so I reached for my face and tried to pull the mask off. When it wouldn't come off, my hands shook and I tried again. This time when it wouldn't come off, my stomach felt weak, and I lost all feeling in my arms. I went over to the mirror and looked at my ugly reflection, and stepped back in fear. I shook my head and said, "It can't be! It just can't be!"

I tried frantically to pull the entire costume off, but I couldn't. I went into the bathroom, took scissors, tried to cut the fabric and it wouldn't cut. I tried to slice the costume off my arm but I began to bleed. I shrieked, "She was right. The costume is me. I am stuck in my own skin!" I fell to my knees and began to cry. "What have I done? I wanted to be popular so badly that I ruined my life. Now no one will ever want to look at me again. I'm so ugly everyone will hate me."

I covered my eyes and cried, "What am I going to do? If this won't come off, then I'll have to hide for the rest of my life. Maybe she will make me her slave." I continued to cry until I fell asleep, exhausted.

The next morning, I woke to my mother saying, "Get up Sydney. You'll be late for school." I jumped out of bed and thought, *It's Saturday. I don't have school.* I went over to the mirror to see my hideous self and when I looked in the mirror, I froze. I looked normal. *What happened? It must have all been a dream. It seemed so real that it couldn't have been a dream.*

Mom walked into my room and said, "Don't forget about the Halloween dance tonight. We have to go pick you out a costume."

"Didn't I go last night?" I asked.

"Last night was Thursday," Mom said. "We can go to that costume shop over on Elm Street if you want. I know how important it is to you to have a good costume and make more friends."

I sighed and said, "I think I won't dress up this year."

Mom's head bounced upward and she asked, "What?"

"Maybe being popular isn't as important as I thought. I'm just happy to be myself."

Mom stared in amazement. "All right with me... I've only been telling you that for two years. I guess I'm a better parent than I thought, if you're finally listening."

After she left the room, I fell to my knees and thought, *That dream was so real and scary.* I said to myself, "I promise I won't ever be jealous of any of the kids at my school again. I'm glad to be me and that it was all a bad dream."

After I stopped being envious of the popular kids, I made many new friends because of my change in attitude. I figured out that it wasn't they that were the problem; it was me not believing in myself.

The Hourglass

Danielle Morey

7th Grade, Mason Middle School,
Mason, Ohio

Everyone has moments when they want to give up in life, and wish they could start over. Most people get the chance and don't realize it. I found out that life changes so quickly that it's like an hourglass. When you're at your darkest moments and the sand is about to run out, it's as if your hourglass gets flipped and you're able to start over.

The first time I experienced this was when I was ten years old. "Come on, Sparky," I said. "Let's go for a walk." I grabbed my Golden Retriever's leash and headed out the door. We walked along the same route that we always did, through our subdivision, along a busy road and then back home. As we were walking, I was listening to the birds sing, without a care in the world.

Sparky saw a squirrel crossing the road and bolted toward him. The leash slipped from my grip and I screamed, "No, Sparky, not in the road!" A car slammed on its brakes and hit Sparky, throwing him several feet in the air. I ran to him as the driver stopped and got out of his car. With tears in my eyes I held Sparky as the driver whined, "It happened so quickly. I couldn't do anything."

Sparky stared off into the distance in shock, while I sat helplessly quivering. I hugged him one last time; then he faded and died in my arms. My stomach felt as if it were turned inside out while I sat there wailing, until Mother came and took me home. It was as if a part of me died that day along with Sparky.

The next day, Mother came to me and said, "I know how badly you feel; I do too. Sometimes in life, things happen, and we have no control over them."

"It was my fault," I cried. "If I had been holding that leash tighter, none of this would've happened."

Mother said, "I know right now you feel it was your fault, but it wasn't. It was no one's fault. I'll tell you what, we'll go tomorrow and look at other dogs. There are so many pets that need a good home."

My shoulders drooped and I looked at the ground and cried. "I don't want another dog. I'll never want another dog."

Mother held her arms out and I ran to her. She hugged me tightly and said, "Time heals all pain. You'll feel better soon." I cried in her arms, still feeling like my world had fallen apart.

About a week later, I went for a walk near a pond by our house. Still depressed, I thought, *I hurt so badly inside. I'm sorry you died, Sparky. It was my fault. I should jump in the pond and not try to swim. If I drowned, then I wouldn't feel this pain and I could see Sparky again in heaven. I feel like I want to die.*

I edged toward the water, then heard a light sound pattering behind me and turned my head. I looked and saw a small baby duck standing there, staring at me. His fuzzy feathers were rough and he looked as if he had been in a fight.

Startled, I asked, "What are you doing here, little guy? Where's your mother?" I extended my hand and moved a little closer. He tucked his head in toward his stomach and backed up. Unsure what to make of me, he quacked in a weak ridiculous tone that sounded like a muffled bike horn. I looked more closely at him and noticed dried blood on his matted, dirty body. "Did your mama get eaten by a fox?" The baby duck stood there staring into my eyes, as if he were pleading for help.

I ran home and got some crackers, came back and fed them to him. I smiled as he ate and then said, "I'm going to name you Quackers. Don't worry, boy. I won't let anything happen to you."

I went back and fed Quackers every day for the next two months until he was big enough to be on his own. That was the first time I felt like my hourglass had nearly run out and was flipped full again.

Years passed, and shortly before high school graduation, my best friend Jennifer came to me and said, "I got accepted at Arizona State. I'm so excited! I can't turn this opportunity down. You understand, don't you?"

I said, "We promised each other that we'd always stick together, even after we were married. You can't go."

Jennifer frowned and said, "I have to go. It's not like we won't see each other again. I'll be home when school's not in, and after college we'll still live near each other, just like we always planned."

I nodded, looked away, hugged Jennifer and said, "I'm going to miss you."

She said, "I'm going to miss you, too."

Later that year she went to Arizona State, and I went to a local community college. I was severely depressed and missed my friend badly. Things were worse when, in her last year of college, I got a letter that said, "Dear Maddy, I met a guy last year who's the one for me. He asked me to marry him after we get out of college. His parents own a business in Arizona and I love it here. I know we always said we were going to live near each other, so I was wondering if you would like to move here."

I dropped the letter on the ground and froze for a second. A tear rolled down my cheek; I knew there was no way I was ever going to move to Arizona and start over. My stomach turned and I felt like I was going to throw up. I knew from when Sparky died what it was like losing my best friend, and felt that the depression from losing Jennifer would never go away. That is, until my hourglass was flipped again and I met the love of my life, George.

Being in love with George was the greatest feeling I had ever had in my life, and when he asked me to marry him, I didn't hesitate one bit. We had two incredible, romantic years together, with my hourglass so full it was ready to burst; I thought it would never empty again. Shortly after our second anniversary, I found out that your hourglass never stays full, and it can be emptied with just a few simple words.

The doctor came in with a frown on his face that made me feel uneasy. He took a deep breath, relaxed his arms and said, "I've reviewed your test results and I wish I had better news." I swallowed the lump in my throat as he continued. "I'm sorry, Mrs. Henderson. You can never have children."

My mind went blank and I shook my head slowly in denial. In an instant, my hourglass went from being filled to the brim to having just a few fleeting grains of sand left.

George and I both struggled with depression over the next two years while waiting for the opportunity to adopt. Along the way, we tried to flip each other's hourglasses with encouraging words and love, but it didn't work. The pain of not being able to bring another life into the world and not knowing the love from nurturing a child was almost too much to bear. I questioned my life many times, wondering what I had done that was so wrong as to make me deserve this.

When we got the phone call that they had found a little boy of three and his one-year-old sister who were in desperate need of a family to take them, I jumped high into the air and screamed in joy. My hourglass was suddenly filled to the brim again.

We all built a unique life together, vacationing at national parks and spending time at our favorite beaches. We never took for granted one moment together, and felt blessed that we were given such a wonderful life. My hourglass was full until after our children were grown and I got another phone call that almost emptied it completely. It was from my father who was crying and said, "Your mother has died of a heart attack. I don't know what I'm going to do." My knees went weak and I began to cry. I spent the next two years helping my dad fight his depression, until he passed away too.

My hourglass stayed low until I got great news from my daughter. "Mom, I'm pregnant. You're going to be a grandmother." My eyes lit up and I felt as alive as I ever had in my life. When my first granddaughter was born, I had tears of joy in my eyes, and life once again had meaning. When my second granddaughter and my grandson were born, I was so busy helping my daughter, I couldn't think straight. The serenity I felt seeing my grandchildren grow and develop was indescribable.

My hourglass stayed full for a long time, until the doctor came into my husband's hospital room and said, "I'm sorry, Mr. Henderson. You have liver cancer. There's nothing we can really do for you, George." My heart felt like it had stopped and I couldn't move or speak.

George looked me in the eyes and said, "Don't worry, dear. It's going to be all right. I'll beat this thing."

George died ten months later and I felt like my guts had been ripped out. Without George, it was if my hourglass had one small speck of sand left that was just about to pass through to the other side.

I was so lonely, I knew I had to do something fast. I decided to volunteer at a local children's charity, which gave me a reason to go on. For six years I was blessed with doing the greatest thing you can for people: helping children. I felt great about myself, and again my hourglass was full.

At the age of eighty-two, I became ill and knew my time was near. I woke up early in the morning and was unable to get out of my hospital bed. My stomach felt like it had a knife turning in it, and I knew there was nothing anyone could do to help. I spent the early part of the day staring at the ceiling of my room in great pain. I looked back on my life, remembering all the great times I had had with a smile on my face, and the pain faded. It was pleasing to know that I had had such an incredible life and had lived it to the fullest.

When evening came, I felt my heart stop and looked up. I said with my last breath, "Oh God, take me now. Turn my hourglass over and fill it full for the last time, and never let it drain again."

And he did.

Little Voices

Cal Noah

7th Grade, Spencer Middle School, Spencer Iowa

Most everyone that lived through the Great Depression of the 1930s has their own horror story. But when I look back on mine, I can't believe it played out the way it did. Hope is a funny thing that can get you through the worst of times, and when it's gone, you have nothing left. I relive the turning point in my life every day, as if it were a recurring nightmare. Some people would call my story fate, or destiny. At times I've called it many things: chance, luck, and even divine intervention. What happened sticks with me in the pit of my stomach, and never goes away.

When the stock market crash hit in 1929, I was thirteen years old. Living in Raleigh, South Carolina, in a small three-bedroom house wasn't so bad in the early years. But when 1932 came, our family's world was torn apart. I had three brothers and three sisters, and I knew it couldn't have come at a worse time.

Father had worked steadily through the Roaring Twenties as an assembler at a furniture plant. I had never heard him complain once about his job, because he was a thankful and proud man; that is, until April of 1932. He came home late one evening from work, and sat down at the kitchen table with his hollow eyes staring off into the distance. We all gathered around, and he said, "I was let go today. Nearly a hundred of us were released. I don't know what I'm going to do! I've been building furniture my whole life."

Mom, standing in her worn-out blue dress, put her hand over her heart, then said, "It'll be all right, dear. We've survived this long, we'll get through it."

My stomach felt weak and my body tensed up; my limbs felt lifeless. Over the last two years, I had heard too many stories about displaced families and people living on the streets for me to take Mom's words of hope as fact. Being the oldest, I quickly blurted out the first thing that came to mind. "I'm sixteen now. I can get a job and help out as much as possible."

"My plan was for all my children to get a good solid education, and I won't have my son supporting the family," Dad said.

"It's all right," I pleaded. "I can go to school and work at the same time. And it would only be for a little while, until things get back to normal."

Mom smiled at my persistence and said, "It wouldn't hurt for you to work, Don, I guess."

I smiled back, with Dad still in a daze. "Then it's settled," I said. "I'll start looking tomorrow."

Dad cleared his throat and piped up with, "I'll start looking tomorrow too." Early the next morning, Dad and I went out looking for any sort of labor positions we could find. Unfortunately, thousands of people were looking at the same time.

When we got home that night and sat down for supper, Dad said, "It's worse than I thought out there. If there is any work, it's taken before they even put up the 'help wanted' sign. Most of the work is day-to-day, too."

"We'll have to keep trying," I insisted. Dad smiled at me, said the blessing for our meal and prayed for help. After he was done, we all dug into my mom's special cooking.

Over a year later, when the summer of 1933 came, so did the second Dust Bowl in the Midwest. With Dad and me working only once in a while at odd jobs, and still looking for steady work, things became desperate. Dad had lost all hope, and Mom held us together with the few encouraging words she could muster.

June 23, 1933, was when Dad sat down with Mom at the kitchen table and said, "I've tried everything, dear. The bank is coming at the end of the week to take the house."

"I asked my father for more money to help us get by," Mom said. "I know he sent all he could last time. He's struggling too. The whole country is struggling. All we can do is pray."

Overhearing this, I walked into the kitchen and said, "I'll find work tomorrow. You'll see."

"One of us better do something soon," Dad said. "We haven't had a decent meal all week. What do we have left?"

"A half of a loaf of bread and some cereal," Mom said, trying not to show her worried frown. I went to sleep that night hungry, just as I had the last four nights in a row.

The next morning I got up early, before anyone else, and walked into town. When the market opened, I stood outside and looked through the window into the refrigerator case. Inside was a prize turkey, displayed with a sign that said "$3.99." *I have to do it,* I thought. *I'm so hungry, and the bread lines will never do. Besides, my family needs it more than me.*

I walked into the store and looked around, trying to be as inconspicuous as possible. I pulled a bag out of my pocket that I had brought just for the occasion. When Mr. Luzio was looking the other way helping another customer, I took a deep breath, reached into the case and placed the turkey into the bag. I ran out of the store while Mr. Luzio yelled, "Stop, thief!"

I ran all the way home, to find Sheriff Green and Mr. Luzio on my front porch speaking with my dad. Dad waved for me to come to him. Still with the turkey in my hands, I walked up to our house with my stomach twisting and turning, knowing what was inevitably going to come next: jail. *At least I'll get three meals a day,* I thought.

When I got to the porch, Dad asked, "Son, how could you? I'll beat you until you learn the meaning of honesty."

"I'm sorry, Father," I said. "I'm so hungry that all I could think about was us losing the house."

Mr. Luzio's face turned down while Sheriff Green's stayed stern. "I didn't know you were even in foreclosure," Mr. Luzio said.

"The bank is coming Friday," Dad said, looking away.

"I saw the writ come through yesterday," Sheriff Green said. "I'll have no choice but to come with them Friday, James. I'm sorry."

"None of us would ever steal, especially not my son," Dad said, frustrated and torn between family and honesty. "It's the times, I tell you. When is Roosevelt going to get this country straightened out?"

Mr. Luzio sighed and said, "I'll tell you what. If you return the turkey, we'll forget this thing ever happened. You've been a good customer, and besides, how will you pay your grocery bill that you owe me if Donny is in jail?" He smiled, hoping to ease Dad's mind, knowing what he was going through.

I handed him the turkey with misted eyes and said, "I'm sorry."

Mr. Luzio nodded and said, "It's all forgotten."

"Only one problem," Sheriff Green said. "When everyone finds out you let him go after stealing, you'll have the whole town in your store taking things. If they know you won't press charges, it could get to be common-place."

"You're right," Mr. Luzio said.

"I'm afraid you'll have to leave town for a little while," Sheriff Green said. "I'll spread the rumor that you went to jail." He wrote something down on a piece of paper and handed to me. "Here's the name and address of a man I know who owns a successful food plant and slaughterhouse in Virginia. Tell him I sent you and that you need a job, but tell him nothing else. He's an old friend who would do almost anything for me. The midnight train goes directly by the town on the paper."

"You may as well, son," Dad said. "We have nothing left here."

I thanked both Mr. Luzio and Sheriff Green then packed my bag. I jumped the midnight train, riding in a cargo car until I got to Virginia the next day. I went to the address the sheriff gave me, and stood outside an iron gate, unable to believe my eyes. The house must have been ten bedrooms, with a huge library that looked out over a pond with a river flowing into it. I rang the bell at the gate and a guard came out of a small shack that was a few yards away.

He walked up and asked, "May I help you?"

"Yes," I said. "My name is Don Crawford, and Sheriff Green sent me here to talk to Mr. Helmer about getting a job."

The guard laughed then asked, "Do you know how many people come here every day asking to speak to Mr. Helmer?" I shook my head. "Dozens," he responded. "They all have the same sad story about how they need a job. Mr. Helmer is very busy and can't be disturbed."

"But I was told to come—"

All my hope was ripped out of me when the guard cut me off and said, "You have two seconds to leave or I'm going to thump your skull."

"But—" I started to say, and the guard started to unlock the gate with a diabolical look on his face. "I'm going," I said. As I walked away, I felt nauseated and anxiety-stricken. I began to breathe heavily and didn't know what to do. I spent the night sleeping in the woods, getting eaten by mosquitoes. I went back to the house every day for the next week, until the guard told me that if I came again he would beat me up, and then call the police and say I tried to break in.

I spent the next three weeks living in a makeshift tent, with hundreds of other homeless people, in a park near the river that everyone called Hooversville. The living conditions were unspeakable, with no work available in the area. During that time I lost twelve pounds, and I hadn't had a bath in weeks. I spent every morning standing in soup lines, having one meal a day, if I was lucky. The worst part was that I hadn't heard from my family, and I knew they were worse off than I was.

I decided to try one more time at Mr. Helmer's house, so I went there right after sunset. When I rang the bell, the guard came to the gate hastily, just on the other side of where I was standing. He said, "I told you not to come back." He jabbed his club through the bars and hit me in the face. I fell to the ground, then got up with my lip slightly bleeding, and stumbled away.

A few minutes later, I found myself at the bridge near Mr. Helmer's house, looking over the side. I stepped up on the ledge, looked up toward the sky, and said, "I've tried everything, so forgive me for this." I took one step over the side with my foot dangling, ready to jump to end my life. My heart raced as I thought, *It's my only choice. I have to go through with it.*

Suddenly, I saw the lights of a car approaching. Startled and scared, I pulled my foot from over the side and stepped down, as the car stopped about fifty yards from me and a well-dressed man stepped out. He stood there looking over the edge just as I had. Perplexed, I walked toward him while he stood almost unaware of my presence. When I got next to him, I asked, "Are you all right?"

"I think so," he said. "You're going to think this is odd, but I heard a voice inside my head that told me to go to this bridge and stand. I have never had anything happen like that before so I felt compelled to do so. I don't understand why I heard that little voice." He stood confused, still staring at the water.

"I wish I had your problem," I said. "I've been trying to speak to Mr. Helmer, who lives in the house at the top of that hill, for four weeks now." I pointed toward the hill, while the man's face lit up like a Christmas tree. "Sheriff Green from my hometown in South Carolina sent me to see him, but the guard won't even let me talk to him."

The man took a step backward and almost fell. He turned as white as a ghost and dropped to his knees. "My name is Frederick Helmer, and I'm the one you've been trying to see. I've known Richard Green since we were boys. He was my best friend growing up. Who are you?"

"My name is Donald Crawford. Sheriff Green sent me here to get a job from you."

Mr. Helmer stood up, swallowed hard, then took a deep breath. "For the last month I've had trouble sleeping. I thought it was from the times. It breaks my heart to see everyone struggling so. I do what I can, but it's so hard right now. When I heard that little voice inside my head, I thought I was going crazy."

My eyes bulged and I couldn't speak. *A little voice,* I thought, *how bizarre.*

"If you need a job, son, you've got one," said Mr. Helmer. He reached into his pocket and pulled out fifty dollars. "Get cleaned up and find a place to stay. Report to work at my plant tomorrow morning at eight o'clock."

"You won't be sorry, sir," I said. "Thank you so much."

"It's the strangest thing," Mr. Helmer said. "It was as if I was told to come to meet you. I guess there are some things in life you can't explain."

He left after that, and I started work the next day. Shortly after that, I found out that my grandfather had sent the money to my mom just in time, so that they could keep the house. Dad found work at a factory a little while later. And me, I went from being one step away from suicide to becoming a vice president at one of the largest food-producing companies in the country in only twelve years. When I look back, I think, *Thank God for little voices.*

The Snow on My Cheeks

Amber Ramey

7th Grade, Prairie View Middle School, Henderson, Colorado

When you live in Colorado, you experience all the seasons, including warm summers and cool falls. But my favorite season has to be winter. Seeing deer tracks in the first fresh blanket of snow covering the Rocky Mountains always makes me feel glad to be alive. And the first snow means one thing: skiing season. Growing up at a ski lodge since birth, I was on skis as soon as I could walk. My mom had gone to the Olympics twenty years before, but now that she was unable to compete due to an injury, she put the fire and willpower into me.

When I was fourteen years old, I didn't have much of a life outside of training. Being home-schooled contributed to my nonexistent social life, which didn't seem important at the time. Even in the summer, it was conditioning almost every day, and practice on a ski simulator. Skiing was my life; when that first snow hit my cheeks on my first downhill run of the season, it was like being in heaven, and all the ten-hour days seemed well worth it.

The first snowfall also brought the dreaded tourist season. I will admit that it was nice to have new faces around for the first few days, except for the snotty snowboarders. Snowboarders always acted like they were better than the rest of the world, and went around the lodge like they owned the place. Their arrogance was evident by the way they were always talking down every sport but snowboarding, and were they ever rude! I was sure I wanted nothing to do with them — that is, until I met Jason Swenties.

I'll never forget that year. That was the year it snowed so much that a week before Christmas, we were snowed in. And with Mom being one of the

133

top ski instructors in the state, she made more in those two weeks than she made the rest of the winter. Every truck and road crew member worked day and night for a solid week to make sure all the tourists could get to the lodge, and I'm glad they did.

It all started when Mom said, "Come on, Elizabeth. We need to go into town to get you a new ski jacket. Your dad's working on the lifts, so we can't be long. I'm sure there'll be a lot of coaches from the Olympic Development Team here next week. I want you to look your best if one spots you. Make sure you get your make-up on; remember, look top-notch at all times."

"You know how I hate wearing that stuff," I complained. "But I guess I will."

After I got ready, we went to one of my favorite stores, Mike's Ski Shop. It was in an old converted log cabin, over a hundred years old, which had been added onto to accommodate the huge business rushes during the winter. Mike's had everything imaginable for the snow lover, and was by far the best in the area.

When we got out of the car, the cold wind hit me, plastering a grin on my face and reminding me that I would soon be on the slopes. And when we walked in, the smell of old cedar and hot chocolate resonated right through my body. *I love this time of year,* I thought.

After we looked at all the picked-over jackets, Mom said, "Not a good one in the bunch. I'm going to check the other side of the store. I'll be right back."

I continued to finger through the jackets; then I looked up and saw three boys off in the distance, looking me over. *Great,* I thought, *my least favorite thing in the world, snowboarders.* I nervously picked up a spider jacket and nonchalantly started looking at the fabric. One of the three guys walked over to me, casually leaning with his arm on the rack from which I had just taken the jacket. He was about sixteen years old and was tall and skinny. He had long dark hair, pulled back, just like most of the snowboarders did.

"So, you from around here?" he asked. "My name's Ryan. Everyone calls me Cal, cause that's where I'm from, California."

"What's it to you?" I asked.

"Oh, come on, baby," he said. "Tell me your name. You look like the type that would go out on the hills with a few spectacular snowboarders like me and my boys over there. We're the best there is." He pointed to his friends and they laughed.

"No thanks," I said. "I'd never do anything with a snowboarder, especially not you. I'd appreciate it if you'd leave me alone."

His friends laughed again, and he said, "That's all right. I see a really hot blonde over there that I'd rather talk to." He lifted his nose and walked toward the girl he was referring to.

Boarders, I thought, *they're all a bunch of rude, inconsiderate jerks.*

Startled, I heard a voice from behind me say, "Sorry about that. I heard the whole thing." I turned around to see another guy, about fifteen years old, with light brown, curly hair and brown eyes. He was about five feet eight inches tall and had goggles pushed up over his hair. "Sometimes people can be so stupid."

"Yeah, especially if they're snowboarders."

"Hey," he said. "You shouldn't judge people that way. Some boarders are pretty cool."

I laughed and said, "Yeah, on another planet. All the ones I've met aren't."

"You must not have met very many," he responded.

"I've met dozens, maybe even hundreds and they're all the same, full of themselves, thinking they own this mountain."

"You shouldn't stereotype people," he retorted. "Just because you've had a bad experience with a few boarders doesn't mean they're all like that."

"Ha!" I laughed. "I've been living on this mountain my whole life, and I know snowboarders as well as anybody. They all think they're the greatest gift to mankind because they participate in a slow sport where you have to do a few jumps. I'd love to get them on a pair of skis and see how they did then. I'd like to see how they felt after they trained for ten hours a day."

"Many boarders do train as hard as some skiers," he said.

"Yeah, right, and tell me it's not going to snow the rest of the winter."

"I'll tell you what," he said, "meet me at Fighter's Mountain at seven o'clock tonight for a race. At seven, everyone will be in for dinner. I'll go on my board and you can go on skis. We'll race down Double Diamond. That is if you think you can beat me."

"What are you going to do, bring all your brain-dead friends so they can intimidate me before I go down?"

"I don't have any friends like that; they wouldn't be my friends if they were. It'll be you and me; that is, if you're not scared."

I gritted my teeth, took a deep breath and said, "You must be out of your mind if you think you can beat me on Fighter's Mountain, on a snowboard!"

"Oh, you are scared," he mocked.

Ready to burst with rage, I said, "I'm going to teach you a lesson! I'll be there at seven sharp."

He reached his hand out and said, "It's a deal. My name's Jason Swenties, by the way."

I briefly shook his hand. "My name's Elizabeth Robinson and you'll be sorry you ever raced me. I'm an expert skier, not some flunky that comes up here once a year. One race down and that's it, so get ready to eat my snow!" I strutted away with my arms swinging and my eyes on fire. *The nerve of him,* I thought. *There isn't a snowboarder in the world that's going to beat me on skis.*

When I found Mom, she had a jacket all picked out and it fit perfectly. We went home with me burning inside, hardly able to wait to finally put an obnoxious boarder in his place.

Later that afternoon, I approached my dad and asked, "Can I go to Fighter's Mountain tonight and ski?"

"What's up?" he asked.

"I'm going to meet a guy there and teach him a lesson about skiing. He thinks he can beat me down Double Diamond on a snowboard."

"That's a good one," laughed Dad. "It's not a date, is it?"

"No way," I growled. "I have to show him up, and that's it."

"I'm all right with it, then. You'll be getting practice in, and that's what counts." I smiled and started to get my equipment ready.

When we parked, I noticed Jason standing off to the side, holding his board, waiting for me. "Is that him?" Dad asked.

"Yep," I answered and grabbed my bag.

"He's a good-looking kid," Dad said.

I raised my eyebrows and gave Dad one of my "get real" looks. "I'll call you when I'm done."

Dad nodded and got into the car. As he pulled away, I walked toward Jason and said, "You're lucky these slopes are lit so well. I'd hate for you to hurt yourself because you couldn't see."

"Wow!" he exclaimed. "Not even a hello or anything. Maybe snowboarders aren't the rude ones."

"Ugh," I grunted, "let's get this over with."

"So, is there some prize, or just bragging rights?" he asked.

"What did you have in mind?"

"I'll tell you what: you win and you get bragging rights, I win and I can kiss you."

"What?" I grumbled, "no way."

"Oh come on, take a chance in your life," he provoked. "You said you're going to win anyway."

"I am going to win," I boasted. "Let's see, though. If I win, I get bragging rights and you have to wear a sign on your back for one day that says 'skiers rule.' You'd probably rather die than do that, and your snowboarder buddies would disown you if you wore that sign. Yeah, that's fair. And if you win, you get to kiss me."

"Deal," he said, shaking my hand.

I mumbled under my breath, "Man, boarders aren't too bright either."

We got our equipment ready, lined up and prepared to push off. "This is going to be great," I boasted. I took a deep breath and the crisp, cool Colorado mountain air tickled the back of my throat. As I let it out, I said, "Ready, one, two, three, go." We both shoved off, with me in the lead. I zoomed way ahead of him, working as hard as I could to build up my speed. I blissfully moved back and forth on the skis as if trying out for the Olympics. After the first hill, I was way out in front and smiled with glee. *This fool is going look like the idiot he is,* I thought.

The snow on the second hill was compacted more than I thought, and had started to turn to ice. I tried slowing down and overcompensated with my rotation. I got off balance, fell right on my side, and did a tumble.

Jason blasted past me as I tried to get up. After I got back up on the skis, I looked down the hill and he was already at the bottom, waiting for me to come down. I finished my run and pulled up right next to him. I dropped my poles and threw my goggles in the snow. He smiled as I said, "I can't believe it. I haven't fallen in two years. How did you know you'd beat me?"

"I didn't," Jason said. "I knew the slopes would be packed down really well and the course would be fast, but I didn't think you'd fall. I figured if you did beat me, then I would take the loss politely and gracefully, to show you all snowboarders aren't jerks. I just wanted to see you again, and if I had to wear a paper saying 'skiers rule,' then oh well. It would be worth it for a chance to kiss you."

"Hmm," I grunted. I closed my eyes and sighed. "Get it done and over with." Jason moved closer to me and my heart raced. Instead of feeling something soft on my lips, I felt it on my cheek, like the first downhill run of the season when the snow hits your face. His lips were soft and soothing and reminded me of a warm towel touching my body when I was wet. A tingle filled my limbs, and all the resentment left my body. He pulled away and our eyes locked in a placid gaze. I stood speechless, knowing that it was my first real kiss.

"You only get one on the cheek," he said. "If you want to get the real thing, you'll have to get to know me better."

I smiled, and we spent the rest of the evening together talking and sharing stories.

That was two years ago. Since then, we have had a great relationship together, calling and texting almost every day. Jason turned out to be the nicest guy I ever met. He was right that I shouldn't have stereotyped or judged a type of people all the same way, because he was nothing like the other boarders I had met. I learned that I should find out about a person first before I make assumptions about his character. Now, my second favorite thing of the ski season is feeling the snow on my cheeks from my first downhill run. My first is feeling the lips on my cheeks of a snowboarder named Jason who loves me, just like the first day we met.

Leviath

Annie Webb

7th Grade, Norco Intermediate School, Norco, California

When I woke up that morning, I had no idea that my life, and the world's destiny, would be in jeopardy. I had always felt that there was something strange about my life and my parents, but I could never figure out what.

I was seventeen years old, with dark hair and skin and a tall, lanky body. My appearance helped me fit right in with the people of Egypt, even though my mom was from the U.S. and my dad was Egyptian. I had no idea why they had given me an American name, with us living where we did.

I walked into the living room, and Porta was standing there with a smile on his face, ready to greet me. Porta had been my sitter since I was born, and was always there when Mom and Dad were away on business. He stood six feet four inches tall and had the body of a weight lifter. He had dark straight hair and a warm but serious smile. "Good morning, Kyle," Porta said.

I frowned and said, "Mom and Dad are gone on business again. Why do they have to go on such short notice? Lately they've been gone so much."

"Now, now," Porta said. "I don't want to hear any complaining."

"I'm sorry," I moaned. "It's just... I've been having these strange dreams, and have felt like there's something wrong lately."

"Hmm," he muttered. Right then his phone rang and he held it to his ear. "I see, sir. Today is the day. I understand, sir. I've been training for this all my life. I know what to do. I'll put Kyle on."

Porta's face turned white and he tightened his hands. He handed me the phone, and Mom said in a shaky voice, "Hi, Kyle."

"What's wrong?" I asked.

"Porta will explain it all to you," Mom said. "Remember that whatever happens, both your father and I love you so much."

"Mom!" I yelled. In the background I heard a large crash, and the phone went dead. "Mom, Mom, please."

Porta took the phone from me and said, "Follow me." I followed him to the side of the staircase, where he took from the wall a picture that had been hanging there since I could remember. He removed a piece of the wall and pushed a button in the middle of a tile that was rooted deep inside. The tile started to glow a fluorescent blue, and a humming noise filled the air. I stepped backward in fear and turned to Porta, while he stood focused on the wall.

A large section of the wall slid away like in a scene from a movie. "Follow me," he said, with no emotion at all. I walked through the wall and into a room about the size of a classroom at school. The room had tables and chairs that looked hundreds of years old in the middle of it. Along one wall were bookcases filled with old leather-bound books and scrolls. Along the opposite wall were two modern computer set-ups with mainframes and several monitors. The room was bright and clean, like an operating room at a hospital. I said, "What the…" when Porta pushed another button.

The ground began to shake, while he stood unconcerned about our safety. "Put your hand out," he said. I stood dumbfounded, and again he said, "Put it out." I extended my hand, and a scroll on the bookshelf began to glow. My mouth dropped wide open when the scroll floated off one of the bookshelves and right into my hand. The ground stopped shaking the instant the scroll touched me. One of the chairs at the table slid out by itself and Porta said, "Sit. This is your destiny."

I sat down with my heart pounding as though it would explode. I set the scroll down and it opened on the table by itself, right in front of my eyes. The writing on the scroll lit up in bright red letters and I began to read.

"Kyle, your father's true name is Rah. You come from a long line of Egyptians known as Protectors. Since the beginning of time, Protectors have battled evil in the underworld, which is called Taut. Every protector has a special power, which separates them from the rest. The power given to you now is in your mind. You must learn how to use your thoughts to make things happen. This power is very great, so use it only for good.

"After three thousand years, a powerful Destroyer named Leviath has been released according to prophecy. He has captured your father and mother and they are in desperate need of your help. All of mankind could be at risk. You are a man now, and must save the world from a terrible fate. This symbol, which is Leviath's weakness, is the only thing that can defeat him. It will render him powerless for only a short period of time. Use it wisely, and good luck."

An old Egyptian symbol appeared on the scroll; it looked like the letter H, but had several other curves on it. The scroll closed and I said, "This can't be happening."

Porta nodded and said, "It's all true. You've felt it inside since you were a little boy."

I closed my eyes tightly and said, "Yes, I have felt it. I understand now." I thought about the scroll sitting on the bookshelf. I opened my eyes and it floated back and set down right where I pictured it in my mind to be.

Porta smiled and said, "You have begun to master your powers, I see. We must hurry and get you to the portal to the underworld at the great pyramids." He took me from the secret room, sealing it up as tight as it was before. We went out to his car and started driving toward the pyramids, which were three hours away. As we were driving down the highway, a bolt of lightning hit an overpass and it crumbled to the ground several hundred yards in front of us.

Porta said, "I see the destruction of the planet has begun. We must get to the pyramids as soon as possible. Use your mind to clear the road." I closed my eyes and thought as hard as I could, then opened them. Instantly, Porta and I were standing outside of the Great Pyramids of Gaza.

"Brilliant," Porta said. "I see not only are you powerful, you are intelligent with your powers as well. I am the only one who knows where the portal is. That's why I have had this name my entire life. We must hurry."

We ran to the side of the pyramid to one of the stones at the bottom, and Porta bent down. "Oh, no," he said. "The sandstorms have covered the stone where I can access the portal." I closed my eyes and thought of Porta and me standing in front of the stone with the sand removed. I opened my eyes, and the sand slid to the sides in piles immediately. A slight tremor shook the ground, and he said, "We have less time than I thought. There may be a huge earthquake soon."

Porta put his hand up against one of the stones and his ring began to glow. The portal opened up before our eyes. We stepped inside, and everything began to spin. The next thing I knew, we were standing on a path in a dark cave. At the end of the corridor was an opening, which we walked through. Standing there on the other side in an open cave was a dark figure dressed in a black robe. He stood eight feet tall and had a red face. He had jet black hair and his slanted eyes resembled something you would carve on a pumpkin. He grinned toothlessly at me.

"Welcome to the underworld of Taut," he scoffed.

"Are you Leviath?" I asked.

"You know I am," he said. "You can feel my presence inside you. I've been waiting for this moment for three thousand years, and they send a boy to defeat me. This must be a joke."

"This is no joke," I said. "Free my parents now and go back to where you came from, and I will spare your life."

"Spare my life," he mocked. "The underworld has waited for this moment for centuries. You and your people will be eliminated and we will rule your world."

I closed my eyes and pictured a sword in my hand, and me striking Leviath dead. I opened my eyes and lunged at Leviath with the sword in my hand.

Leviath laughed and stepped aside. "You have no powers over me. You are a mere child compared to me. And you, Porta, are useless. The underworld should have sent better minions to take care of your people on earth a long time ago."

I turned to swing the sword at Leviath again and it turned to sand, which fell to the ground. His voice boomed, "I've had enough games! You will die where you stand!"

I closed my eyes and pictured the symbol from the scroll burning on Leviath's forehead. I opened my eyes, and saw the symbol pressed deep into his forehead. It began to burn beneath his skin, while Leviath screamed in agony and fell to his knees. The walls of the cave shook and every creature screeched in the underworld, feeling his excruciating pain. I quickly closed my eyes and pictured Leviath in chains that couldn't be broken, lying powerless in the center of the earth. A hideous voice said in the background, "We've tried everything and those chains cannot be broken. He will lie there for all of eternity."

I opened my eyes, and a huge chain wrapped around Leviath as he screamed in pain on his knees. The earth opened up, and he fell in screaming, "No!"

The earth closed back up and Porta said, "You did it!"

I smiled and said, "He will never bother mankind again." I closed my eyes and pictured my parents and Porta unhurt, standing beside me at home in my room, just before bed. I opened my eyes and our bodies started to disintegrate. We reappeared in my bedroom, just as I had pictured it.

Dad said, "You did it, son! I'm proud of you. You saved our world." Mom and Porta both congratulated me too.

I woke up the next morning thinking it had all been a dream. I pinched myself, knowing it wasn't a dream — it was real. Leviath never bothered mankind again, and I went on as the Protector of the modern world.

Eighth Grade Students

Don't Go Into the Basement

Rachael Gulch

8th Grade, Springfield Middle School,
Holland, Ohio

When Mom died two months ago and left us without a father or any close relatives, I worried about what was going to happen to me and my brother Jack. As I was sixteen years old and Jack fourteen, we weren't even close to being able to take care of ourselves. When the court said we had a great-aunt who I had never heard of living in the Midwest, I was relieved that foster care wasn't our only option.

Jack and I had cried almost every night since Mom's car accident, and when we finally showed up with a state worker on my great-aunt's doorstep, I knew this was our only hope for some sort of a stable life again. As we stood, desperate, on the porch of her hundred-year-old Victorian house, my stomach turned and a chill went up my spine.

"It's sort of creepy," Jack said.

I eyeballed him with my lips pursed and my hands by my sides. "Let's make the best of this," I said as the state worker knocked on the door. A few seconds later, the door flung open, and there stood a little old lady with gray hair and a frail body. She was about seventy-five years old and weighed no more than one hundred pounds. She was dressed in an old, faded, blue plaid dress and shoes that looked like they were forty years old.

"Come on in," she said. "I'm your great-aunt Greta. You can just call me Aunt Greta." We walked in, and I turned my head and exhaled quickly from the strong smell of moth balls, which made me gag.

"I'm Gwen Washington, from the state human services," our case worker said to her. "Pleased to meet you."

"Nice to meet you," Aunt Greta replied.

"This is a very nice house you have," Mrs. Washington said. "All the paperwork has been taken care of, and everything checked out. I guess this is goodbye, until my follow-up visit in a month. You kids have my number if you need anything." Mrs. Washington smiled and left, leaving us standing awkwardly face to face.

"Your room, Melanie, is at the top of the stairs, first door on the right," Aunt Greta said. "And yours, Jack, is across the hall. I have two rules in this house. Pick up after yourself and don't go into the basement. The basement is my room, which I keep for myself. If you can't follow these rules, then I'm going to have to ask you to leave. Do you both understand?"

We both nodded our heads and said, "Yes."

"Most of your stuff is supposed to arrive tomorrow," Aunt Greta said. "You can go up into your rooms and get situated. Dinner is at five, and I'll have your list of chores tomorrow."

Jack and I went and looked at my room first. Our eyes met and widened together. "Look at this flowered wallpaper," I said. "It must be seventy-five years old. And the bed and dresser are antique, probably turn of the century."

"She's old," Jack said. "Just be happy we didn't have to go to foster care again."

"I don't know," I said. "There's something about her that I don't like. And what's that about not going into the basement? That's creepy. "

"All I know is I'm going to follow her rules," Jack said. "I'm not going back into state care and that's final."

"Yeah," I agreed. "I guess you're right."

After we sat down for dinner, a strange noise that sounded like someone pounding a sledgehammer on the walls came from the basement. Jack and I looked over at Aunt Greta and I asked, "What was that?"

"What was what?" she asked.

"That sound as if someone was banging on something," Jack said.

"I didn't hear anything," Aunt Greta said. "It must be your imagination. Are you two all right?"

"We're fine," I said. "It's just… that noise."

"There was no noise," she said. "You must be hearing things." Jack and I looked at each other, with our eyes wide open and blank looks on our faces. We finished dinner without hearing another sound from the basement.

The next morning, I woke up and went downstairs and into the kitchen. I opened the refrigerator and stuck my head into it. I jumped a foot into the air, then swiveled around, when I heard the same banging coming from the basement, but louder than the last time. I walked toward the basement door just as Aunt Greta was coming through it. "What was that noise?" I asked.

"What noise?" she asked.

"That loud banging," I said.

"I didn't hear anything," she insisted. I frowned, shook my head and looked away.

A week passed, and Jack and I continued to hear strange banging noises from the basement. Meanwhile, Aunt Greta watched our every move, as if she didn't trust us one bit. Eight days after we arrived, she called us into the living room. She said, "I have to go to the store and grocery shop. I want you two to behave and follow the rules. And whatever you do, don't go into the basement." We both nodded, and she left.

Not two minutes after she left, we heard the banging sound again. Jack sighed, walked over to the window, totally ignoring the sound, and asked, "Do you want to go outside?"

I walked over to the basement door, put my ear up against it and said, "I know you heard that noise. I wonder what it was."

"I don't know and I don't care," Jack said.

"This place is too weird for me," I said. "I have to know what's going on downstairs." I took a deep breath, swallowed, and reached for the handle of the basement door, just as Jack said, "Don't! You know the rules."

I twisted the knob with all my might, but the handle wouldn't turn. I exhaled and said, "Don't worry. It's locked. Where does she keep the key?"

"I don't know," Jack said again. "And I don't care. She's not that bad, you know, and I'm not going back to the state. Forget about the basement."

I squinted at Jack and said, "I wonder."

Later that day a moving van pulled up in front of the vacant house next door. The movers started unloading furniture and boxes and taking them into the house. Aunt Greta looked out the window and said under her breath, not realizing we were listening, "I don't trust them. They're probably like all the rest."

"Like all the rest of what?" I asked.

Aunt Greta let go of the curtains and swung abruptly around. She puckered up with a piercing look and said, "Never you mind. It's none of your business. You two go do the dishes and behave yourselves."

"What's going on?" I asked. "And what are those noises coming from the basement?"

"You mind your own business, and I told you not to worry about the basement. I told the state that I didn't want you to come, and when they said I was the only one that could take you, I was kind enough to say yes. I've been kind to you, so don't ask any more questions."

Jack intervened, "We won't, will we, Melanie?" I nodded and went into the kitchen.

For the next week the noises continued, until I couldn't take it anymore. I sneaked around and watched Aunt Greta daily for three days until I finally saw her put the key to the basement door into a sugar bowl in the cupboard. Shortly after that, she came to us and said, "I'm going to the grocery store. I'll be back in an hour, so don't get into any trouble." We both nodded.

Ten minutes after she left, Jack and I went into the back yard and sat down. From over the fence I heard a voice say, "Have you seen my cat? He was around here a minute ago."

Jack and I looked up and saw a woman in her early forties, with blonde hair and blue eyes. She was slim, fit and quite attractive in her designer jeans and new blouse. "What does your cat look like?" I asked.

"She's a tabby with a tint of orange on her backside, with black feet."

"No, we haven't seen her," said Jack.

"My name is Olivia. I moved in a week ago."

"My name is Melanie and this is Jack. Pleased to meet you."

Our eyes met with warm smiles as she extended her hand. We shook as she asked, "Have you lived here long? How's the neighborhood?"

"We've only been here a couple of weeks," I said. "Our mom died in a car accident, and we came here to live with our great-aunt."

"I'm so sorry to hear that," Olivia said. "If there's ever anything I can do for you, don't hesitate to ask."

"Thank you," I said. A lonely feeling came over me, and a memory of Christmas shopping with my mother flashed into my head. "I miss my mom so much," I said. I turned, holding back my tears, and said, "Excuse me," and walked into the house, with Jack following.

A week passed, and the noises kept coming from the basement, with Aunt Greta going down there every day as if nothing was going on. She went to the grocery store again, and Jack and I went into the back yard while she was gone. From over the fence we heard, "Hi Melanie, hi Jack."

We looked over at Olivia and I said, "Hi."

"It's a lot of work moving," Olivia said. "How are you and Jack holding up?"

Jack sat quietly and I said, "We miss our mom. It's been hard living here."

"Is everything all right?" Olivia asked.

Bursting with loneliness and the desire for someone to talk to, I said, "My aunt is a little strange. She's abrasive and... she's always watching what we do."

"Is that all?" Olivia asked.

"No. She always goes into the basement and we're not allowed down there," I said. "There are always noises coming from down there too."

"What kind of noises?" Olivia asked.

"Banging noises," said Jack.

"I know where she keeps the key, but I'm scared to go down there with just us two," I said.

Olivia's eyes sparkled and her kind smile comforted me. "It's probably nothing, but if it makes you feel better, I'll go down and check it out with you."

"I don't know," Jack said. "She said not to go down there."

"I have to know what's down there," I said. "Come on, let's go, Jack." He nodded and Olivia met us at the front door. We went into the kitchen and I grabbed the key from the sugar bowl, and then we went to the basement door. My hands shook and my legs felt like lead, as Jack and Olivia watched me put the key into the lock. I opened the door and took a deep breath. We went through the door, and I blinked heavily from the dust floating about as we stood on the landing.

I looked down and saw that the staircase went straight down, not allowing us to see into the basement. The creak of Olivia's first step down was like nails on a chalkboard and made the hair on the back of my neck stand straight up. Jack grabbed my arm and said, "We better not." The banging sound we had heard so many times before echoed through the air, making me shake.

Olivia walked quickly down the stairs while Jack and I followed at a slower pace. When we turned the corner of the staircase, my heart was thumping, and I expected something to jump out at me. Olivia stood with her eyes focused, with a look of total elation on her face. "Finally, after all these years, it's finally mine!"

Jack and I gazed across the basement and were bewildered to see a single rose in a glass case. It was the most beautiful vibrant purple I had ever seen in my life. The flower was the size of a softball and almost didn't look real. Olivia went to the case and opened it. She reached inside just as we heard a click behind us. I turned to see Aunt Greta standing there with her teeth clenched and her hands gripped tightly on a shotgun pointed right at Olivia.

We started to shake, then stepped backward as she said, "You touch that flower and you'll die right where you stand!"

Olivia pulled her hand out of the case and said, "Please, you've had it so long. I've been looking for it for years. Give it to me, please."

"Get out!" Aunt Greta yelled.

I took a step toward the stairs, quivering with fear, as Olivia said, "No, help me, please."

Aunt Greta said, "Not a chance," and walked her out of the basement and then the house, with the shotgun pointed right at her head. After getting Olivia outside, she locked the door behind her. Aunt Greta loosened her grip on the shotgun and said, "I can't do this anymore. I'm too old," and started to cry.

Jack asked, "What's going on?"

Aunt Greta said, "I'm not your great-aunt. I'm your great, great, great, great-aunt. That rose you saw is one of only three in existence. It allows the person that has it to live an extra hundred years unless someone does bodily harm to you. I'm a hundred and seventy-nine years old. People have been trying to steal it from me for years. If it gets into the hands of an evil person and they live that long, they may destroy the world. That's why I agreed for you two to come here. I don't have much longer to live. I was hoping you were good people who one day could take over for me, protecting the world by not letting the rose get into the wrong hands."

Jack and I stood silently with our hands sweating. "I was mean to you, and watched your every move, to be sure you two were worthy of the responsibility. You're my last hope." She looked at the floor and dropped her arms. "I'm so tired and so old. I'm ready to give up." I walked toward my aunt and hugged her, and Jack joined in.

"We'll protect the rose as long as we live," I said.

Aunt Greta looked into my eyes and said, "I know you will."

After our embrace was over, I asked, "What was that weird banging we heard down there?"

"That was the hot water pipes," Aunt Greta said. "They've been doing that for years."

I looked at Jack, started to laugh, and then said, "We thought… we thought, oh never mind. I'm just glad you're not some sort of weirdo."

She laughed and said, "Not hardly."

We had to move, because Olivia would have never given up trying to steal the rose. Aunt Greta died five years later. Jack and I wanted no part of living for nearly two hundred years and always worrying about someone stealing the flower, so we buried the rose with her and told no one. We figured there is good and evil in the world, and if you use your life to promote good, you'll never be sorry. We both lived a good life after that, and never once regretted burying the rose.

Someone's Crying Somewhere

Jane Kang

8th Grade, Falcon Cove Middle School, Weston, Florida

Everyone has that one special person they meet who changes their life forever, and you never know when or where you'll meet them. Susan was independent, caring and brave, oh so brave. She knew her day would come soon, so she tried to spend her last days as happily as she could. She never regretted what she did or said throughout her life. I remember every detail of every moment I spent with her, even though I only met her twelve days before she died in my arms.

My parents were always very good to me, but being a fourteen-year-old girl who was slight in stature, with a father who pushed me into sports, was discouraging. Though he never spoke it in words, he made it all too clear that he had always wanted a son. The fact that he and Mom tried for so long for another child made me feel that I could never be good enough once my brother was born.

As I waited outside the delivery room, my stomach was twisted in knots like an old frayed shoelace that had been tied too many times. With a gleam in his eye and a smile on his face, Dad spoke the dreaded words right after he burst out of the delivery room. "Come on in and meet your brother, Jen."

I followed Dad into the delivery room, where Mom was out of breath and looked like a woman who had just run a marathon. She lay there holding my brother, and said, "He's beautiful, just like you when you were born. Do you want to hold him?"

I gulped and Dad said, "I have a son. I finally have a son. We've named him James."

The nurse who was standing in the back of the room saved me when she said, "He barely cried once; how lucky you are. I hate to break up this special moment, but James has to go to the nursery to be checked out by the pediatrician. You two can go down in a few minutes and see him there, and Mom needs her rest." Mom handed James to the nurse, who whisked him away in a wheeled hospital crib.

"You two are going to get along so well," Mom said. "I know it. Why don't you go down to the nursery, and your father will be down in a minute." I nodded, then left and got on the elevator.

As I stood in front of the window peering at James, a weak but confident voice surprised me. "Is he your brother?" I turned around to find a girl about my age sitting in a wheelchair with her small skeleton-like arms holding onto the wheels. She wore a knitted hat, and between the small holes I saw no hair. She looked weak, torn and pale. *Cancer,* I thought.

"Yeah," I said proudly as I turned back toward James, ignoring her physical features.

"By the looks of him, he's seven pounds and won't be as sociable as the others." Startled, I didn't know whether to be offended for my brother or not. "He'll most likely have dirty blond hair and baby blue eyes. He won't play many sports, but instead, a musical instrument. My name's Susan, by the way." She had a great smile, one that could brighten up the whole room.

"I'm Jen. How do you know what my brother will be like?"

"The weight is easy, and he wasn't crying when he got here, which is a sign he barely will. I'm mainly guessing on his appearance, and his fingers are long and skinny, which shows musical talent." She paused. "What's his name?"

"James. What are you doing in the hospital?" I knew why, but I asked anyway.

She chuckled as if it were a joke, pointed to her head and said, "Cancer. Duh, isn't it obvious? Leukemia, to be specific. I like you. You're funny and somewhat stupid."

"I'm not stupid. I just didn't want to ask it that way." I blushed, then smiled.

A nurse came up, looked at Susan and frowned. She didn't have to say anything for Susan to understand. "More tests?" she asked.

"You know it's a weekly thing," the nurse said regretfully.

Susan gave me a weak smile and asked, "Will you be coming back tomorrow?" I nodded, as Susan hung her head and the nurse started to roll her away. I glanced their way and Susan turned around, holding up a pinky in a "promise" sign. I held mine up too.

For the next week, I went to see Susan every day. I pushed her wheelchair back and forth to where the babies lay. She especially loved the newborns, because she liked guessing what their personalities would be like. To her, that brought joy, and the more I spent time with her, the more I wanted to know why.

On the tenth day, I walked into her room, and she was in bed quietly reading. "Want to go see the babies?" I teased.

"Not today. Let's stay here." She continued to read, ignoring my presence. A minute later she looked up into my eyes. "Your eyes are pretty. They're like a deep pool of sky, just in that small area. I hope James will have eyes like you."

"Is something wrong?" I put my hand on her forehead to check whether she had a fever. It didn't feel hot or even abnormal. She was usually all fun and games, but it seemed as if a vacuum had taken the excitement out of her. I decided to ask her the question that had bothered me so long. "Why do you like babies so much?"

"Because I can't have any of my own." She paused. "Life's short, Jen. Do you know how many babies are born in a week? About 2.5 million. That's close to four babies per second. It's too bad one of them will never be mine. Ever since I was little, I played 'mommy' and pretended to have a child of my own, but now my days are limited." She was at the point of tears. "I'll never get to hold a child in my arms and call it my own. The doctor's tests say I only have days left. I'm going to enjoy every one of the 2.5 million babies I can before I go."

A single tear fell from her face silently. "Seeing all those babies stopped me from crying so many times when I hurt so badly inside." Another tear came streaming down her pale skinny face. It dripped on her book, leaving a mark. I held her hand, and then comforted her by stroking her back.

She said she only had a few days left to enjoy what she loved most, and yet she was lying there. I wanted to do something special for her, something that would remind her to be happy and that she could have a baby of her own somehow. Then it hit me, like a cold winter wind on a January morning. I felt guilty because I left early, but I figured this special project would be worth it.

It took paper cuts, glue, scissors, more paper cuts, and, of course, babies. I worked late into the night making a scrapbook for her with pictures of all kinds of newborns from around the world. I knew I couldn't get 2.5 million, but I was going to get as many as I could.

On the eleventh morning I went to Mom and asked, "Can I hold James?" She smiled and handed him to me. I sat down in the rocking chair and said, "I was so worried that when James came, Dad would like him more than me. I know he always wanted a son."

"The day you were born, your father was so excited he could hardly speak. He didn't eat for two days afterward. No matter how old you are or where you are in the world, you'll always be his little girl."

"I know," I said. "Susan made me realize how precious life is. She could never hold a baby of her own and I have a beautiful baby brother. I feel so lucky. I love you, James." I kissed James, and Mom smiled as I rocked him, in awe of his beauty.

When I went to see Susan that day, she was sleeping in bed. I wanted to see her face when she opened her scrapbook, so I waited for over an hour. I sat on the lounge chair and began to look over the work I had done. It contained fifty pages, and each of them had a different baby. Each page listed the baby's name, weight and where he or she was from.

When she woke, her eyes met mine and it was if I could feel her pain. I tried to smile as I energetically said, "I made this for you." She could barely move and her skin was pale. She tried to smile to mask the pain for me, but couldn't.

I sat down beside her, opened the scrapbook and started showing her pictures of the babies that I had worked so hard on. She grinned and weakly said, "That one's going to have dark hair and brown eyes. He'll go to college and be an engineer one day." I turned the page and she tried to continue. "And that girl is going to have strawberry blonde hair and blue eyes. She's going to be a singer. I can tell by her neck." She swallowed hard and couldn't speak.

I turned the page and tried to go on for her. "This one's going to have red hair with freckles. She'll have light skin and take an office job so she can stay out of the sun. This one's going to have jet black, straight hair and be over six feet tall. He'll love to fly and become a pilot one day." I looked back at Susan, who had dozed off into a tranquil sleep.

I sat looking down at the scrapbook, until a nurse walked in and said, "I'm sorry, but you'll have to leave. Visiting hours are over and her family is going to spend some time alone with her. "

I set the book next to her bed and started walking out. I looked back and saw needles being injected in Susan's skin. My stomach twisted in pain, and a tear rolled down my cheek. I couldn't stand needles and to think that Susan had to go through that every week was unbearable. I walked out, unable to look back.

On day twelve, I rushed to her room to find her mom, dad, brother and sister all by her side. There were some other people in the room whom I had never seen before. I took a step backward toward the door, feeling out of place. Susan's mom said, "No. Please join us."

I made my way through the room, to see Susan with the scrapbook I had made her by her side. When our eyes met, she smiled with the same smile I had seen on the day we met. "I love the book." I went to her and she said, barely above a whisper, "It's the perfect goodbye present."

"Goodbye present? You have at least a few more days," I exclaimed.

Susan's mom shook her head. "Her white blood cells have decreased and the cancer cells have taken over."

"Stay with me here today," Susan said. She took my hand in her own and kissed it softly. "Someone's crying somewhere, and I don't want it to be you. I don't want your beautiful eyes to be full of tears when I go."

She closed her eyes softly and I hugged her. I had to be strong for her, so I tried to hold back my tears. I told myself she was only sleeping and she would wake up soon. But her heart slowed, and she would never wake up again.

At the funeral, there were nearly a hundred people, probably ones she had deeply touched, like me. I waited until the right moment to tell everyone how strong Susan was, and why she had had such a great love for babies. I finished by saying, "Someone's crying somewhere, and Susan didn't want it to be us. She wanted to be strong and live her last moments happily, and I looked up to her for that. I hope to see her again when my time comes, with tears of joy."

The Brann Affair

Ben Lewis

8th grade, Ionia Middle School, Ionia, Michigan

I stared down blankly at the page as I sat in my one-bedroom apartment, hoping an idea would pop into my head. Being an unemployed writer in the Portland area had hit me hard, so when I got the call to freelance for the newspaper, I was ecstatic. I touched the keyboard and thought, *That's it. How perfect.*

The seconds turned into minutes, until I looked at the clock and thought, *A full hour for this story, whoa. I'm glad that's done. It turned out pretty good, if I do have to say so myself. I need some air. I think I'll walk down to the coffee shop and get a latte.*

When I got to the elevator and pressed the button, I heard from behind me the all-too-familiar voice of my nemesis, John Sherlock. "If it isn't Zach Brann. How are things going? Have you found work yet?"

I bit my lip, holding back what I truly wanted to say, and paused. I took a deep breath and said, "As a matter of fact, I have. I'm doing freelance for the *Portland News.*"

"I've been writing in that paper for years," John said. "Did I mention that my second novel just hit the bestseller list?"

"Three times," I said. The elevator door popped open, saving me. "I have to go now. I have to get my first story over to the editor by tomorrow." I stepped into the elevator as fast as I could and pushed the button; the door shut without either of us saying another word. I thought, *Man, I can't stand him. I wish he didn't live in the same apartment building. And he always brags about his success. Oh well. I'm not going to let him ruin my day.*

The next day I went to the editor, Jerry Hepson, who had hired me, and handed him my piece. He read about two paragraphs and said, "A similar story was already submitted for today's paper by John Sherlock. It's being typeset as we speak."

"That's impossible," I said. "I just wrote that yesterday."

"You're a little too late," Jerry said. "I have room for another piece if you want to get it to me the day after tomorrow. I'll send over the specs."

"Thanks," I said. "I'll make sure it's perfect."

The next morning I went and bought a newspaper and thumbed through it until I came to John Sherlock's column. I started reading it and thought, *This is my story, almost word for word. What's going on? I'll get to the bottom of this.*

I went to John's apartment and saw him just down the hall. I called out his name and he slowly turned, as if he had been awakened from a trance. He moved his large frame ominously toward me. "Yes, Zach. What do you want?"

"How could you steal my story?" I asked. "I saw it in today's paper, almost word for word."

"What are you talking about?" John said. "I wrote that story two weeks ago."

My eyes bulged out of my head and I said, "That's impossible. I wrote it two days ago."

"I know what you're doing," John said. "I know you were unemployed for quite a while, and times are hard for you right now. Believe me, I've been there. If you need me to lend you some money, I will. But you can't make a wild accusation like that. A story will come to you, don't worry."

I shook my head to clear it and said, "I'm going to write the best story I ever have. Mr. Hepson told me he'll print it the day after tomorrow. Then we'll see who the better writer is."

I stormed back to my apartment and typed feverishly. An hour later, I sat back and thought, *Wow! One of my best ever, for sure. This time I'm going to save it under my pictures just in case. That way John can never find it if he's snooping somehow.* Then I went and did my laundry at the laundromat and went grocery shopping.

The next morning I got up and went down to the newspaper office. I went into Mr. Hepson's office and handed him my story. He raised his eyebrows and started reading it. After two paragraphs he said, "I can't use this."

"Why not?" I said. "It's one of my best ever."

"John Sherlock turned in a story just like this one and it's going to print tomorrow."

My hands dropped to my sides, my face went blank and I said, "I don't understand. He couldn't have turned in a story like this. I just wrote it yesterday."

"I know you really need this job," Mr. Hepson said. "But if you're stealing his work, I'm going to have to terminate our agreement. John has been writing for us for years. I've seen your work, and I know you're talented too. You don't need to do that. I'll give you one more chance to come up with something original."

"I don't understand," I mumbled. "All right, you'll have the story the day after tomorrow." I left confused and unsure what to do. When I got onto the elevator I thought, *Am I going crazy? Can John read my mind? I don't know what's going on, but I'm going to find out.*

I knocked on John's apartment door, and when he opened it I stood with my arms crossed. "How'd you steal my story?" I asked. "Mr. Hepson said you turned in a story that was just like mine."

"You're crazy," John said. "Man, once you have a little success, everyone tries to take your work as their own. Why don't you come up with some of your own material? If you come up with something good, maybe I'll even put a good word in for you with Mr. Hepson." He shut the door, leaving me standing there.

I said through the door, "I'll write a better story for Mr. Hepson than you ever have in your life. You'll see."

I walked down the hall and pushed the button for the elevator. As I stood waiting, I thought, *This can't be happening. I know I wrote those stories. How did he get them done before me? Is he telepathic? I'll find out exactly what's going on.*

I went to the local electronics store and bought a camera with a motion sensor on it. I went back to my apartment and started setting it up, smiling like a madman. I hid it in a small clock and thought, *If he is doing something, now I'll know for sure.*

I sat down at my computer and started typing. An hour later I was done, and sat back in my chair grinning with my arms folded. *I'd better save it under my pictures again, just in case,* I thought. *I'm going to put an alert on it to see if it was viewed as well.*

I went to the park and sat outside for an hour or so, and then went to the mall, giving John plenty of time to take the bait. I went back home late at night, and went right to my computer. My stomach turned and my palms started sweating as I turned on the computer. I pulled my story up on the computer and sure enough a pop-up came up that said, "Viewed at 7:35."

"I knew it," I said. "The rat took the bait, and now I have him."

I went over to the camera and played back the tape. John was on the camera, going through my computer with a device that helped him find my password. He said to himself, "I hope this one is worth all the trouble."

"I got you," I said. "You're a thief." I went to the Portland police and showed them the video. They agreed to meet me the next morning at the newspaper office.

The next morning, when John walked into Mr. Hepson's office, his eyes opened wide as he saw me and the police sitting there. "I knew you were stealing my stories," I said.

"You're crazy," John said. "I never stole one of your stories."

"Am I?" I asked. "Look here." We played him the tape, and he stood watching as if he were a child entranced by a TV show.

When the tape was done, Mr. Hepson asked him, "How could you? You're fired."

Detective Kennedy said, "We had complaints that he stole both of his novels from a struggling writer as well. We could never prove it, because they weren't copyrighted yet. He made all his money off of other people's work. What a shame."

John said, "I... I... forget it. I want to see my lawyer."

The police took John away. He was later convicted of breaking and entering and piracy. The tape I made ruined him, and he was never able to get a job as a writer again.

I got a full-time job as a writer for the newspaper, with a nationally syndicated column. I went on to write five novels with my newfound confidence. One of them was about my experiences with John Sherlock. The conclusion at the end of the book about my trials and tribulations with John was this: "Sometimes hardship comes before success, and cheaters never prosper."

Lana's Eyes

Nicholas Lozen

8th Grade, L'Anse Creuse Middle School South, Harrison Township, Michigan

I am Lana — Lana the hawk. I am what you pink-flesh humans call a "prairie falcon." Human — the very word brings agony to my soul. I didn't always hate humans. In difficult feeding times, their beasts of metal and smoke provided an easy meal of road kill on the great flat rock they call a highway. Now, if I hear the word *human*, I'm filled with fury in every bone in my body.

Six months ago, life was difficult, but better. I was a single mother raising three chicks named Minos, Nero and Freya. Daily gliding above the spiraling thermals, straining my eyes in the thick forest, trying to provide my chicks with any type of meal, was no easy task. The forest floor had been picked clean by all the other Raptors, and with three screaming chicks that hadn't eaten in two days, I had no choice but to go to the great flat rock.

When I arrived, I hovered above, hoping for any morsel of fresh meat to give to my young. Suddenly a red beast of metal and smoke roared down the great flat rock, discarding an apple from inside. My heart pumped as movement from the brush off to the side caught my eye. A small field mouse looked around and then ran onto the great flat rock toward the apple.

I thought, *Wait for it, wait for it.* Blood pumped fiercely throughout my body as the mouse sniffed the apple and then looked around nervously. *Now!* I swooped down with full force, a glimmer of hope in my eyes. The mouse turned, wide-eyed just as my talons scraped the pavement, seizing the mouse's tail.

The next thing I knew, a large black fiend snarled down the great rock right at me. My eyes froze and I quickly tried to fly away. I got a few inches off the ground and felt a great force strike me. I was jolted to the other side of the great flat rock, careening out of control. I landed roughly on my side, letting go of my catch. I shrieked angrily, "Oh no, my babies' meal!"

I attempted to stand, but winced, looking down at my wing, which was twisted the wrong way. "Mommy! You hit a bird," a high-pitched voice exclaimed.

"Oh that poor thing," lamented another.

I heard ringing in my ears as I thought, *Minos... Nero... Freya. I'm sorry.* Everything went dark as I faded into unconsciousness.

The next thing I knew, I was in a cage, with several strangely dressed humans watching my every move. They fed me and provided me with medical care, until my wing was better. Finally an odd-looking man came in and said, "My name is David and I will be your trainer, Cloudbreak."

"Cloudbreak?" I squeaked. "My name is Lana. It's been Lana since the day I was born."

David pulled me from the cage, put a glove on and attached a rope to my leg as I squawked, protesting vehemently. "Up," he commanded pointing at his wrist. I refused to move and again he said, "Up!"

"You must let me go," I screeched. "My babies need me." I took off to fly, only to find the rope pulling hard on my leg.

David said again, "Up!"

I yelled, "Why is it I can understand most everything you stupid humans say, but you can't understand animal talk? You must let me go. Mino, Nero and Freya need me!"

David kept saying, "Up." I flew until total exhaustion set in. I finally jumped up on the perch and asked, "Now will you let me go?"

David gave me piece of meat and said, "Good girl, Cloudbreak."

Every day was the same routine, with me asking about my family and David scolding me for being loud. I soon found the only way to be fed and stay healthy so I could return to my young was to do exactly what David told me.

Soon I was loaded onto a truck in a smelly cage with all my fellow birds. Valerie was a female Hoatzin from South America, whose cage was right next to mine as the truck moved down the great flat rock. I was surprised when she said, "Your first presentation! Don't be nervous."

"Forget my presentation," I said. "I need to go home to my family."

Donald, a barn owl with only one leg, said, "You may as well forget leaving. The humans use us for their pleasure."

"I will not be used for pleasure," I said. "I must leave at once."

Donald said, "It's hopeless. You're better off doing exactly what they say."

"Never!" I protested.

Soon after, I felt my cage being taken out of the truck to an outdoor pavilion. Just before David opened the door, Valerie said, "Good luck." I squawked in anger.

David took me with his glove on, and set me on his arm. I looked up and saw them everywhere... dozens of them... human offspring. They ooh-ed and ah-ed as I jumped off my perch. "This is Cloudbreak," David explained. "She's not used to the public yet, so let's be calm." I hated David's guts, so I did what any sensible bird of prey would do; I tried to fly away in a fury.

All the children laughed at my antics as the rope made me feel like my leg was going to pull off. David commanded, "Up." With no other choice I perched on his arm waiting for a treat.

He fed me and then the questions started. "What does he eat? How fast can he fly? Is he a boy or a girl?" A boy with a brown hat on asked, "What if she pecks you in the face?"

David said, "She would never do that. She's too well trained. Besides, she likes me. "

So you think, human, I thought. "Payback!" I screeched, stabbing him in the cheekbone with my sharp beak. Howling, David leapt backward. I perched on his exposed arm just above the glove, and squeezed and ripped his arm with my talons as hard as I could. David screamed in pain and removed the glove. Taking advantage of my only chance, I took flight with the glove still attached. I soared free through the air, as I had before I was captured, out of breath from the added weight.

I didn't stop until I was just on the edge of the forest I knew so well. Exhausted, I settled down for the night. Waking up, I angrily pecked at the straps that bound me. After the longest time I screeched, "I'll never get home."

A porcupine heard me, wobbled up from the bushes and laughed, "You'll never get that thing off."

"I've come so far," I said. "I must get back to my young. You must help me get this thing off or my babies will die."

"Help you! You would eat me if you could."

"I promise if you help me, I'll never forget what you did," I sniffled.

The porcupine's face softened. "Come," the porcupine said beckoning me with one claw. I hopped over to him still sniffling. With one swipe of his sharp claw, I felt the bindings that had held me for so long fall away. I thanked the porcupine and flew away, soaring on the thermals with the wind at my back. My blood pumped freely as I realized that I was liberated once again.

When I got back to my nest, it was right before dusk. My heart raced as I saw Freya still in the nest. She had grown so much and if I had not been held captive by the humans she would be ready to leave the nest by now. I cried out to her, and noticed that she had three bloody cuts across her chest.

"Freya," I cried. "Wha-what happened?"

"M-m-mother, is that really you?"

"Yes," I cooed, stoking her with the tips of my wing feathers. "Where are your brothers?"

Freya coughed. "They got hurt, Mommy, r-real b-bad."

"Tell me what happened," I said softly.

Freya took a shaky breath and said, "After you were gone we all thought you were dead, so Lorelei took care of us. She told us how you two were friends since birth. She tried as best she could, but she wasn't half the hawk you are."

"Then what?" I whispered.

"A couple of bobcats got into the nest," Freya said. "Lorelei fended them off… but they teamed up on her and killed her."

"And Minos and Nero?" I asked, almost too afraid to find out.

"They, they… ate them, Mommy," Freya sobbed.

"What about you?" I asked, with tears rolling down my cheeks.

"I was too scrawny to eat, so they slashed me and left me to die."

"But you won't die," I exclaimed. "I'll heal you up… and everything will be all right."

"I'm going to see Minos and Nero, Mommy," Freya muttered shakily.

"No!" I cried and held her against my chest. I felt her last breath against my breast as her tiny heart stopped beating. I sat there holding my dead daughter in my wings, unsure how to react. I wept, thinking, *Humans! How I hate that word. Don't they know we have babies that we want to see grow up just like they do? When will they ever realize that we have feelings and shouldn't be caged for their pleasure? It seems that humans will never learn to take care of this planet. I wish they'd understand we need it too.*

Movie Star Murder

Isabella Piccinini

8th Grade, Larson Middle School,
Troy, Michigan

Being one of the greatest detectives in the world had definitely taken its toll on my health. The long, anxiety-filled, sleepless nights, and not having an appetite while on huge cases, had left me weary and haggard. At thirty-five years of age, with slightly graying hair, I shouldn't have been concerned about the five thousand a day plus expenses I was missing out on. And with seven best-selling mystery novels under my belt, money should've been the last thing on my mind. But with my slightly paranoid tendencies and my always-racing mind, I worried about money just like everything else.

As I approached the entrance to board the plane to go abroad, I took a deep breath. *Just what I need*, I thought, *relaxation*. I stared at the floor while walking through the jetway, desperately trying to stop being myself for one minute. I reached into my pocket and pulled out a pill I had just for the occasion. *A mild sedative is perfect for me so I can control my thoughts on the plane.*

I swallowed the pill without any water, scraping it on the back of my throat. The bitter aftertaste of the sedative engulfed my tongue. *Those taste horrible,* I thought. *I don't think I could get through the flight without them, though.* I kept staring at the floor until just before I got on the plane. *Don't do it. Please don't look up.*

I looked up and thought, *The boy in front of me is approximately twelve years old, wishing he was older. I can tell this by his shorts and music t-shirt, which is usually the style of young college students. He must have an older brother he wants to try to keep up with, because his shoes would be worn by a much older person. His hair looks dirty and not well kept, which tells me one of two things: either he doesn't care about hygiene, or he's crying out for attention from his parents. From his wristband and the way he walks, I can tell he must be from the southern part of Boston. Many of the kids wear wristbands like that there. He's probably going abroad to see a relative, dressed like that.*

I sighed and thought, *I promised I wouldn't do this to myself on this trip. Those sedatives are so mild they barely help at all. I hope they kick in soon.* I sat down in my aisle seat, with the boy I saw on the jetway and his parents sitting one row back.

The boy said, "I don't see why I have to go to London. It was Jerry who decided to go to college at Oxford. If he was normal, he would've gone to school here like everyone else. I could've stayed home by myself. I'm almost thirteen, you know."

The boy's father said, "Yeah. You're almost thirteen and you act like you're seven years old half the time. No way would I let you stay home alone, even if you were eighteen."

The boy exhaled heavily and said, "You never give me credit for anything. If it was Jerry, you'd let him stay."

"No, I wouldn't," the father said. "Just sit back and relax. Can't you turn your iPod on or something, so I can have some peace and quiet? It's a long flight, and if you're going to carry on like you normally do, I'm going to go crazy."

I smiled and thought, *Spot on about the boy, Quinn. Sometimes the way your mind works is a curse, and sometimes it's a blessing.*

A young woman and her ten-year-old son sat down next to me. On the other side of the aisle, another woman and her teenage daughter sat down closest to the window. A man who looked very familiar sat on the aisle seat across from me. *That's John Winkler, the famous actor,* I thought. *I never forget a face or a name. I'm sure he wants to be left alone, just like I do. I won't say anything.*

The woman next to him said, "I know you. You're that actor that was in the movie *Chains.* Can I have your autograph?"

"Sure, if you promise to let me rest the entire trip," John said. The woman nodded and gave him a piece of paper and a pen from her backpack under her seat. John signed the paper and handed it to her.

After the plane took off, I fell asleep. I woke up an hour later when we hit turbulence. I shook my head and thought, *I'm going back to the doctor and getting a stronger sedative next time. I do feel a little better, though.*

My thoughts were erased when an attractive blonde flight attendant asked, "Can I get you a coffee, sir?"

I looked at her name tag and said, "Stacy, no coffee for me. It makes my mind race. I'll have an orange juice, if I could."

She smiled and handed me my juice and a sandwich with a bag of peanuts. Then she turned to John Winkler and scowled, "And you, sir?"

John coyly smiled and said, "I'll have a coffee with the special meal I ordered," and then winked.

Confused, I glanced over at John and Stacy and started to deduce the facts when she asked, "And you two?"

The mother next to John said, "We'll both have Cokes."

Stacy poured John his coffee and handed it to him. She gave him his special meal from beneath the cart and poured the two Cokes. She handed them to the ladies with their sandwiches and peanuts, and then started to move her cart down the aisle. As Stacy was moving away, John took his finger and stroked her leg just below her knee. Of course, I was the only one who saw this. Stacy turned to John with a look like an evil serpent. She took a deep breath, didn't say a word, and moved the cart two rows down, continuing as if nothing had happened.

Perplexed, I thought, *They must know each other in some way. He's an actor, and he does have a reputation as a player. She's a beautiful woman.* I paused. *No. I promised myself this was going to be a vacation.* I took a book out of my backpack and started reading, trying to empty my mind.

Five minutes later, my mind started to wander. *Almost every time I read a book, I find the story mundane. They're so predictable. I always know who did it halfway through the mystery. I wish other writers besides me could make it interesting.* I continued to read, until a large, athletic-looking man walked toward us down the aisle. He was just over six feet tall and had short, straight, dark hair. He looked to be about twenty-nine years old, and was dressed casually in jeans and a soccer shirt.

Just as he was almost next to us, he stumbled and lost his balance. He caught himself with one hand, grabbing John's seat right next to his head. I faintly heard a plunking sound like a rock being dropped into water. The man quickly said, "I'm sorry. It's this darn turbulence."

"Watch your step next time," John said.

"Sorry, sir," the man responded, and continued to walk toward his seat. I looked down at John's table and noticed a few droplets of coffee that had splashed onto his pull-out table. John quickly wiped up the coffee with his napkin and took a sip.

"Hmm," I mumbled. I shook my head and thought, *Just read your book, Quinn.* Shortly after that, Stacy came back and picked up our cups and threw them in the garbage. John got up and went to the bathroom.

Fifteen minutes later, a woman went to a different flight attendant and said, "That man has been in the bathroom forever."

The flight attendant went to the bathroom door, knocked on it and asked, "Is anyone in there?" As I was only a few seats from the bathroom, I put my book down and listened. After no one answered several times, another flight attendant walked up with one of the crew from the cockpit. They used a special key to unlock the door and then tried to push it open. When they got it partially opened, one of the flight attendants shrieked, "Oh my gosh!"

A professionally dressed man came over and asked, "Is there a problem here?" He flipped out a badge and said, "U.S. Air Marshal, International Division."

The flight attendant said, "That man looks like he's dead in there." Hearing this, I stood up, while some of the other passengers started to panic.

The air marshal said loudly, "Don't panic. I'm Air Marshal William Jenkins. Everything is under control."

Air Marshal Jenkins began to move the body out of the bathroom. I walked up and said, "I wouldn't do that just yet."

Air Marshal Jenkins' face stiffened and his lip curled. "And why is that?" he replied.

"You could be damaging evidence," I said.

"Hey, you're that famous detective Quinn Clark," he said. "I've read every one of your books. What do you think happened, a heart attack?"

I reached through the door and felt for a pulse. I looked at Air Marshal Jenkins and shook my head. "He's dead," I said. "I think we can take him out of there now." We maneuvered him out of the bathroom and into the back area of the plane reserved specifically for the flight crew. We laid him down and I said, "This is John Winkler, the famous actor."

"You're right," Marshal Jenkins said. "It was probably a heart attack. Look at the discoloration around his lips."

"Maybe, maybe not," I said. I grabbed his hand and looked at every inch of it. "His nails are already starting to change color. His skin is awfully pink for a heart attack victim, as well. Usually skin color will be white, or at least lighter, if he had a heart attack. I believe he was poisoned."

"Oh, come on," Marshal Jenkins said. "This isn't a movie or one of your books. You can't tell that by looking at him."

Our eyes met and my face turned to stone. "I've solved hundreds of cases and seen dozens of dead bodies, and I say this man was poisoned!" Air Marshal Jenkins stood up straight and pinned his shoulders back. One passenger stood up and gasped, while several others got up, one screaming.

"Everyone, remain calm," Marshal Jenkins yelled. "The situation is under control!" He turned to me and said, "You're panicking the passengers."

"I'm Quinn Clark, a detective," I loudly said. "Everyone remain calm. Even though Mr. Winkler was poisoned, there is no immediate threat to any of you. This was definitely planned to be made to look like a heart attack."

One passenger asked, "How do you know?"

"Simple," I said. "Mr. Winkler has a reputation as a player and a heavy partier. It would be the most logical conclusion that it had finally caught up to him, but I see it differently. You see, Mr. Winkler was obviously going on vacation, as I am. He was going to a place where he's not as well known, England. Like me, he probably wanted to get away from the everyday grind. I could tell this by the way he gave the woman next to him his autograph and then asked to be left alone. When actors are lucky enough to find work, that's the first thing they want to talk about, to help promote their careers and satisfy their egos.

"Stacy, the flight attendant and John had had a fling at one time. I could tell by the way she scowled at him when she greeted him. This was verified when Mr. Winkler touched her leg and she didn't respond." Stacy's eyes met mine and then she quickly turned away. I pointed at the athletic man I'd seen earlier and said, "When this gentleman over here walked by Mr. Winkler, he dropped something into his coffee, probably a lethal dose of cyanide. What's your name, sir?"

"My name is Frank Bilton."

"Mr. Bilton," I continued, "I heard the splash of the dose you dropped into his cup when you stumbled by. This is also verified by the way the coffee spurted onto the table. It formed a splash of droplets rather than a spill."

"All this nonsense about a spill and a splash is absurd!" Frank yelled.

"Oh, is it?" I asked. "How do you explain the fact that Mr. Winkler died shortly after you dropped something into his coffee?"

"I'm not saying anything," Frank said.

"When we get to London, I think the authorities will want to ask you a few questions," Marshal Jenkins said.

"The fact that you're dating Stacy is more than evident," I continued.

"I've never seen her in my life," Frank protested.

"You saw her just before you got on the plane," I said. "Didn't he, Stacy?"

"No... I don't know that man," Stacy said.

"Really," I replied. "Then how do you explain the fact that there's a fresh smudge of your lipstick on his collar?"

"That's not my lipstick," Stacy said.

"You're wearing Maybelline number 45, Camille Red, and if you look at his collar, it will be a perfect match," I said.

"That lipstick could be from yesterday and could be someone else's," Stacy complained.

"If you look at the smudge you will see that the lipstick is still soft and hasn't hardened," I said. "That means the smudge has to have been made less than four hours ago. The fact that your lipstick is a rare number means that the likelihood of another woman wearing it would be almost nonexistent."

"You can't prove anything," Frank said.

"On the contrary, Mr. Bilton," I gloated. "I saw Stacy take the cup Mr. Winkler was drinking from and wipe it clean with a napkin. His cup was the only one she did that to. I'm sure by now she has washed the cup clean to destroy the evidence. If we pull the napkin from the garbage, I'm sure you'll find traces of cyanide on it."

I stared Stacy down, and she broke down and cried. With her face in her hands she wailed, "All right. It's true. I was in love with John, and he two-timed me, just as he did with every woman he ever went out with. I'm so broken up inside that I haven't been able to eat or sleep. He deserved it."

"Quiet!" Frank shouted. "They can't prove it."

"I couldn't get over John, and used Frank to help me plot my revenge," Stacy said. "It's all true, like Mr. Clark said. I'm glad it's over."

"I think you might want to cuff them to their seats until we get to London, Marshal Jenkins. The police will have many questions for these two."

Marshal Jenkins cuffed them both, and I went back and sat down, while all the passengers clapped. After the noise died down, the boy next to me asked, "How did you know all that stuff, mister? Are you psychic?"

"No," I returned. "You can tell things about people if you pay attention and are aware of your surroundings. Take that woman three rows up, for example. Even though I didn't see her with a book, she definitely loves to read and doesn't like sports. Anyone can tell that."

"How, mister?" he asked.

"When I walked by her earlier, I noticed quite a few things," I said. "I saw her first two fingers were worn at the tips only on her right hand. That's usually from turning the pages in books. She also has an expensive set of reading glasses on her table that only an avid reader would use. The look she gave the man who was reading a sports magazine next to her was unpleasant, and she gave the same look to Frank Bilton when he walked by. She's also overweight, which is usually the result of a lack of exercise. Some people that are overweight are heavy readers."

"You knew all that from looking at that woman?" the boy asked.

I nodded and asked, "You couldn't figure that out?" The boy shook his head. "It's a matter of common knowledge, being observant and simple deduction."

"Maybe for you," the boy said.

"Forgive me, but I need to sleep now," I said. "My mind is racing." I closed my eyes and thought, *This is a vacation. Now I really need to clear my mind.*

The Berlin Project

Jarod Palmer

8th Grade, South Allegheny Middle School, Liberty Boro, Pennsylvania

April 30, 1945, 07:00 hours: In Nazi Germany, in a bunker deep inside Berlin, Dr. Von Gieson stood tall and thin in a lab coat, in a dimly lit underground laboratory with the doors securely shut. His hands rested over his ears, with the loud thunder of Allied bombing rarely allowing him a brief moment of silence. The Allies were quickly approaching. Dr. Von Gieson was awaiting his inevitable fate: a war criminal trial and then execution. Dr. Schuster, a young blond man similarly dressed, rushed through the double doors in haste, carrying a jar of strangely colored liquid.

"Do you have it?" Dr. Von Gieson asked.

"Of course; I told you I wouldn't return until I did." Dr. Schuster handed Dr. Von Gieson the jar. "I'm still unsure of the dose."

"Thank you for your fine discovery," Von Gieson said, reaching into a drawer and pulling out a bottle of wine and two glasses. He cracked the bottle and poured two half-glasses, saying, "Drink, my friend. This bottle was given to me by the Führer himself."

Both doctors took a long drink and Von Gieson went on, "We have no time to celebrate. If we can perfect this serum, then maybe we can rise to rule the world again. General Hulman has given me full authority to create a race of super soldiers that will fight to the death without question. If it works, then the general public, including old men and women, can be injected and fight to the death for the Führer. It's our last hope, my friend, so let us begin."

They walked over to a table with a cadaver on it and Von Gieson said, "We must try it on a living soldier first, before we try to bring the dead back to life." Over in the corner of the room was a soldier strapped to a table, like Frankenstein. "This is Private Edward Van Talsen," Von Gieson said. "He was hit with shrapnel in the leg, and gangrene has set in. He has little chance for survival. Get the dose ready that you believe will work."

Dr. Schuster took a syringe, filled it halfway with the serum, called Policium, and grinned with a twisted smile. "What an honor for all of Germany," he gloated. He attached the needle to the syringe and handed it to Dr. Von Gieson.

"I hope it works," Von Gieson said while injecting Private Van Talsen. Von Gieson pulled the needle out of Van Talsen's arm and stepped backward, a bead of sweat rolling down his middle-aged cheek. Desperation and pain radiated from the doctor's eyes as they stood helplessly waiting for the Policium to work.

Van Talsen began to shake violently, going into seizure. His eyes opened wide, and he suddenly stopped shaking. An evil smile lit up his face, followed by a dead, hollow-eyed stare.

A man with a full rack of medals on his chest walked in with two lower-ranking officers closely following. General Hulman asked, "Any progress yet?"

"Yes, Herr General," Von Gieson said. "He's ready for the test. I will unstrap him." Dr. Von Geison unstrapped the private, with the two lower-ranking officers armed and ready in case anything went wrong. Private Van Talsen stood up with his fists clenched and his eyes ablaze.

"Do you know your name, soldier?" General Hulman asked.

In a deep, raspy, malicious voice the young man said, "I am Private Edward Van Talsen from the 23rd Airborne Division, sir. I serve Germany and the Führer."

"Good," said General Hulman. "Private, I want you to take this pistol and run toward the enemy lines and not stop until every American and British soldier is dead."

Private Van Talsen's muscles swelled as if he were a body builder and growing stronger by the second. He grabbed the gun and immediately ran out of the bunker, screaming, "Kill the Americans and the British!"

"Is it not what you asked for, Herr General?" Von Gieson gloated.

"Remarkable, simply amazing," General Hulman said. "He shouldn't even have been able to walk, let alone run like he did. I believe you have finally done it. All of Germany will revere you two as heroes. All our people will be injected with this, and we will thwart the Allies' efforts once and for all. This is our last chance for survival, so get five doses ready for a special demonstration. The Führer himself will see your great discovery."

Dr. Von Geison and Dr. Schuster both gulped and exhaled nervously. General Hulman said, "Heil Hitler," and extended his hand, then left in a rush to report to the Führer in a bunker several hundred yards away.

■ ■ ■

09:00 hours: Dr. Schuster said, "I can't be sure if the dose goes by weight, injury or what. There's no way to predict the outcome. We really need more time for testing."

"We have no more time," Dr. Von Gieson warned. He carefully placed five needles in a case and shut the lid. He looked up and jumped backward a full foot as the double doors bolted open.

"Heil Hitler," General Hulman said as he rapidly strode in, saluting with pride. With him this time were Colonel Hesterman and four armed sergeants, all loyal servants of the Führer himself.

"Bring in the subjects," General Hulman ordered. The four sergeants went out through the double doors and started wheeling in wounded soldiers, five in all. Dr. Von Gieson looked at the five and hastily said, "I will need time to assess their injuries and to prepare and adjust the doses."

"You have thirty minutes," General Hulman insisted.

Dr. Von Gieson gulped and saluted the general. The entourage left the room while Dr. Von Gieson and Dr. Schuster began to examine the patients. Dr. Schuster looked at one soldier's arms and said, "He's barely alive. I hope this works."

"They're all barely alive," Von Gieson replied. "I guess this will be the true test of whether our five years of work has paid off. Only one officer in the bunch, Lieutenant Snell, I see."

The two doctors stared blankly at each other; with Dr. Schuster breaking the silence. "You know there is another thing we haven't considered." Dr. Von Gieson gazed into Dr. Schuster's eyes as if he knew exactly what he was going to say.

"Creating super soldiers can create super egos. What if one of the soldiers feels that he is above us? With power comes desire for more power. It takes a brilliant person to control it as well as our Führer has. These are only infantrymen, with the exception of the lieutenant, and there is the risk of defiance."

"It's a risk we must take," said Von Gieson.

Dr. Schuster sighed, then agreed. "I know, my friend, I know."

■ ■ ■

10:00 hours: "Is everything ready?" General Hulman asked.

"Yes, Herr General," Dr. Von Gieson said.

"I will inform the Führer at once, so don't make him wait when he arrives," General Hulman said.

"Yes, Herr General," Dr. Von Gieson said.

Dr. Schuster and Dr. Von Gieson carefully placed a needle with an estimated dose of Policium near each patient and nervously awaited the entry of the man they had served unquestioningly for the last several years, Adolf Hitler.

■ ■ ■

11:00 hours: Dr. Von Gieson and Dr. Schuster abruptly turned toward the door as General Hulman, Colonel Hesterman and four armed bodyguards entered the room. An Allied bomb exploded dangerously nearby, shaking the room and the walls of the bunker; a fine line of dirt from the ceiling fell to the floor. Both doctors stood firmly at attention and saluted as Adolf Hitler walked through the door.

Hitler said, "I hear you have good news for Germany."

"Yes, my Führer," Dr. Von Gieson nervously said. "We have finally created a serum that will turn ordinary people into fighting machines. If we can inject the common population, every man, woman and child in the world will become a fierce fighting soldier for you, my Führer." Another explosion rang out in the distance, silencing the doctor.

"Proceed," Hitler said.

Dr. Von Gieson explained, "We will inject these five soldiers, who will inevitably die without the serum. Then we will give them impossible orders to carry out. They will feel no pain from their injuries, and will carry out the orders or die trying."

Dr. Von Gieson injected three of the soldiers with the serum while Dr. Schuster injected the other two. All five of the soldiers went into seizure as before, and came out of it wide-eyed and attentive.

Dr. Von Gieson commanded, "All of you, stand up." All five of the soldiers stood up, ignoring their wounds, muscles bulging. Von Gieson ordered,

"This is your Führer, whom you will serve to the death. I want all five of you to go toward the enemy lines and kill every British and American soldier you can find without question."

Two of the soldiers ran out of the room and yelled, "Kill all British and American soldiers!" Lieutenant Snell and two of the other soldiers began to foam at the mouth, one of the soldiers shaking violently. One of the soldiers yelled, "I am the Führer. I will rule Germany!"

Lieutenant Snell screamed, "No, I am the Führer and will rule Germany!" The other soldier suddenly stopped shaking and lunged at one of the bodyguards. The bodyguard fired a shot at the soldier and it went right into his chest. The soldier ignored the shot and jumped on the bodyguard and started beating him violently. The other soldier and Lieutenant Snell rushed the other bodyguards, while gunfire rang out wildly in the bunker. General Hulman grabbed Hitler, threw him to the ground and lay on top of him, protecting him with his life.

Lieutenant Snell grabbed another bodyguard's neck and twisted it violently, snapping it, making him fall to the ground. The other soldier was shot in the arm, then hit the two remaining bodyguards in the face with raging fists. He killed them with his bare hands. When it was all over, the two soldiers who were shot were bleeding, but still alive, while everyone else in the room lay dead except for General Hulman, Adolf Hitler and Lieutenant Snell.

Lieutenant Snell, unscathed, picked up a dead bodyguard's rifle and shot General Hulman in the head. He moved the general aside to get at Hitler lying safely underneath him. Hitler said, "I am the Führer and I order you to put your weapon down."

Lieutenant Snell, foaming at the mouth, said, "I order you to die! I am the Führer now!" He pulled the trigger of the rifle twice and shot Hitler in the head, killing him. Hitler's body lay limp in the bunker while the three soldiers ran out of the bunker as Lieutenant Snell screamed, "I am the Führer. I am the Führer!" The two soldiers who had been shot kept running toward the front lines until they bled to death, less than two hundred yards away from the bunker.

Lieutenant Snell was blown to pieces by an Allied bomb only thirty minutes later as he ran through the streets, still yelling, "I am the Führer."

From an adjacent bunker, second-in-command General Heinrich Himmler and his advisors entered the bunker and found Hitler dead. Himmler turned to his high-ranking subordinates and said, "We cannot let the world know our Führer died this way. Burn his body beyond recognition."

They burned Hitler's body and Germany ultimately surrendered. The headline read, "Hitler Dead." The story stated that Hitler committed suicide. Only a few people ever knew the truth behind Adolf Hitler's death, and now you know the true story too.

Starry Night

Kayla Rack

8th Grade, South Allegheny Middle School, Liberty Boro, Pennsylvania

Have you ever had that one special place you could go, to get away from everything the world had to throw at you; that one place where nothing seemed to matter, and whatever bad that had happened in your life all melted away?

Johanna and I had been friends for as long as I could remember. We knew each other's deepest darkest secrets, lifetime wishes, and basic train of thought. Both of us dreamed of being best friends forever, and living next to each other the rest of our lives. Whenever I slept over, we would go out on the balcony outside her window, where we could both escape from even the worst of days.

Things were so peaceful on that balcony, and I'll never forget the last night I ever went out there. It was the last Saturday of summer vacation, 2010. The stars shone brightly in the sky and I couldn't keep my eyes off my favorite one, the North Star. The North Star permanently lay like a centerpiece in the middle of the nighttime blackness that always soothed me. I fell asleep so many times staring at that star on Johanna's balcony that if I tried to count them all, my head would spin.

Johanna and I grabbed our sleeping bags, rolled them out and lay on top of them. "Do you ever wonder what it's going to be like when we get older, Fiona?" she asked, while twirling a strand of her chocolate brown hair between her fingers.

I shrugged, "How should I know? I couldn't even tell you what tenth grade's going to be like in two days. I wish I could stay young forever."

"Me too," Johanna agreed.

I didn't like thinking about the future much. It scared me more than anyone would ever know. I think the unpredictability was the worst thing about it. And when fate came into play, it was as if you had no control over your life whatsoever.

I picked up a small twig and threw it over the side of the balcony, as if to throw all of my problems away into the thick dark night. As Johanna and I sat up half the night talking, I had no idea that our friendship was about to change direction as quickly as a hurricane going back out to sea to gain more strength.

It all started on the first day of school. Mom woke me with a nicer than normal voice, saying, "Fiona, sweetheart, I don't want you to be late." I rolled out of bed, showered and tried straightening my hair. It seemed like my endless blonde curls would never cooperate, forcing me to comb it through. I threw on my normal girly-girl outfit consisting of a simple pink and black plaid skirt with a pink blouse.

I strolled toward the bus stop, unaware that my life was about change and I was never going to be the same. I didn't have any classes with Johanna, but shared a lunch period with her. I wasn't able to find her at lunch, and texted her several times with no response.

The second day went by in a blur, with a creepy feeling that she was avoiding me. When I darted into the lunchroom, I scanned our normal table and Johanna wasn't there. I peered toward the corner of the room and saw her surrounded by what we always called the preps. The preps were the girls who wore the latest trends, laughed at pointless jokes, flirted with boys without a clue, thought they were perfect in every way, and didn't hesitate to humiliate others. And did they ever have the reputation at parties, with everything from beer to drugs.

I shook my head and thought, *That's weird. We always made fun of them, and now it looks as if she's one of them.* And when I saw the bracelet that they all wore around her wrist, I knew they had gotten to her. I wasn't sure whether to approach the table and sit down, or turn the other way and sit where we normally did. I chose the second. I ate lunch with my stomach churning, barely able to get any food down.

Later that day, Johanna called me with her voice shaken, almost if she was upset or unsure of herself. I could almost picture her lips trembling as she said, "Why didn't you sit with us at lunch?"

The question caught me off guard, so I hesitated, then said, "You were sitting with the preps. You know how they are."

"Don't call them that," she snapped back. Her sudden change of tone startled me. "They're my friends too. You shouldn't be so quick to judge people."

"You're sticking up for the preps?" I nervously questioned. "What's going on, and why haven't you talked to me in two days?"

There was a short pause on the phone and I had to strain to hear her muted words, "I can get you into our group if you come sit with us tomorrow. I'm sure I can talk to them and see if you can get a bracelet. There's a party Saturday night over at Courtney's. Her parents won't be home, and the whole world will be there. I can introduce you to everyone."

"I've heard about those parties," I cautiously said. "They do a lot of raunchy things there and I'm not into that stuff."

"Come on," Johanna insisted, "you don't have to do anything. You can come along and have fun."

"I don't think so," I said, with my heart almost in my hands.

"Then I guess we're no longer friends," Johanna shot back. That one hurt. It was almost like someone had taken a hammer and slammed it with all their strength into my chest.

"Why?" I asked, trembling, with the phone pressed up against my ear.

"Things change, just like we talked about the other night," Johanna briskly returned. "I hope to see you at the party Saturday night. If not, then I probably won't see you again." She hung up, and my heart went dead just as the phone had.

I stood there and thought, while my eyes misted: *How could someone change so fast in a few days? I guess once the preps get hold of you, there's no turning back. I don't know what to do. We've been friends forever, and if I don't go to that party, she'll hate me.*

The rest of the week, I ate lunch with Johanna, sitting with the preps while my insides turned inside out. When Saturday night finally came, I moped around the house, unsure what I should do. Shortly after eight o'clock, both Mom and Dad approached me with Mom asking, "What's wrong? How come you're not out with Johanna?"

"Johanna and I aren't friends anymore."

"Don't be ridiculous," said Dad. "People get into disagreements all the time and they end up working out their problems. You two will be friends again in a day or two."

A tear formed in my eye and rolled down my cheek. "Not this time," I whined. "Johanna is hanging around with the preps, and she told me if I don't go to this party tonight, then our friendship is over."

"Maybe you should go to the party," said Dad. "It would do you good to meet other people."

"You don't understand," I said. "There's going to be drinking and probably drugs. They do the craziest things there, and I don't want to be part of it."

Mom and Dad both stared at me in awe. Dad cleared his throat and said, "I'm proud of you, Fiona. Part of growing up is making wise choices, and it takes a big person to be able to make a decision like that. I'll tell you what, why don't we all go to the mall and I'll let you pick out an outfit or something, since you have so much common sense."

"No," I said. "I'd rather be alone for a while. I'm going to walk across the street to the park and stare at the stars for a while, if you don't mind. It'll be dark soon and I wouldn't mind sitting for a little bit."

Mom smiled and said, "Sure. I'll come out after a bit to check on you."

I walked across the street, sat on the middle swing and lightly pushed off. My head was spinning with unanswered questions about my life. *What am I going to do without Johanna? What would have happened if I had gone to the party? Why do I feel so horrible, if I did the right thing?* I looked up at the North Star and felt more settled.

The sound of footsteps in the mulch tore my focus from the beauty of the night sky. I stopped my swing and looked around. Standing a few feet to my right was Hillary Patrick, who was in my grade and lived in my neighborhood. Her hair was bright red and her eyes seemed curious. I had never sat with her group of friends at lunch before, and I had never really known her.

"What are you doing?" Hillary asked.

"Oh, nothing," I responded. "How come you're not at Courtney's party like everyone else?"

Hillary laughed, "I'm not going there and getting into that stuff. Not everyone's at that party, you know. I want to be a fashion designer when I grow up, and the last thing I need to do is go to that party. I'm going to have my own clothing line when I get older."

I looked up at the North Star and said, "The sky is so beautiful. It's going to be a starry night."

"Look how bright the North Star is tonight," Hillary said.

My mouth dropped open and I asked, "You like the night sky too?"

"It's my favorite," said Hillary. "It seems like no matter how bad things are in life, the sky always calms me." I smiled and took a soothing breath. "Hey, do you want to go to a late night movie that starts at ten?" Hillary asked. "After, maybe you could spend the night and I could show you some of my designs. They're pretty good."

"Sure, I'd like that," I said. I looked up at the North Star again and it held my gaze.

"Is something wrong?" Hillary asked in a concerned tone.

I smiled, still gazing at the stars, and said, "No, everything is fine; different, but perfectly fine."

The Impure and the Self-Centered

Riddhi Rane

8th Grade, Coppell Middle School East, Coppell, Texas

Sydney, Australia was home to one of the meanest, most arrogant, self-centered girls in the world; her name was Alyssa Cyprus. Alyssa was five feet six inches tall, and had medium length dark hair. At twelve years old, she was much stronger than anyone in her grade at school. She did whatever she wanted to people, and never thought about their feelings.

Alyssa woke up one morning with a scowl on her face and got ready for school. She went into the kitchen where her mother was getting ready for work. Her mother said, "Remember, I'll be out of town today and tomorrow. There's plenty of food in the refrigerator, and Mrs. Jacobs will be here to watch you when you get home from school."

"I'm old enough to take care of myself," Alyssa said.

"We've been over this before," her mother said. "I want you to be good for once while I'm away. If I get another phone call from school when I'm on the road, I'll scream. You know how I hate traveling, but you know how it is being in sales."

"Do you think Daddy will come home soon?" Alyssa asked.

"I know the divorce was hard on you, dear," her mother said. "It was hard on me too. He's looking for work near home right now online. I have a feeling he won't be staying at that job in the U.S. long. He'll be back soon. I'm sure of it. Remember to be good while I'm gone." And she rushed off on her trip.

Alyssa arrived at school angrier than she had been in a long time. When she walked through the school, everyone moved out of her way as they always did, hoping that they wouldn't be the one to feel her wrath. Her bitterness festered inside as she looked around the hallway. *Shelby Jackson*, Alyssa thought, *the perfect person to make me feel better. She's the biggest wimp in the school.*

Alyssa walked up behind Shelby and reached for the books she was carrying. She yanked them out of Shelby's hands and they all fell to the floor. Shelby turned around somberly and was just about to say something, until she saw who it was. Alyssa said with a scowl, "Are you having trouble holding on to your books today, dweeb?"

Shelby bent down to start picking up her things, and Alyssa put her foot on top of one of the books. Shelby's friend Whitney bent over to help and said, "Leave her alone. She didn't do anything to you."

Alyssa hated it when people talked back to her, so she bent over and unzipped Whitney's backpack. She pulled two books out and threw them on the floor too. She laughed and said, "Now you two nerds can pick up your books together, since you're friends and all. If you tell a teacher or the principal about this, I'll wait for you every day after school. In fact, I'll buy a new pair of shoes and write your names on them, just so I won't forget to come see you every day. Then you can see your name every time I kick you in the face."

Alyssa walked away with a slight smile on her face and thought, *I love making those twits squirm.*

When Alyssa got to class, the teacher had not yet arrived. She walked over to a boy named Nathan, who was sitting down getting his things ready. She said loudly, "You're in my seat." Nathan began to say something, and Alyssa cut him off: "I see we're going to do this the hard way."

She took one of his papers and ripped it in half. She grabbed one of his pencils, broke it and said, "That's what's going to happen to you if you don't get out of my seat!" Nathan slowly got up, gathered his things and Alyssa said, "Not fast enough!" and she tore a page out of his textbook. "If you moved quicker, you wouldn't have to pay for the damaged book at the end of the year, nerd." Nathan moved faster and Alyssa said, "That's better."

The girl behind where Nathan had been sitting looked at Alyssa. Alyssa lifted her lip, gave the girl a dirty look and tossed her head toward her, making her jump a little. Alyssa said, "You're pathetic, Courtney."

The teacher walked through the door and said, "Sorry I'm late. Now open your books to page thirty and we'll start there."

Alyssa put her finger on her chest and thumped it and then pointed at Courtney, gesturing, *Me and you after class in the hallway.* Courtney swallowed heavily and didn't say a word. Alyssa antagonized four more kids that day until the principal called Alyssa into her office.

Mrs. Harper said, "I've been getting complaints that you've been bullying kids again, for the third time in the last two weeks."

Alyssa said, "I'll bet it was Shelby Jackson. She's such a liar and a baby."

"I've had several complaints," Mrs. Harper said. "I have no choice but to suspend you. I'll call you mother right now."

"No, don't call my mom," Alyssa pleaded. "Give me one more chance."

"I know you've had it hard at home, because I've talked to your mother many times," Mrs. Harper said. "But you can't keep doing this to other people. You need to stop being so self-centered. Did you ever think about how they feel?" Alyssa shook her head.

"I'm going to give you one more chance. If I get as much as one complaint from this moment on, you're gone and you might not be coming back this time. With the new rules about bullying, I would have no choice but to push for a permanent suspension. Now get back to class. Here's your pass." Alyssa went back to class, and didn't have an incident the rest of the day.

After school, Alyssa stopped at a park along the way. She sat down on a bench all alone. There were three younger kids playing soccer nearby. One of them kicked the ball and it went wildly toward Alyssa, landing right in front of her. One of the boys yelled, "A little help, please!"

Alyssa picked up the ball and started to kick it back toward the boys, and then thought, *I'm not in school. I don't have to watch what I'm doing.* She turned away from the boys and kicked the ball as far as she could in the opposite direction. She laughed and yelled, "You should learn how to control your kicks! That'll teach you a lesson!"

The boy shook his head, mumbled under his breath, "You're an idiot," and went running after the ball.

A few seconds later an old woman with a cane walked to where Alyssa was now sitting on the bench. The woman said, "I see the talk your principal had with you didn't do any good."

Alyssa said, "Lady, I don't know who you are but you better keep your mouth shut unless you want that cane of yours stuck up in that tree." Then she grinned.

"I suppose you would put an old lady's cane in a tree," the lady said. "I knew you were mean, Alyssa, but I didn't realize you were that mean. This is going to be harder than I thought."

"Lady, you better get out of here before something bad happens to you," Alyssa said. "And how did you know my name?"

"My name is Asgarnya and I help the unfortunates of this world. I have heard the cries for help from the people you've hurt one too many times. For the rest of the day, every time you do something mean to someone something bad will happen to you. If you don't learn your lesson by the end of the day, tomorrow you'll know what it feels like to be picked on."

Alyssa said, "Lady, you need professional help. Get out of here now, or I'm going to have you arrested for being ugly."

Asgarnya put her finger in the air and Alyssa's body felt limp. The next twenty seconds were a blur to Alyssa, and when she came out of her daze, Asgarnya was gone. Alyssa cleared her head by shaking it, got up, and walked away, thinking nothing of Asgarnya's warning.

Later that day Alyssa went down by the pier and watched the fisherman bring in their catch for the day. As she was watching, a fisherman walked by and gently brushed her arm with his smelly net full of fish. Alyssa seized the moment and said, "How dare you hit me with your net, you idiot. Are you stupid or something?"

The man was just about to apologize when Alyssa took a step backwards and slipped. She fell and landed with her hand in a bucket of fish that a man had set down. She stood up and said, "Now look what you've done."

The man said, "I'm sorry."

Alyssa got up and said, "Whatever," and walked angrily away.

When she got home, her sitter was there and asked, "Where have you been? I've been worried about you."

"Don't worry about me," Alyssa said. "I can take care of myself. In fact, I don't even need you here, so why don't you go home and do your nails or something." Right then Alyssa bumped her knee into the chair. She grunted and said, "Just leave me alone." She stomped away, went into her bedroom and shut the door.

She stayed there the rest of the day, until she picked up her phone and called a local store. When the clerk answered, she made a loud disgusting noise and hung up. She laughed and then sat down at her desk. She reached for her favorite glass figurine and knocked it over. It fell and shattered on the floor. Alyssa sighed and started cleaning it up. She spent the rest of the night at home in her room, not thinking about her meeting with Asgarnya once.

The next morning Alyssa woke up in a strange place. She rushed to the bathroom where everything seemed foreign to her. She looked into the mirror and shrieked, "No. It can't be. That lady yesterday wasn't crazy. No, please no, anybody but Shelby Jackson. She made me into Shelby Jackson!"

"Hurry up, dear," Shelby's mom said. "You'll be late for school."

Alyssa closed her eyes tightly, trying to make sense of it all, thinking it was just a dream. She opened her eyes and shook her head wildly. She took another deep breath and mumbled, "No. Anyone but Shelby Jackson."

Alyssa hid from Shelby's mother in the bathroom. Shelby's mother banged on the door and said, "It's time to leave for school."

Alyssa said, "I don't feel good. I'm not going to go to school today."

"Not that again," Shelby's mother complained. "I know how it is for you there, but you can't keep hiding from your problems. Try reasoning with the people that pick on you. Maybe that will work." Alyssa gulped and knew she had to go to school.

When she got to school, Whitney walked up and said, "Hello."

Forgetting who she was for a moment, Alyssa said, "What do you want? You didn't get enough yesterday and you're back for more?"

Whitney asked, "What's wrong with you?"

Remembering she was Shelby now, she said, "Oh, I'm sorry. I wasn't thinking right." Whitney shook her head, looked at Shelby weirdly and said, "Come on, we'll be late for first hour."

As Alyssa was closing her locker, another mean girl named Haley walked up. She grabbed Alyssa's arm and said, "Hand over your lunch money. You know the routine."

Alyssa said, "Not a chance," and made a fist and swung at Haley.

Haley moved out of the way and said, "I've waiting for the day you tried to stand up for yourself. This is going to be fun." Haley grabbed Alyssa and said, "I'm going to enjoy this, Shelby," and pushed Alyssa toward the locker face first, holding her firmly.

Alyssa's face slammed against the cold metal of the locker door while the rest of the kids in the hall yelled, "Hit her, hit her, hit her!"

Just as Haley was going to hit Alyssa Mrs. Harper walked up. She separated the two and said, "Both of you in my office, now!" When they got into her office she asked, "What happened?" After they were both done telling their stories Mrs. Harper said, "Haley, you're suspended. Go into the other room until I call your mother." Haley left the room.

Mrs. Harper said to Alyssa, "Shelby, I know how hard it is for you, always getting picked on all the time, and I'm doing my best to stop it. You're a great student and a great kid. I'm sorry it's that way for you here." Alyssa took a deep breath and didn't say anything. Mrs. Harper continued, "You can go back to class, and let me know if you have any more problems."

Three more times that day, Alyssa as Shelby was picked on with demeaning verbal assaults. She spent the rest of the day after that in fear that someone would do something awful to her.

That night, before Alyssa went to bed, she said, "Please, Asgarnya, change me back. I've learned my lesson. I promise I'll never be mean to anyone again. Please, I'll do anything." She went to sleep after that.

The next morning Alyssa woke up in her own bed and went into the bathroom. She looked in the mirror and scowled, "I'm back. I can't wait to get to school today."

Alyssa went to school with a gleam in her eyes. She walked up to Shelby with her teeth gritted, her fists tight and a mean look on her face. Shelby backed up nervously. Alyssa grabbed one of her books and said, "I'm sorry for all the times I was mean to you. I'll never be mean to you again."

Shelby's eyes perked up and she couldn't speak. She stood thunderstruck a moment, then a cautious look came over her face.

"I was wondering," Alyssa went on, "if... maybe... you'd like to do something after school today. Do you want to go to the movies?"

Shelby stood there another moment and asked, "Is this some kind of a joke?"

Alyssa shook her head and said, "I've been the biggest jerk ever, and I want to make it up to you."

"Sure... I'll go to the movies," Shelby said.

Shelby and Alyssa became good friends. She even saw to it that no one ever picked on Shelby again. Alyssa's dad moved back to Australia and got remarried to her mother. And Alyssa kept her promise and was never mean to anyone again.

The Hunt

Abigail Scheirer

8th Grade, South Allegheny Middle School, Liberty Boro, Pennsylvania

As soon as I walked into the gas station, I knew he was there. The smell of him was like a garbage dump on a hot summer day. Just another keen way I was trained to tell one of them was around — my enhanced sense of smell.

I walked down the aisle, searching for a man who no longer belonged to this world. There he was, standing over a bag of chips, wishing he could taste at least one morsel of salt. I laughed to myself, knowing he couldn't. The man seemed to have been in his mid-thirties when he died, and wore an old pair of ripped jeans with a gray button-down shirt; a walking corpse that no one could see, except me and a few other ghost hunters.

I paid for my gas, carefully not giving away who I was or why I was there. The fact that the troubled dead couldn't recognize us as ghost hunters until we wielded our weapons was one of the few advantages we had.

As I walked outside, the cool fall breeze rippled through my hair while I thought, *What a great night for a hunt.* I patiently waited outside until he left, wanting to see if he headed toward the bridge. When he came out, he turned toward the bridge, just as I had expected.

I knew that he was the ghost of Dunstan Bridge, and that his name was Brad Marshall. He had died less than a mile from the bridge. I mumbled "hmm" under my breath as I reached for the dagger I always kept carefully by my side. My dagger, which had faithfully served me so many times, was no ordinary knife. It was a special weapon given to me by the head ghost hunter himself, Zaruous. It had a spiritual energy that no ghost could combat. One stab through the heart, and any troubled ghost would be sent straight to the depths of hell.

The blade was eight inches long and the handle was made of ivory, with small hand-carved inscriptions by each hunter who had used it. It had been passed down for thousands of years and I was the latest recipient. The only time a ghost recognized me as a hunter was when the knife glowed in my hand. Other hunters had other weapons, but my dagger fit me just fine.

My name is Bayard, and since my mother and father died when I was an infant, I was recruited as a child. I have had twenty-one years of continuous training, teaching me one thing: to kill evil ghosts, which have been around since the birth of time. When an evil person dies, his soul is sent to hell. But when hell won't take them right away because they have so many at once, the ghost is forced to roam the earth, wreaking havoc on all of mankind. And that's where I come in. One stab through the heart with my dagger, and hell is forced to take them.

I knew that since ghosts can never roam far from their home, the Dunstan Bridge had to be close. I had done my research and learned that over the last thirteen years, six people had died on or near that bridge, and it was no coincidence to me. Ghosts couldn't directly touch or kill someone, but they had the power to do other things.

One death was caused by a deer running in front of a car, which went over the bank before it reached the bridge. Another death was a suicide, a man in his thirties who jumped into the icy river below. Then there was the night when two teenagers stopped in the middle of the bridge and got spooked. They burned their tires taking off into the other lane and collided with an oncoming car. The two teenagers, and the woman driving the other car, were killed on impact. Also killed was a child who had somehow wandered onto the bridge and into an oncoming car. That one made me the angriest, and now, revenge for all the havoc the ghost had inflicted on mankind was surely going to be mine.

I carefully followed the ghost until he finally arrived at the bridge. I never had an advance strategy. It was get in, kill the ghost and get out, and then move on to the next one. This time, as I sat in my car watching, just fifty yards away from the bridge, I had an unnerving feeling that the ghost knew I was there.

I took a deep breath, reached for the case with the dagger in it, and got out of my car. I walked toward the bridge as if I were an average person out for a stroll. I walked to the center of the bridge and stood looking around. Trying to trick the ghost, I said loudly, "I may as well end it now. Life isn't worth living without Kirsty." I took a step up on the ledge and said, "Kirsty, this is for you."

I smelled the awful stench again, then looked to my side and saw the ghost of Dunstan Bridge walking toward me. He was probably going to do something to make sure I went through with it. When he got just feet from me, I pulled the dagger out of its case and it started to glow. I lunged at him, trying to stab him in the heart.

He jumped back and said, "I knew who you were the moment I saw you in the gas station. You're all the same and you can't fool me. I know that once you reveal yourself to me, I can kill your mortal body with my bare hands, or with an inanimate object. I've killed three of you so-called ghost hunters in my time, and you're going to be the fourth."

"I wouldn't count on it," I confidently said.

At that instant, a car turned the corner toward the bridge with its head-lights on, startling me. The ghost quickly jolted toward me, hitting me on my arm with a two-by-four he had hidden behind his back, and knocking the dagger from my hand. I winced in pain as I looked down at the dagger, which was now lodged between two wooden planks in the center of the bridge. The ghost moved toward me as the approaching car honked its horn.

I moved toward the dagger, then stepped backward as the car pulled into the other lane to avoid me. It drove right over the dagger. The ghost swung the two-by-four, grazing me across the side of my head. I wobbled backward, woozy from the blow, while the ghost stepped between me and the dagger.

"What are you going to do now?" he asked. "When will you ghost hunters ever learn not to come after me? Do I have to kill a hundred of you before you stop?" The ghost swung the two-by-four again and hit me square on the side of my arm. I stumbled, then twisted my ankle and fell.

The ghost stood over me, with my only hope ten feet away in the center of the bridge. I slid toward the dagger in great pain and he stepped in the way again, saying, "Oh no you don't. You'll never touch that knife again!" He jumped on top of me with the two-by-four clenched in both hands. "I killed another ghost hunter with this same board," he gloated. "He had a sickle as his weapon. You people never learn that when you have a weapon, I can have one too. You shouldn't have showed me that knife so early."

He shoved the two-by-four under my throat, then leaned forward with his full weight on the board, choking me. I gasped for air, struggling to get loose, to no avail. I began to black out, knowing I only had seconds left. My eyes shot open and a burst of energy entered my body when I saw the famil-iar sight of the glare from my sister Alaura's sword in the moonlight, flashing behind the ghost. She swung her special weapon with all her might, decapitating the spirit.

The ghost's head rolled toward the center of the bridge near where my dagger was. His body turned to dust, and a loud, ungodly screech filled the air. A black outline of Brad Marshall appeared where his body had been, and another larger, darker figure hovered over him. Brad screamed, "No, please, no!" The larger figure sucked Brad's soul into a small prism-like object. Brad screamed one last time and then the figure disappeared before our eyes while I was still gasping for air.

"It's about time, sister," I said. "What took you so long?"

"I had to sneak up on him or he would've heard me," Alaura said. "Are you all right?"

I coughed again and tried to breathe normally. I stood up, limped toward Alaura, and stumbled. "I think I'll be all right. My ankle is sprained, and my arm is throbbing."

Alaura picked up the knife and handed it to me. She put her arm around me and helped me walk toward the end of the bridge. As we got to the end, she said, "I heard there's a ghost in Florida at an old Victorian house where three people died. What do you think?"

"I think I'll take two weeks off, partner. Well, maybe one," I said.

All is Fair in Love and War

Christine Shepard

8th Grade, Gahanna East Middle School, Gahanna, Ohio

As he stood before the familiar battlefield in Iraq, every aspect of his existence exemplified "The Star Spangled Banner." From his Timberland boots, to his army-issue helmet, to the tattoo of the American flag on his arm, Frank Williams was a solder first and a person second. The fact that this was his second tour of duty meant nothing to him but a chance to prove again that he loved his country.

He turned to his friend since high school, Jordan Shuttle, and asked, "Are you ready?"

Jordan nodded and they both rushed the line of insurgents while firing. The rest of the outfit followed, while the sound of uninterrupted gunfire filled the air. One shot here, two shots there, until the line was secured and the rebels were all dead. After six hours, it was back to the safety of their makeshift camp for some grub and a little shuteye. Before bed, one of the corporals yelled, "Mail call," sending hope throughout the camp.

Frank rushed to the corporal and asked, "Is there anything for me?" The corporal nodded and handed him a letter. Frank went to his tent and sat excitedly as he opened the envelope. A thought surfaced of his wedding day, when he had taken his vows. With a smile on his face, he began to read: *Dear Frank, I cannot go on living this lie any longer, pretending to love only you. Unfortunately, my feelings for you have changed, and I love someone else. My heart now belongs to him. Don't blame the war, or yourself, for our separation. Blame me, for falling for another man. — Julia*

Frank gritted his teeth, looked out at the dry sand and the barren land and thought, *If I hadn't been gone, this never would've happened. It's all for what? So a few people can live better. It's not worth it.* Frank sighed; his stomach felt like it had a knife in it. He had known that getting married while he was on active duty would make his marriage harder, but he had never expected this. But then again, he was no fool, and he had known about them.

I should go shoot him right now, he thought. *Then Julia would have to love me instead of my best friend. How could I have ever stayed friends with him, knowing what I know about them?* He remembered when he had first found out, just two days before they were sent to Iraq. *How could he live with the lies while still serving beside me all this time, as if nothing happened? He's such a cheat, and so is she.*

Frank spent the night plotting his revenge, and was sure he'd go through with it no matter what the cost. He thought nothing less than death could mend the cuts that were slashed deep into his soul. He planned on shooting Jordan in the head the next morning on the battlefield and blaming it on the rebels. He thought it was a perfect way to get his best friend and his wife back all at once for the pain they had caused him.

Frank and Jordan stood at the front lines the next day, Frank's eyes beaming with malice. They rushed the line as gunfire rang out. Frank was almost ready to turn his rifle on Jordan when Jordan fell to the ground. He screamed, "I'm hit." He moaned in pain as Frank went to Jordan's side. "Please help me, Frank, please."

"Help you?" Frank laughed. "Help you, like you helped my wife? I've known about you and Julia for over a year."

Jordan's face turned white and he said, "I'm sorry, Frank, but I love her."

"Well, she doesn't love you," Frank lied. "She sent me a letter yesterday saying how sorry she was about what had happened, and how she was going to tell you it was over between you two. She never did love you. You were nothing more than a fling."

Jordan's face turned blank and he said, "No!"

Frank whispered in a devilish tone, "Die, you piece of garbage, for what you did to me, die. All is fair in love and war, so die." Frank fired his gun, hitting Jordan in the chest. Jordan took his last breath while a satisfying grin was pinned on Frank's face. Frank mumbled, "Now I can be happy, you cheater."

Jordan's body was shipped back to the United States, and he was given a hero's funeral. When Frank returned home, his heart had hardened, and his resentment toward his wife festered inside him. Julia stayed for a little while, then broke it off and filed for divorce because he had become so mean. Frank lived the rest of his life miserably with the guilt of what he had done to Jordan on the battlefield. He tried to cover his pain and guilt with drugs. He overdosed four years later, dying angry and alone.

The devil laughed when he died, and said, "You were right, Frank Williams. Everything is fair in love and war, and that's one of my favorite statements. Many a man has been doomed, using that statement as an excuse to do my work. And you have the rest of eternity to think about it."

Different

Megan Sekulich

8th Grade, South Allegheny Middle School, Liberty Boro, Pennsylvania

Most fourteen-year-old girls want to have friends and live normal lives, but I'm different. My name is Ella Betters, and I am the furthest thing from normal you can find. After I had to leave four different schools because I was too much of a distraction, home schooling was Mom's only option. I was fine with having no friends and being by myself, but Mom couldn't stand it. She wanted me to have a normal life like hers, but that was never going to happen.

As we sat in the car outside yet another school, for another hopeless try, she said, "Don't tell anyone you can talk to spirits, and maybe no one will know. Try and fit in this time, please."

"Grandma says it's a gift just like she has," I said. "She says she loves to talk to spirits. She said spirits roam the earth with unfinished business until they can be set free. She's helped save so many lost souls."

"Not another word about it, and I mean it," Mom demanded.

"You know I can't ignore them."

"Try, for your sake and mine," said Mom. "Now go in there and try, and have a good day."

I got out of the car and walked into my first class. I sat down and a girl smiled at me, then said, "My name is Kylie. What's yours?" She twitched once while waiting for my answer.

"I'm Ella Betters, pleased to meet you." We shook hands, and I smiled back. "The first day of high school is always nerve-wracking," she said, twitching again.

195

"You have no idea," I mumbled under my breath.

Our first teacher started class by saying, "I'm Mrs. Raymond, and English this year will be quite challenging." Suddenly, next to Mrs. Raymond I saw an old woman in a dark outfit that looked like it was from fifty years ago. I sat up straight in my seat and looked away.

The spirit walked toward me and asked," Are you Ella Betters?"

"Yes," I whispered.

"My name is Grace Radison, and I died nine years ago. Mrs. Raymond is my granddaughter, and I need you to tell her something for me," Grace said.

"Please, not now," I said.

Mrs. Raymond turned toward me and asked, "Did you say something? Let's see," she looked at the seating chart, "Ella."

"No ma'am, I didn't say anything."

As Mrs. Raymond continued speaking, Grace said, "I need you to tell Shelly, my granddaughter, that there's a chest with family heirlooms in the house her mother still lives in. It used to be my house, but I died before I could tell her about them. Those items are more valuable to our heritage then you'll ever know. Those things have been passed down to each generation for over two hundred years. They're hidden in the cellar behind a panel in the wall. It's the last unfinished thing I have left here. You must tell her, so I can pass to the next life."

"Stop," I blurted out.

"Stop what?" Mrs. Raymond asked.

"Oh, nothing," I said.

"One more interruption, Ella, and I'm going to have to ask you to go to the principal's office."

I nodded, then turned to Grace and whispered, "If you leave me alone, I will tell her after school. I promise."

"All right, Ella, down to the office," Mrs. Raymond said. She wrote out a slip and I took it to the principal's office.

After Principal Jenkins called me into his office, he said, "How fitting. It's Mrs. Raymond's turn to hold detention in her room today. You have an hour there after school." I knew better than to tell him why I was talking in class, and didn't argue one bit. I wasn't visited by another spirit the rest of the day, until I got into Mrs. Raymond's room during detention.

After I sat down, Grace came to me and asked, "Are you going to tell her?"

"Leave me alone, please," I said.

Mrs. Raymond said, "I can see you're going to be spending a lot of time in detention, Ella. You know there is absolutely no talking here."

"Talk to her now," said Grace.

I sighed and asked, "Can I come to your desk, please?"

Mrs. Raymond said, "As you wish."

I approached Mrs. Raymond and said in a low tone, hoping no one else would hear me, "There's an old chest that's hidden in your mother's cellar behind one of the walls, with old family heirlooms in it."

Mrs. Raymond's eyes popped open, and she looked ready to foam at the mouth. "How dare you make up such a ridiculous story as that? I'm going to ask Principal Jenkins to give you two weeks after school."

Grace quickly said, "Tell her it's in the fruit cellar behind the wall to the left. There are four nails holding the board in place that she can easily pry out. If she doesn't believe you, tell her I used to always call her Pumpkin and take her to the park on her orange bike."

I exhaled heavily and said, "Grace said, if you don't believe it, remember when she used to call you Pumpkin and always take you to the park on your orange bike."

Mrs. Raymond's eyes narrowed as she asked, "How do you know that? You're in a lot of trouble, young lady."

I whispered, "I can hear and see spirits." I must not have whispered softly enough, because a boy in the front row repeated what I had said, and the entire classroom began to laugh.

One boy said, "Oh, I'm scared. You can see dead people."

Another girl followed with, "You're crazy."

Mrs. Raymond gritted her teeth and said, "Out in the hall, now." She took me out into the hall and slammed the door. "Ella Betters, I don't know what you're up to, but I've had about enough. How dare you research my family and use it against me?"

Grace said, "Tell her she had a pink dress for her confirmation, and one of the buttons was missing."

I repeated, "Grace told me that you had a pink dress for your confirmation, and one of the buttons was missing."

"I don't know how you knew that," Mrs. Raymond questioned. "But I still don't believe you."

"Please, Mrs. Raymond," I begged. "Just look behind that wall so your grandmother can pass to the other side."

"Hmm," Mrs. Raymond mumbled, then said, "Let's go back inside."

When I walked into the classroom the entire group laughed while one boy said, "Oh, I can see dead people too, Mrs. Raymond. Your great-grand-pa wants to tell you to let me go home. Should I leave now?"

"That will be enough from all of you," Mrs. Raymond said. "I think you can go home now, Ella, while the rest of you stay."

I gathered my books, while one boy said, "I can see dead people too. Can I go home now too?" Everyone laughed as I walked out of the room.

When I got outside, I called my grandmother to pick me up. When I got into the car she asked, "How was school?"

"Not good," I said. "Sometimes I wish I was never born. I saw one of my teacher's grandmothers and she wanted me to give her a message so she could pass. Everyone laughed at me again. I don't know if I'll be able to ever live it down."

"Not everyone will understand your gift," Grandma said. "I know many people still call me a kook. But the main thing is that you're helping others. Hang in there, and you might be surprised how things will work out." Her words weren't much help. I felt as empty inside as an abandoned building.

The next morning, when I went into Mrs. Raymond's room, I sat down and Kylie said, "Good morning."

I replied, "You haven't heard. I'm crazy and you shouldn't talk to me."

"I don't care what everyone says," Kylie said. "I sure have my problems. I've been in counseling for two years now and my parents think I'm nuts. I have acrophobia and can't even go up one step on a ladder without being afraid of heights. I twitch a lot too. Maybe I'm the one that's crazy, way more than you'll ever be. It's not like I have a lot of friends anyway, and people usually don't want to talk to me. Besides, from talking to you, I think you seem pretty nice."

Mrs. Raymond took attendance and then called me into the hall. Her eyes misted and she said, "I don't know how to thank you. I went over to my mom's house and pried that panel away like you told me. There was a chest back there with all sorts of things in it, that was passed down from generation to generation. There were things in there that dated back to before the Constitution was written. Our family immigrated here before we were even a country. The things in that trunk are priceless." As Mrs. Raymond hugged me, Grace appeared.

"Thank you so much for helping me," Grace said. "You don't know how difficult it's been for me all these years. Tell Shelly I love her and I'm at peace now, because I was able to leave this world."

Grace disappeared and I said, "Your grandmother is in a better place now. She said she loves you, and called you Shelly."

Mrs. Raymond hugged me while choking back her tears. She stepped back with a hint of a smile on her face and said, "Come on. Let's go back inside. I'll make sure no one ever makes fun of you in my classroom again." We went back into the room, and she was very protective of my gift after that.

I helped two other people at the school with lost loved ones that semester, and Kylie and I became best friends. She didn't care that I could see and hear dead people, and I didn't care that she had problems too. My grandmother was right. My gift was all about helping others, and Mrs. Raymond never forgot what I did for her.

I Am Rich

Simone Shaffer

8th Grade, Downing Middle School, Flower Mound, Texas

I stared at myself in the mirror, last years' tight clothing from ninth grade barely fitting. The same plain jeans and black V-neck had to have been noticed at school as one of my only outfits that still fit. I sighed and shoved the resentment down once again about how unfair life was, while ruffling up my short dark hair, getting ready for school. "My hair's never right," I mumbled.

I grabbed last year's hoodie and backpack off the counter, then trampled out the door. The slow walk to the bus stop to wait in the cold for the dreaded ride to school was never pleasing. Mum had already left for work, and she took my younger brother James with her, dropping him off early at school in the old Milano. A quick stop on the way to visit my dad at the hospital was her usual routine.

When the bus pulled up, I reluctantly got on. Chad said, "Good mornin', Ello," as he always did.

I muttered, "Good morning," while ignoring the obvious glances from the other kids. After I stumbled to the back of the bus and slammed down into a seat, I stared out the window and sighed. *It wasn't always like this*, I thought. *Before Dad got sick and went into the hospital, I was one of them, a rich kid living in an affluent neighborhood, looking down on others. And now I'm a poor kid living in a rich neighborhood, whose dad is dying. How things have changed.*

Mum had tried her best since Dad got ill, but living in that neighborhood was a stretch to begin with. With her at the hospital all the time, James and

I were basically on our own. So many times on the bus, I wanted to scream, but held back because I knew it wouldn't do any good. The same echoing thoughts riddled my brain. *If Dad dies, I wonder what will happen to James and me. I wonder if we're going to be homeless. I can't keep thinking like this. It'll be better once I get to school, I know it will.*

With the emotions about my father blazing inside me, I was almost in tears by the time the bus pulled into the lot. I mustered all the strength I could and walked inside the lunchroom, looking around to find my safe place.

"Glomp!" Brie screeched from behind me, as I whipped my head around to see her with a huge smile on her face. She rushed over to me, gave me a big hug and said, "Come on." I grinned, my stomach settling a bit.

We went to our normal table and sat down. Everyone was there. Mick asked Brandon, "Did you see the new episode of *Regular Show* last night? Pops was hilarious."

"Yeah," Brandon agreed. "Mordecai and Rigby were so funny, too. I couldn't stop laughing."

Natasha continued to draw, and Sage kept doing her homework, as if Mick's words had never been spoken. I smiled, looked around at our table and thought, *These are my friends. They're the reason I'm not a crying mess. To them I'm me, not a poor girl with a dying father and a working mother trying to hold things together. Most of them come from the other side of town, and that's probably why they don't judge me like the people in my neighborhood do.*

My problems at home faded away when Brie said, "Let's all go to the mall on Saturday and walk around."

"All right," I said, and everyone else agreed in unison.

"Where's Jack?" Brie asked. "Late again?"

"Probably," I responded. "You know him."

The first warning bell rang, and we all got up and scurried to class. Most of the day flew by as I focused on school, trying not to think about the loneliness and pain I was going to have to endure later at home. During sixth-hour English class, it was as if Mrs. Cook had read my mind when she said, "Sometimes, writing about things can make you feel better. I'm going to cut you guys a break today. I want you to write a three-page story about the most difficult thing you've ever done in your life. Hand it in at the end of class, and absolutely no talking."

I didn't need to think twice. I loved my family, but the reality was always embedded in the back of my mind that soon my dad would be gone. I carefully began to write as if a heart was on my desk and I was a surgeon with a scalpel performing surgery. My stomach tightened and I squeezed my pencil with all my might as anger, fear and pain filled my body. I began to write feverishly, not holding anything back. The next thing I knew the bell rang, and sitting in front of me was the most incredible paper I had ever written, with my emotions bleeding off the pages.

I handed it to Mrs. Cook and went to Jack's locker to meet him. Just before I got there, he came down the hall the opposite way. As our eyes met, all my troubles faded away. I had been waiting all day to see him alone, and finally my wish had come true. He put his arm around me and said, "Hey Ello. I missed you."

My smile melted into his as we went into a full hug. "Me too," I said.

Our circle of friends grew, then dissipated as Natasha said, "I'll call you later."

I smiled and said for reassurance, "Don't forget." She put her thumb up, while Jack slipped his arm around my shoulder heading toward our busses. He walked me to my bus and gave me a peck on my cheek. I smiled, kissed him lightly on the lips and waved when I got on the bus. I plopped down on my seat in the back for the lonely ride home, staring outside all the way.

When I got home, I went into the kitchen and threw my stuff on the table, not thinking twice about whether I made a mess or not. After all, there was no one there to care if I did. I was heading for the safety of my room when my phone rang. I answered, "Hello."

"Hey Ello," Aunt Elaina said. "Your mom asked if I'd come by and check on you two after school. I'll be over after James gets home, and I'll have your favorite subs. I hope you're hungry."

"Thanks," I said enthusiastically in a false tone.

"See you soon," said Aunt Elaina.

About thirty minutes later, James burst into the house and put his backpack down on the floor. He went to the couch, sat down and said, "I hate eighth grade. I hope it'll be better when I get to high school."

"It will," I said.

"I never felt this way when Dad was here," he complained. "It's not fair. It's just not fair." He punched the couch and put his head down with his arm over his forehead.

I looked at James and knew his feelings all too well. The arguments that he and I had had growing up were now completely gone, since Dad had gotten sick. It was almost as if we needed each other too much to fight. I went to where James was sitting and gave him a hug. "I miss Dad so much," he said.

"I do too," I calmly said. I took a deep breath, knowing I was James' big sister and had to be strong and hold it together for him. "We're going to see him tomorrow."

"I know," James said. My head joggled around when Aunt Elaina knocked on the door and came in. A huge ear-to-ear grin covered my face when my niece Alyssa walked in too. She was another reason why I had to remain strong and not give up.

I fell to my knees, and she ran to me with her arms open. She slammed into my arms, squealing and laughing as I picked her up off the ground and twirled her around. My heart fluttered, and a thick feeling hit me right in my throat. I set her down and heard her little four-year-old voice squeak out, "Guess what?"

My eyes widened in pure delight. "What?"

"Mommy bought me a backpack today just like yours, for school next year. It's the same color and everything."

"She did?" I excitedly said.

"Yup, and I got pencils and pens too." Alyssa turned to James and hugged him. James let go, and Alyssa said, "Mommy brought you dinner."

"I know," I said.

"Sorry we can't stay," Aunt Elaina said. "Don't forget we're all going to the hospital tomorrow."

"I know," I said.

After Elaina and Alyssa left, James and I went into the kitchen and started gobbling down the subs she had left us. Two bites into the meal, my phone rang, and I answered with a mouth full of food. "Hello."

"Alyssa is crying because she says she misses you," Aunt Elaina said. "I told her we'd be seeing you tomorrow but she started crying anyway."

"Oh, you only left a few minutes ago. Put her on the phone." Aunt Elaina handed her the phone and I said, "I miss you so much."

"Me too," she whined.

"Promise me you won't cry, and tomorrow we'll play cards like we always do."

"Okay," she sniffled.

Alyssa handed Aunt Elaina the phone and she said, "We'll see you tomorrow."

"Okay," I said, and retreated to my room to start my homework. Throughout the evening, I got phone calls and texts from Natasha, Brie and Jack. The night wasted away, until about eleven o'clock when Mum got home. I acted like I was asleep when she snuck into my room to see me for a brief instant before the next day started with the same routine. She carefully prayed over me with a tear in her eye, "Help keep our family safe, please."

I kicked off the covers and hugged Mum with all my strength. She started humming a tune while we swayed back and forth. "I'm scared," I said.

"I'm scared too."

As Mum held me, the events of the day rattled through my brain as fast as a high-speed train in the open country. *I may be seen as a poor, helpless girl whose father is dying, and whose mother is hardly home, but I'm none of those things. I am rich with the things that truly matter. I have friends who care, a boyfriend who loves me, a niece who needs me, and a Mum who would do anything for me and is trying her best. Even though at times I feel so empty inside, I have to go on, if not for myself, then for others. I am rich beyond belief in life, love and laughter, and it's a proven fact that all the money in the world can't replace that.*

I got through the toughest time of my life that year and never forgot what truly mattered again.

Ninth Grade Students

The Descent

Craig Spearman

9th Grade, Vandalia High School,
Vandalia, Illinois

I woke to screams, as my eyes flew open to dimmed, blinking lights at the end of a small room. I didn't remember a thing, not who I was or why I was there. People rushed by in a panicked frenzy as they ran for the lights. A tranquil, soothing man's voice broke through the madness. "Passengers, please make your way calmly to the front of the transport."

Confused, I stood up, and the smell of smoke hit me. *Where am I?* I thought. I walked toward the lights, bumping shoulders with the stragglers, trying to get to the passage to figure out what was going on. When I made it to the doorway, I was cut off by a sealed metal door with the rest of the stragglers. A bright red light flashed and then disappeared, and all was silent. The screams and excitement were now replaced with blank looks on everyone's faces. The sudden sound of twisting metal from behind the door made me jump backward and fall into a seat that was off to the side.

A sudden thundering roar and a brilliant white light filled the room, making me feel like my eardrums would shatter and I would go blind. I stood as the smoke cleared, and felt my body being pulled toward the bright light. I slid along the floor, unable to move, being sucked into a vacuum tube tumbling about.

Everything went black, and the next thing I knew, I was sitting on a small passenger transport steam ship, heading for the clouds. A loud explosion jolted me sideways, as the front of the ship burst into flames. I shivered in fear as I was ejected from the transport, still in my seat. My heart jumped into my throat when I looked down and realized I was three thousand feet in the air and going into a free fall toward a secluded desert area.

I took a shuddery breath and looked up to see the few remaining fragments of the ship falling right above me, on fire. While I plunged to my inevitable death, I closed my eyes tightly, trying to remember what this was all about. *I was on a mission on this planet,* I thought. *It was something to do with infiltrating an organization not too far from where I am now. Or no, it was about testing out some new piece of equipment.*

My mind went blank, and I must have passed out. The next thing I heard was a girl's dim, high-pitched, airy voice in the distance asking, "Are you sure he's still alive? It was you that said he fell from that transport." I felt a slight pinch right by my knee, above my thigh.

My eyes flew open in pain, to see a dimly lit area with a ripped-up tarp above me, held up by narrow rafters. Looking down at me were two girls, one wide-eyed and the other with a smug look on her face. "Told you," one of the girls said.

I peered down at the source of my pain and saw a twisted piece of dark metal buried straight down into my leg. I started to hyperventilate when one of the girls, named Yuffie, who had mocha-colored skin and blonde hair, said, "Calm down and take deep breaths. It's not as bad as it looks."

The other girl, named Bayliee, who had shoulder-length jet-black hair and olive skin, knelt next to me. "You're lucky, you know. You could've died. Falling through the cam net probably slowed you down a bit."

"I'm going to take it out now," Yuffie said.

"Okay," answered Bayliee. "I'll hold him down." I screamed as Yuffie pulled the piece of metal from my leg, causing me to black out again.

Two days later, I woke up with a bandaged leg and a pounding headache. Yuffie and Bayliee were by my side. Dazed, I asked, "What happened, and where am I?"

"You had two run-ins with death in a few days, and you managed to pull through," Yuffie said. "You fell through one of our hangars. The Desert Tigers you know, DTs. Your transport ship was shot down on the way to your next mission to do a test fire of new equipment. Your name is Brandon Hues, and you're one of us."

"You don't know us?" Bayliee asked. I shook my head, confused and unsure whether I could trust them. "I'm a medic, and Yuffie is a mechanical engineer. We've only known each other half our lives. Sleep now, and you'll be better in a week."

I closed my eyes and mumbled, "I remember a little now," and fell back asleep.

A week later I was up and about as best as I could be. The next thing I knew, I found myself on a fighter ship with Yuffie and Bayliee. Yuffie said, "This is Hawke. He's our captain and pilot. This is Jainah. She navigates, runs the bridge and is the copilot." Hawke stood about six feet tall and had shoulder-length dark hair. He was well built and had the toughness of a true leader. Jainah was short and cute, with bouncy brown hair.

"We're going to be way past our base," Hawke said. "Normally we have a subsonic flagship named the *Tiger-D* that can help us pick up and drop off, but not today. We're flying out in this new Phantom Stealth to a planet named Alveria in the Faltron quadrant. Our mission is to intercept a ship, capture or destroy it and take the stolen cargo on board."

"There has to be a catch if they're giving us a new ship," Jainah said, while spinning around on her chair.

"We have no idea what type of cargo it is," Hawke replied. "All they said is that it was something suspicious and out of the norm. They said it was sensitive and had to be taken at all cost, even if it means our lives."

Hawke frowned and pulled Yuffie aside. I could barely make out Hawke asking, "Are you sure he's going to be all right?"

"He'll be fine," Yuffie confidently said.

We flew at light speed one for about an hour. I looked out the window and saw three moons with a planet off in the distance, and a small black blob cruising in space in front of us. Hawke said, "It looks like a military supply ship, based on the markings on the wing. I'm sure once they break through our cloaking device and spot us, they'll break through the planet's atmosphere for cover. We don't have much time."

Jainah nodded and pushed a button on the console, and a screen popped up. On the screen was an enlarged image of the ship that was in front of us. It had a large phoenix flying upward, surrounded on all sides by a moon. "*Rising Moon,*" snarled Hawke.

"Never thought we'd run into them again," Bayliee said with a slight grin on her face. "Do you remember them now, Brandon?" I shook my head and she went on. "The Moons are a mercenary group that highjacks other ships and raids colonies. They even take part in contract kills. They have a stronghold in a large part of the galaxy. "

Hawke's eyes and voice turned to fire. "Jainah, switch us to stealth and come down on them from the clouds. Yuffie, take Brandon to the jumper and go with him."

"Right!" everyone yelled in unison. As Yuffie waved for me to follow, I felt the slight pitch of the ship's ascent.

"The jumper is a secondary shuttle large enough to hold two people and a small amount of cargo." Yuffie plopped into the pilot seat and turned on the engines. The cockpit lit up, a loud humming filled the room, and a monitor appeared with Jainah on it.

"Okay guys, wait for the light to come on and then launch. Go through the smoke: there'll be a hole just below the atmosphere. Good luck, you two." Jainah signed off with a smile.

"When we get there," Yuffie said, nervously twirling her hair, "I'm going to stay in the jumper. It shouldn't be hard to find, whatever we're looking for." She looked around briefly before asking, "So do you remember anything now?"

I sat down in the seat next to her and said, "Yup. I have a sister named Erika, and my birthday is January 5. Hers is the same day, but she's a year older."

"That's good," she said. "It's coming back to you."

A bright light came on the monitor. Yuffie took hold of the controls and the countdown started from ten. The right side of the monitor showed the mini-hanger's doors opening. Our ship rolled over, straight down, and fired a laser shot at the enemy vessel, piercing its body. The jumper flew out of the opening and broke through the clouds at first, with our ship barely visible on the monitor.

As we descended into the planet's atmosphere, the enemy ship jolted into the atmosphere in front of us and burst into flames, lighting up the entire sky. "Hang on!" Yuffie yelled as she pulled in tight, barreling toward the center of the huge mass of smoke coming from the enemy vessel. Swiftly we made our way in, and Yuffie put us down softly. She opened the door and said, "Good luck, and remember you don't have much time, so hurry."

I nodded and stepped out. The smoke cleared, and all around me was warped metal littering the floor. I looked across the room and spotted something that looked out of the ordinary. I walked up to it and took the tarp off to reveal a large tube. Inside was what looked like a water tank with air lines everywhere; connected to the life support was a girl, her face calm and dreamlike. She looked strangely familiar.

"Brandon."

I whipped around, facing the voice, to see a figure sitting in a chair behind the tube. "I see you found your sister."

My memory fell back into place. My sister Erika was an ambassador to the Inter-Galactic Planetary Society. She was the only one that could stop an all-out war in the universe. Erika had been on her way to a meeting amongst the galaxies when she was kidnapped by the Rising Moons. The Rising Moons would stop at nothing to conquer the universe, and they would never give her back.

I was one of the top retrievers for the DTs. A traitor had hit me on the head before I was in the room with the bright lights, causing me to lose my memory. When I was sucked onto the ship through the tube, I didn't know where I was. I was on that transport for a rendezvous with several other great retrievers from the universe to try to get Erika back. Later, when the ship was attacked, I was ejected for my safety.

Now I stood face to face with Phoenix, the most evil leader the Rising Moons had ever had. Phoenix was over seven feet tall, with green skin. His head was larger than mine, and he wore a black cloak with the Rising Moon logo on it. I stepped forward, and Phoenix said, "Join me now and we can rule the universe."

"Never," I said. "I'm here for her." I looked down and saw green blood dripping from under Phoenix's cloak, beginning to form a puddle on the floor. He dropped his arms, which were covering a large piece of metal that was protruding from his chest, just over his heart. He must have been on the bridge when the vessel was hit.

"If you won't join us, then she won't live," Phoenix sneered. "The universe will be ours either way." With a shaky hand, he fired his laser weapon and barely grazed the side of the tube. A crack slowly appeared in the tube and then expanded the entire length of the glass. Phoenix laughed ominously and fell to the ground, moaning and coughing up more green blood.

Water had started to seep out of the tube when Yuffie came up behind me and said, "Hurry. We must go." We pushed the leaking tube into the back of the jumper. Yuffie took off just in time as an explosion rang out, cracking the hull of the well-disguised ship of the Rising Moons.

"Mission accomplished," Yuffie said.

I sat down, overflowing with joy. "Everything is clear now. Erika can go to her meeting and save the universe. And me, I can go back with the Desert Tigers where I belong."

Letting Go

Sadie Shattuck

9th Grade, Ionia High School, Ionia, Michigan

It's hard to believe that your whole life can change in an instant, and a single event can have a huge impact on the way you live the rest of your life. My grandfather had been my best friend since I could remember, and even though he was seventy years old, you would have never known it. With my mom and dad divorced, he was the one who taught me how to play basketball and baseball. And whenever I asked him to play a game, he was there with a smile on his face, asking, "So, do you think today will be the day you finally beat me?"

It had been five years since that awful day, which has haunted me ever since. I've been through it a thousand times and remember it like it was yesterday. God knows I've blamed myself a hundred times unjustly, and I can't stop thinking it was my entire fault. The therapist told me over and over again that it wasn't my fault and that blaming myself is a normal way for me to cope.

We were driving down a busy road when I was twelve years old, on the way to get ice cream, when I asked, "Do you want to hear a joke?"

"Now, Milo," said Grandpa. "I always want to hear a joke, that is, if it's a good one."

I smiled and looked over at Grandpa, and he looked back. I asked, "What did the monster say when he ate the four cylinder engine?"

"I don't know," Grandpa said.

"I could've had a V-8."

"Ugh," Grandpa said. "That was horrible."

"I got one more," I said. "A woman walks into a psychiatrist's office and says, 'Doctor you have to help me. Every time I go to bed, I have this huge fear that something is going to come from under my bed and get me. I can't sleep.'

"The psychiatrist said, 'I have a Ph.D and I'm one of the best in my field. I can cure you if you come twice a week for six months. I only charge a hundred and fifty an hour.'

"The woman said, 'I'll have to think about it.'

"Six months later, the psychiatrist saw the woman in the grocery store and asked, 'How come you never came back? I could've cured you.'

"The woman said, 'I went to a dude ranch for a vacation and I told a cowboy about my problem. He said he'd cure me for a bottle of whiskey and he did.'

"'He must have been really smart,' the psychiatrist said. 'What did he do?'

"'The cowboy told me to cut the legs off my bed so the frame would be flush to the floor. Then nobody could possibly be under my bed.'"

We both started laughing. Suddenly a car ran a red light, and my smile was interrupted by a loud bang. I was jolted to the side of the door, slamming my head into the window just as the airbags went off. We spun around in a circle three times as I held on for dear life. We hit a tree on the side of the road, and everything went dark.

I woke up a few seconds later and shook the cobwebs from my brain. I had a small gash on my forehead, and blood was flowing down the side of my face. I turned to Grandpa and saw that he was crushed inside the car, with his legs under the dash.

My heart felt like it had stopped, and I thought I was going to throw up. I knew Grandpa was in great pain, but his face had an almost surreal smile on it. I asked, "Are you're all right?"

"No, Milo," Grandpa said. "I'm not all right. I can see a bright light, and I feel faint."

My eyes started to water as I cried, "Please Grandpa, stay with me."

"Don't be sad for me," Grandpa coughed. "I've lived a good life, and I have no regrets." He coughed up a mouthful of blood and said, "Look for the cobra from my friend, and his numbers will help you find what I left you."

"What do you mean?" I asked. "Save your strength, you're delirious."

"I love you, Milo," he said with his last breath, while his eyes stared forward and remained open.

"No Grandpa, please!" I cried. The next thing I knew, I was in a hospital bed with Mom next to me, crying.

For the next year, I was in a dark depression. I held deep inside me what his last words were, not telling anyone. I thought, day after day, that if I hadn't told that joke, he'd have been watching the road more closely, and it wouldn't have happened. Or if I hadn't asked him to go get ice cream, he'd still be alive.

I slowly came back to life after that first year, and five years later, at the age of seventeen, I had become almost functional. My nightmares about that day had faded, until one night when I went to bed extremely tired. I dreamed clearly of Grandpa's face at his death and his last words echoed in my brain. I woke up in a deep sweat, panting heavily.

The next day I went to Mom and said, "I still miss Grandpa. I never told anyone this, but before he died, he said something really weird to me. He said, 'Look for the cobra from my friend, and his numbers will help you find what I left for you.'"

"Are you sure?" Mom asked. "And why have you never told anyone this?"

"I thought he was delirious just before he died. Until last night, when I saw him say it again in my dream, I didn't think much of it. Besides, I've been trying to forget about it for five years now."

"I wonder what he meant by that?" Mom asked.

"Let's go ask Grandma if she knows anything," I said.

We went over to Grandma's house and sat down with her. When I told her what Grandpa said before he died, her eyes began to water and she said, "I don't know anything about that riddle. Charlie Grader was his best friend though. He was a huge car enthusiast, but I don't think he liked snakes. Maybe you should ask Mabel, his wife. Charlie died two years ago and I never told you because…well because I know how hard you took it when you're Grandpa died. I'll call her and see if you can talk to her."

The next day Mom and I went to Ms. Grader's house and sat down. I told her what my Grandpa said before he died. Ms. Grader said, "It sounds puzzling to me. I know Charlie never liked snakes, but he sure loved cars. I know his favorite was a Cobra. He owned one when he was younger and bought another one two years before he died. I sold it after he was gone. Your grandfather and Charlie were such good friends, he had a picture of a cobra hand drawn by an artist and gave it to him on his birthday."

"A cobra," I said. "I wonder if that's what he meant. Can I see the picture?"

"Sure," Ms. Grader said. "It's still hanging in the den." We walked into the den and Ms. Grader said, "Here it is."

We looked at it closely. It was a picture of a red cobra, reared upright. He looked mean, with muscles bulging and his teeth were sticking out, as if he was ready to strike. At the bottom of his body, where he touched the ground, were four wheels with smoke coming off the tires.

"It's really cool," I said. "It looks like a snake car." We looked closer at the picture examining every inch of it. I smiled enthusiastically and said, "Look at his collar. It has numbers on it just as Grandpa said, 19165."

I looked at Mom and both are eyes widened. "I don't know what it means," she said. "But it must mean something."

"I don't know either," Ms. Grader said. "If I think of anything, I'll let you know." After a slight pause she lowered her voice and said, "Why don't you take the picture, Milo. I don't have any use for it, and it's your mystery to solve. Your grandfather was a great man, and I think he'd want you to have it."

"Thanks," I said.

We left shortly after that, and went right to Grandma's house and showed her picture. She was as confused as we were, and had no idea what the numbers meant. For three days, I racked my brains, trying to figure out what Grandpa meant about the numbers, and came up with nothing. I was ready to give up until I thought, *I know. I'll ask Ivy. She's my best friend, and she's smarter than anyone I know. If she can't figure it out, then no one can.*

Ivy was five feet five inches tall and twenty-five pounds overweight. She had brown hair and a picture-perfect face. She was a straight-A student, and tutored other students on a regular basis. When I called her and explained the situation, she agreed to come right over.

When she came over, she sat down on the couch and I handed her the picture. She looked at it closely and said, "It's awesome, so colorful too."

I said, "You know what my grandpa said. Do you have any idea what those numbers could mean?"

Ivy grabbed a piece of paper and a pencil and said, "Let's see if we can figure this out. I guess it could be a classic code, you know, A=1 B=2. Let's give it a try. 19165, 1 would be A, 9 would be I, 1 would be A, 6 would be F and 5 would be E. That spells Aiafe. Does that mean anything?"

I shook my head with frustration and said, "No."

"Let's try it backwards," Ivy said. "Efaia, does that mean anything?"

"No," I said again. "We'll never figure this out."

"Be patient," Ivy said. "Wait, let's try this. 19 is S, 1 is A, 5 is F, and 6 is E. Safe, that must mean something."

"Grandpa wanted me to be safe, safe from what?" I asked frowning in confusion.

"No, silly," Ivy laughed. "Did your grandpa have a safe, you know, something that he would keep valuables in?"

"I don't think so," I said. "Let's go and ask my grandma."

When we went over to my grandma's house and sat her down on the couch, I was bursting with excitement. I was shaky and could hardly get the words out. "I think we solved Grandpa's riddle," I said. "Did he have a safe?"

My heart dropped to the floor and I wanted to sink into the ground when Grandma said, "Not that I know of. He was always in that library of his fiddling with something. I never knew what he was up to."

"Can we go in and look around?" I asked.

"Help yourself," said Grandma. "I've barely touched a thing in there since he's been gone."

When Ivy and I got into the room, it looked cluttered. There was a huge oak bookcase, with books stacked full to the very top. There were also two file cabinets in the corner, with a TV and a stereo on the other side of the room. The desk sat in the middle of the room, with a few papers still stacked on it. "Boy, your grandpa must have loved reading," Ivy said.

"He did," I said. "Just like me."

"The most obvious place for a safe would be behind a picture," Ivy said. She walked over to a large picture on the wall and took it down. We stared at the wall, hoping for any clue to help us find out what the numbers meant, and there was none. She sighed, put her hand to her chin and said, "The next most obvious place to look would be behind the bookcase." We took every book out of the bookcase and stacked them in the corner on the floor.

Ivy and I looked at the back of the bookcase closely and I said, "Look, a compartment with a latch." I grasped the metal latch and unhooked it. My throat felt like it had a golf ball stuck in it as I opened the compartment. Our eyes lit up and we smiled as we looked through the compartment, seeing a handle and a spindle on a safe door.

Ivy touched my shoulder and asked, "Can it be that easy as those numbers being the combination of the safe?" I shrugged my shoulders and put both my hands out. "Let's try 19, 16, 5 first." Ivy carefully turned the spindle, stopping precisely on each number. I took a deep breath and tried opening the safe. The handle wouldn't budge, so I looked at Ivy for help. "Let's try 19, 1 65." She turned the spindle carefully again, until she was done with the combination, and then looked at me. I took another deep breath, tugged on the handle and pushed it down, and this time the door popped open.

I screeched with joy as we both took a half a step backward. I reached my hand into the safe and pulled out an envelope with my name on it. Ivy said, "Open it."

I opened it and read out loud, "Dear Milo: If you're reading this then that means I've passed away, and you've solved my puzzle. It also means that you've learned to trust others. I know you could have never figured out the combination on your own without the help of many people. Take a few seconds and think about all the people that have helped you in your life so far."

Thoughts of Grandpa, Grandma, Mom, teachers from the past, friends, and even neighbors, all entered my head and then faded away. I continued to read. "At some point in your life, you'll need to grow up. You don't always need to be as you were. Letting go once in a while is the best thing you can do to stay happy. Look at all the times I let go and played games with you. They were the happiest times of my life, and you made me feel like a kid again."

A tear rolled down my cheek, and my stomach felt all knotted up as I continued. "Don't be sad for me, because I've had a great life and lived it to the fullest. I've met so many wonderful people along the way and tried to thank every one of them. Live your life to the fullest, just as I have, and don't take a single, day for granted. I don't want you to dwell on my death because I'm sure we'll meet again one day. I'll always be in your heart, as you will be in mine. Go out and make me proud, because I love you." It was signed, "Grandpa."

I fell to my knees in tears. Ivy put her hand on my shoulder and said, "He was a great man. You're lucky to have had him as your grandpa."

I stood up, wiped my eyes and said, "I feel different. I feel free. I know it wasn't my fault he died now. He's right. I need to let go of the pain inside myself and move on, just as he would've wanted. He'll always be with me in my heart. I'm going to take his advice and let go. I'm going to live my life to its fullest, and let go every once in a while until we meet again."

Tenth Grade Students

Witch Doll

Elise Tallis

10th Grade, Romeo High School, Romeo, Michigan

The mournful faces of rag dolls surrounding me mirror my own as we sit on our shelves. The innate look of hopelessness has been my only companion for the last five years. I looked down at the rough little stumps of fabric that are now my hands and think back to when I used to be flesh, blood, and bone instead of cotton, cloth, and thread. Those who frequent the little shop that serves as our prison rarely notice us as we lie trapped between the remembered pleasures of life and the desperate wish for release. After all, who would want a bunch of rag dolls as badly stitched and mismatched as us? If we had only listened!

It all began five years ago, not long after my move to Salem in search of a job. I had heard of a small company, which created costumes, that was on the lookout for a new designer. I thought, *If I could land this job, it would be a dream come true.*

With all the confidence I could muster, I walked into the outer office clutching my portfolio. The manager called me into his office and looked over my designs, until one in particular caught his eye. It was one of my favorites; a petite maid outfit in Halloween-based orange and black, which transformed with a few well-placed snaps and buttons into an authentic looking witch's costume. He pointed to it and said, "Recreate this on a doll. If it looks as good in real life as it does here, the job is yours." I left with the giddiness of success burning through me, wanting to get started right away.

When I got outside, I could barely contain myself, with joy singing through me, and let out the loud whoop of triumph that fought to be free.

My euphoria quickly turned to embarrassment when I saw a petite brunette woman in a green sundress staring me down with an amused smile on her face. My face tightened as I brought my arms down and straightened my blouse. She giggled and tilted her head. "You definitely are not from around here, are you?"

I cleared my throat and dug my hands deep into my pockets, "Ahem… no, miss, no, I'm not. I just moved here recently."

She stepped closer, her smile warm and inviting, and held out a delicate, fine-boned hand. "Welcome to Salem! My name's Maggie."

Her hand was dwarfed in mine as I gently shook it. "Hi Maggie, I'm Georgia. Do you know of any stores around that sell dolls? You know, the kind that a little girl would play with." At her quizzically lifted brow, I could feel the flush creeping up my neck as I hastened to assure her, "I… um… need it for my job."

She laughed kindly and told me of several toy stores where I might find the type of doll I needed for my project. I thanked her and started to leave, when she placed a restraining hand on my arm. "Georgia, near some of the other stores there is an antique toy store named Druna's. Please don't go there. The lady that owns it is weird, and many people claim she's a witch!"

I covered my mouth to hide my skepticism and smiled at her. "A witch, huh? I don't believe in that type of stuff."

Somberly, she studied me and sighed. "Just don't go in there."

"Well, um, it's getting late," I said. "I better get going." She looked deep into my eyes and was about to say something; instead she shook her head and turned away. "Goodbye," she said, and hurried off.

People around here are a little odd, I thought, and I walked toward the first store.

After searching through all the shops, I could not find what I needed. At last I came to the antique store that Maggie had warned me about. It seemed harmless, almost warm and inviting. The ancient hinges announced my arrival with a protesting squeak as I entered. The discordant ticking of several grandfather clocks filled the small space, but seemed to be muted by the dim light where dust motes floated in and out of the shadows. My eyes were immediately drawn to several hand-stitched cloth dolls, each one more ragged and forlorn than the next.

It was the one on the end that lured me in. Smaller than the others, her long dark hair fell across big gray button eyes. She looked jaunty compared to the others, almost as if she dared me to pick her up. As I held her in my hand, my gaze was trapped in hers and a shiver went down my spine when her eyes appeared to gleam as if alive.

"She's a pretty one, is she not?"

Startled, I whirled around to find a woman, stooped with age, standing next to me. Where had she come from? Composing myself, I cleared my throat and nodded, "She's perfect. How much?"

"Promise me you'll take good care of young Alice and she's free."

I looked at the doll she called Alice, promising just that, and she was true to her word. I thanked her profusely and left the shop, elated at my good fortune.

At home I worked long into the night, until Alice had been transformed. Gone was the bright-eyed conspiratorial look and in its place something dark and mysterious beckoned. I held her out at arm's length and studied her. She didn't look like Alice any longer.

"No, definitely not Alice. Hmmm, maybe more like Malice!" Her eyes seemed to shine brighter with that, as I set her down carefully by my design sketches.

The next morning, I was puzzled to see Malice wearing the witch version of the costume. I could've sworn I'd left her in the maid design. I noticed the collar was slightly torn as well. Glancing at the clock, I hurried to repair the minor damage and had almost finished when the doorbell rang. Startled, I pricked my finger, cursing softly when I got a spot of blood on her cheek.

I hastened to the door, only to find the sheriff standing there. Stunned, I looked at a picture he held of Maggie, horrified to learn she was missing. I told him of my meeting with her the day before. It seemed I was one of the last people who had seen her. I quickly told him of all the stores I had visited while he made a list. He told me I should plan on sticking around. With one last curious glance into my living room, he tipped his hat and left.

It was as I was closing the door that I heard a noise from my bedroom. I climbed the stairs as quickly as I could, thinking it was my neighbor's cat, which must have sneaked in through the balcony again. My breath caught in the back of my throat when I saw what, or rather who, it was. Malice. My Malice. A living, breathing, fully grown Malice!

I froze as her eyes locked on mine. The depths of her clear gray eyes burned orange like hot coals. The longer I looked into her eyes, the more distant I felt from myself. It was as if I were watching the scene unfold like a bad horror movie. Powerless, I could do nothing but obey her commands as she gathered up a few of my things and threw them at me.

"We're leaving," she hissed. "Take these, put them in the trunk of your rust-bucket automobile, and let us be gone from here."

I did as she bade me. In a daze, I followed her out to the darkened garage and went to the trunk of my car. My heart stopped, and then pounded frantically when I opened the trunk to find the blood-soaked body of Maggie lying twisted in death. The sound of Malice's grating chuckles went up my spine like nails on a chalkboard.

"She got what she deserved! Miss Goody-Two-Shoes sticking her nose where it doesn't belong!"

I stared in horror, trapped, until the ringing of my cell phone jolted me to my senses and broke the hold Malice had over me. Reacting on instinct, I shoved the suitcase at Malice and didn't wait to see her fall before running to the driver's side and jumping in. Quickly I slammed home the locks, frantically turned the key and slammed my foot on the accelerator. The thud of the car as it peeled backwards out of the drive told me that Malice hadn't yet regained her feet. I spared her no backward glance as I took off down the road that separated the thick forest from the peaceful homes that faced it.

I felt nauseated as I thought of poor Maggie lying in my trunk. I swallowed hard as I gripped the wheel tightly and went around the bend in the road, the morning sunlight making it difficult to see through the shadows cast by the tall pines. A flash of color caught my eye and I jerked the wheel to avoid hitting whatever had run onto the road. It wasn't enough to keep me from slamming headfirst into a tree, which stopped my car with a bone-jarring crunch as my head hit the windshield. My vision hazy, I could do no more than whimper as I watched Malice tear the door from its hinges.

"Poor Georgia!" she cackled. "I'll rid you of your pain."

Pinned in the wreckage of my car, I could only watch as from the pocket of her dress she drew a small rag doll form with no face. Reaching into the car, she drew a finger through the blood that ran down my face and then smeared it on the doll's face while she chanted a strange language. My body grew cold and my sight blurred. And then I was looking at the mangled remains of my body as Malice clutched me in her fist.

"Good work, Alice, my dear," rasped an old woman's voice.

"For you, Mistress, any time."

Their cold, soulless laughter was the last sound I heard before Malice stuffed me into her pocket and they made their way back to the shop to set me on the shelf.

If I had only listened! If only any of us had listened.

Index of Authors

Index of Author Schools